The LOOSE

ENDS

LIST

CARRIE FIRESTONE

LITTLE, BROWN AND COMPANY
New York Boston

Little, Brown and Company

Hachette Book Group
1290 Avenue of the Americas, New York, NY 10104

Visit us at lb-teens.com

Little, Brown and Company is a division of Hachette Book Group, Inc.
The Little, Brown name and logo are trademarks of Hachette Book Group, Inc.

The publisher is not responsible for websites (or their content) that are not owned by the publisher.

First Edition: June 2016

Library of Congress Cataloging-in-Publication Data

Names: Firestone, Carrie, author.
Title: The loose ends list / Carrie Firestone.
Description: First edition. | New York ; Boston : Little, Brown and Company, 2016. | Summary: "Seventeen-year-old Maddie O'Neill Levine and her zany family accompany their terminally ill matriarch on her 'death with dignity' cruise, where Maddie falls in love, makes new friends, and struggles to find the strength to let go of her beloved Gram"—Provided by publisher.
Identifiers: LCCN 2015021095 | ISBN 9780316382823 (hardcover) | ISBN 9780316382816 (ebook) | ISBN 9780316382847 (library edition ebook)
Subjects: | CYAC: Family life—Fiction. | Death—Fiction. | Cruise Ships—Fiction. | Grief—Fiction. | Love—Fiction.
Classification: LCC PZ7.1.F55 Loo 2016 | DDC [Fic]—dc23 LC record available at http://lccn.loc.gov/2015021095

10 9 8 7 6 5 4 3 2 1

RRD-C

Printed in the United States of America

For the unlikely revolutionaries
The ones who are brave
The ones who change the world

I TOUCHED DEATH with my fingertips. It wasn't cold or hard like I had heard. I knew it was coming before I touched it. It scattered funny, random objects: a trumpet, a sapphire, a Jules Verne book, a macaroon, a worry doll, a snow globe, and 531 bottles made of paper. There were other things, but those were my favorites.

-ε·° ONE ·°ɜ-

WHEN GRAM CALLS, I ignore it. Lizzie and I are at Starbucks waiting for Kyle and Ethan to get out of lacrosse practice. We're working on our Loose Ends lists, and they're just getting good. I scroll through mine while Lizzie sticks her straw into another iced tea lemonade. It's uncomfortably hot for May.

One. *Save enough lifeguarding money to pay for a road trip.*
Last year I blew all my money on a stupid designer bag that now has ink all over the inside.

Two. *Have an alone day with each of the E's.*
I love my three closest friends deeply, but those girls glom onto one another like puke under a toilet seat.

The noise, the drama, and the differing opinions can be maddening.

Three. *Learn how to cook an entire meal to perfection so I can survive on my own.*

Mom bakes constantly, but she doesn't cook. And Dad's Thanksgivings are amazing, but most nights we get hummus and lentil chips. I want my uncle Wes to design a menu and teach me to cook from scratch.

Four. *Discover a new constellation.*

Dad and Jeb and I have been studying the sky since we were curled-up marsupials wrapped in Dad's sweatshirt. Jeb enjoys stargazing because he's a stoner. I like it because I appreciate vastness, and it's the only thing I have in common with Dad.

As much as my friends make fun of it, my astronomy hobby helped me get Ethan last winter during a sledding party. I have a well-known weakness for team captains, and I had been eyeing Ethan since he landed that esteemed lacrosse title, beating out Lizzie's precious Kyle. I jumped on the sled behind Ethan, and we flew into a snowdrift. I wrapped my legs around his, and broke the silence with, "Look, it's the Big Dipper. Isn't it cool?" He looked up, and I kissed his cheek.

I pointed out four constellations that night before he kissed me back on the lips. It tasted like beer and watermelon gum, but I had snagged Ethan, the hottest captain of them all.

Five. *Rewatch all the eighties movies during a weekend marathon,* preferably with Abby, since she's the only other one willing to eat massive amounts of junk food without complaining about fatness.

———————

Gram calls again.

"It's just my grandmother," I say. "She's probably at Saks. She hates my graduation dress and won't give up on trying to find me a better one." I take a swig of iced chai. "Okay, I have a few more loose ends and then we can finish with something big."

"Isn't a road trip big enough?" Lizzie also missed out on the doomed road trip last summer, after her dad found out about a certain topless selfie. Gram says Lizzie leaves nothing to the imagination, which is pretty ironic coming from an elderly woman with a library full of VHS porn.

Six. *Find a drive-in movie theater somewhere in Connecticut and watch from the car in my pajamas.*

I plan to do this with my friends because Ethan will just try to bone me again.

———————

Seven. *Let Ethan try to bone me again.*

The first time was a disaster. Ethan had an "accident" the second we got into his twin bed. I try not to dwell on the details, but it was gross, and his apologizing no fewer than five thousand times annoyed me so much I had to leave. Now he's insecure and telling me it happened because I'm so pretty.

———————

As irritating as he is sometimes, I'm staying with Ethan for now because he's firmly in my social circle and it would take way too much energy to avoid him all summer.

Eight. *Prepare for City Living.*

My phone vibrates. Gram.

"God, my grandmother gets obsessive when she's shopping." I ignore again.

"She is so funny," Lizzie says. "My grandma watches *Wheel of Fortune* and goes to Target when she needs an adventure."

"Yeah. My grandmother gets mud wraps in remote jungles when she needs an adventure," I say. "You should see her boyfriend, Denny. He's my mom's age and wears diamond rings on both pinkies."

"I can't stand jewelry on men," Lizzie says.

"This guy is drippy diamond rich. Actually, Drippy is a good name for him." I grab Lizzie's phone. Her list is pretty conventional. *Learn how to do a proper shot. Lose ten pounds.*

"Lizzie, this is more like a to-do list. You're so boring."

"Maddie, I've been trying to do a shot for months, and it always comes out my nose. Perfecting my shot technique is definitely a loose end."

"Okay, but please get rid of *lose ten pounds*. You're already skinny, and that's a waste of a good one."

"Hey, you wrote *change hair color*. That's equally lame."

"I crossed it out. I do need an edgier look for New York, though.

I was thinking of going strawberry blond." I wrap my unruly Medusa curls into a bun.

"No way. That would totally wash you out. My stylist says blue eyes, light skin, dark hair. Keep it brown."

"Your stylist lives in Connecticut," I say as my phone vibrates. It's a text from Gram. I need to talk to you right away. It's urgent. My stomach sinks. Gram has never texted me before. I run outside to call her.

"Gram, what's wrong?"

"You don't return my calls now? Are you too popular for your grandmother?"

"You just freaked me out. You never text me."

"You wouldn't answer your phone. I happen to know that thing is glued to you at all times."

My heart is still racing. "Can you not do that again, please?"

"So what are you doing that's so important?" Gram says.

"I was making my Loose Ends list."

"What's a Loose Ends list? Sounds fascinating."

"It's a list of the things I never got to in high school that I want to do before college."

"Like blow jobs?"

"Oh my God, Gram. You're disgusting."

"So, I need you all to come to my place tonight at seven sharp."

"But it's Friday. I have to drive everyone to a big party." Gram knows I'm the permanently designated driver of a powder-blue minivan.

"Hon, I have something important to share, and I need the

family here. Somebody else will have to drive your bimbo cheerleader friends." There's a strange urgency in her voice.

"You're making me nervous." Gram always has surprises up her sleeve, but she usually blurts them out before she can build any anticipation. "Did you call Mom?"

"I got your father. He said they would be here. I had to bribe him with Indian food and theater tickets, mooch that he is." Gram thinks Dad is a weird, socially awkward freeloader and that Mom ended up with him because she has the emotional fortitude of a newborn panda.

She's kind of right.

It's a good thing I haven't had to rely on my parents for much more than stargazing and shoe shopping. Gram takes care of everything. We shop, eat out, visit museums, take amazing trips, and meet famous people. Once, just to piss off Dad, Gram got her board member friend from the planetarium to give Jeb and me a private show.

Gram always delivers. So I will play her little game and go to her mystery meeting.

"Fine, Gram. I'll be there. Can you give me a clue?"

"No." She hangs up.

"I have to go into the city." I grab my stuff and hug Lizzie good-bye.

"Wait, what are you talking about?" Lizzie yanks my T-shirt.

"My grandmother needs us for some surprise announcement. I have a feeling she's engaged to Drippy."

"Why do you have to go into the city for that? Even the college people are coming to this party." Lizzie's whining. "Can you at least come later?"

"I have no idea when I'll be back. This is bizarre, even for her."

-ξ○ζ-

I find Rachel, my neighbor and former best friend, watching TV in our living room. Our mothers have been friends since we were in utero. Mom spends her afternoons at Rachel's house drinking while Bev eats. They accept each other unconditionally and dwell in the underworld of the American housewife, sipping cocktails, eating cupcakes, and watching prerecorded episodes of Kathie Lee and Hoda.

My friendship with Rachel became a struggle in fourth grade. My Barbies were not compatible with Rachel's LEGOs. We tried. We even built a LEGO yacht for the Barbies, but they just couldn't get comfortable.

By seventh grade, I had found Lizzie, Remy, and Abby. We dressed one another up like Barbies, and called ourselves the E's because our names ended with the *E* sound. We group texted and had sleepovers, studied together, and made appearances at all the parties.

There was no place for a Rachel among E's.

Of course, our mothers were devastated. They labeled me a snot and Rachel a victim of exclusion and bitchiness. So we sat them down one afternoon, when they were all tanked up on gin and banana bread, and explained the situation.

"Mom," Rachel started, "I am not a victim. I have friends. Most of them are boys, but that's because boys are the only ones who get my computer games. Maddie and I need to go our separate ways right now. We will always be friends, but our interests are diverging."

"Good word, Rach," I said. "I promise we'll reverge—"

"Converge," Rachel interrupted.

"Converge, when we're adults and have children and our interests don't matter anymore." And that ended that. We still hang out, just not in public. Rachel is a stargazer, too, because she's obsessed with *Star Trek* and always on the lookout for alien life-forms.

"Rach, Gram's up to her old cryptic tricks." She looks up from her box of donut holes. "She wants us all to go to her apartment tonight for an announcement."

"Maybe she's getting another tattoo." Rachel knows Gram.

"I hope not. I saw her ass a couple weeks ago, and the seahorse is sagging like someone whacked it with a flyswatter."

Dad comes up from the basement. "Astrid wants us at her place in two hours. I'm guessing she's going to announce her engagement to that Denny."

"The one with the pinkie rings?" Rachel wiggles her pinkies.

"I was thinking engagement, too," I say. "I'm calling him Drippy from now on. Can you imagine the wedding? Who gets the bigger diamond?"

Mom comes downstairs in a perfectly pressed dress, with her full makeup face on.

"Here, Rachel, take these to Bev." Mom takes a picture of cinnamon scones on a tray for her Pinterest page and wraps the tray in plastic.

I text the E's: Family emergency. Can't drive. Will try to meet you later. I ignore the flurry of responses. My friends aren't used to me bailing before a party. Ignore. Ignore. Ignore. The E's are panicked chickens with no head.

─§∘TWO∘3─

JEB MEETS US in Gram's lobby. He's a sophomore at Pratt, an art school in Brooklyn, where he listens to angry music and paints twisted crap. He looks ridiculous in his skinny jeans and silver hoop earrings.

It's even hotter in the city, and Dad is more sweaty and disheveled than usual. Mom gives Jeb a heaping bag of groceries and hugs him like she's welcoming him back from two tours of duty.

"Mom, stop. I saw you last week." Jeb has little tolerance for Mom. He should be nicer to her. The woman spends half her life baking him cookies.

"Nice to see you, too, Jeb," Dad says.

Mom's sister, Aunt Mary, walks in with my twin cousins, Brit and Janie, who are back from their first year at college. Brit is a whiny, homely brat who has nothing better to do than stalk Janie and me online. Janie is an honorary E because of her name and because she's funny and fun and fascinatingly urban.

"I guess Mother isn't getting enough attention," Aunt Mary says. We cram into the elevator. Aunt Mary is Brit in thirty years. Her black cloud of negativity nearly suffocates us all on the ride up to the penthouse floor. I don't blame my uncle for leaving her.

The elevator opens into Gram's living room, which is sleek and pristine with white furniture and painted white floors. There are color-coordinated collections on the walls, the shelves, and the tables, gathered from all corners of the globe, and each attached to a different adventure. Only Astrid North O'Neill would set a carved Swiss music box next to an Argentinian peyote jar and a Chinese oracle shell, all because they share a shade of eggplant.

Mom's younger brother, Uncle Billy, pours white wine. His husband, Wes, gets up from the piano.

"Baby girl, look at you." Wes kisses my cheeks. He's tall and dirty blond and ruggedly handsome. Janie and I never quite understood how Wes fell for our skinny, sullen, four-eyed uncle.

"Where's Gram?" I ignore another text from Abby.

"We have no idea. Titi says she's staying locked in her room until everyone gets here," Wes says. Gram's housekeeper walks out of the butler's pantry carrying a tray of macaroons. Aunt Mary pulls her aside and berates her with whispers. Titi shakes her head repeatedly, sets down the cookie tray, and escapes to the kitchen.

Brit is texting and completely ignoring Great-aunt Rose. Granted,

Aunt Rose tells the same ten stories over and over again, but Brit could at least have the decency to pretend she's listening.

"I'm assuming pinkie ring Denny isn't here yet," Wes says.

"I've renamed him Drippy," I say.

"You'd think Billy could find something to say to his own damn family." Wes nods toward Uncle Billy, who is sitting on the piano bench studying *The Wall Street Journal*. "I mean, make an effort at least. Look at Aaron charming the pants off Mary."

Dad nods enthusiastically as Aunt Mary makes a face. Dad has no family to speak of—he was an only child, and his parents are dead. They were antisocial, so Dad barely knows his relatives. This is my whole family, for better or for worse.

"Do you like Brit's outfit?" Janie says, stuffing a macaroon into her mouth.

Wes laughs a little too loudly at Brit's ensemble of pleated, high-water khakis and metallic gladiator sandals.

Titi rings a little bell and instructs us to go into the library. She slides the fake bookcase wall in the living room to the right, revealing a hidden passageway where we used to act out all kinds of Anne Frank, Underground Railroad dramatizations. I follow Janie into the library, where Gram's longtime lawyer fidgets with a stack of papers. We sit in a semicircle of chairs arranged in front of the desk.

"Eww." I elbow Janie and point out the lawyer's crusty scalp.

Gram walks in and stands behind the desk. She pauses for a moment, taking in the visual of her entire family seated before her.

"Okay, Mother, what's up?" Aunt Mary breaks the silence.

"Hello, beloved family, and thank you for coming." Gram welcomes us like she's giving a speech to a foreign delegation.

"Where's Denny?" Aunt Rose calls out. "I hear you two are getting married."

"Oh stop, Rose, for God's sake." Aunt Rose looks wounded. "Give me more credit than that. I was only seeing that buffoon because he had great opera seats. I told you after Martin died I would never marry again, and I won't." She shakes her head. "Now, listen. I called you all here for a reason."

"What's the reason?" Aunt Rose yells. Wes stifles a laugh.

"Rose, let me speak." Gram beckons the lawyer to join her. She links her arm through his. He towers above her petite frame.

"Okay, here I go. Kids, I brought you here because I'm sick. Well, I'm basically dying. I have pancreatic cancer, and in case you don't know, that's one of the bad ones."

My stomach drops. A thick lump forms in my throat, and I can't breathe.

All the blood exits Aunt Mary's face. "Why are you telling us like this?"

"Mary, I wanted to tell you all at the same time. I just found out a couple weeks ago. I needed time to make some big decisions."

We sit, motionless, until Dad breaks the silence. "Well, thank God we're in the best city in the world for medical care," he says. "We'll get you into Sloan Kettering this week. My buddy is a top-notch oncologist there."

"I don't want to see your friend, Aaron. Could you just let me say what I brought you here to say?" She takes a deep breath and smiles. "I've booked us all on an eight-week cruise. It leaves right after Maddie graduates." She looks at me. "I'm still working on finding you a dress, by the way."

I can't tell if she's trying to be funny, if all of this is a sick Gram joke.

"Mom, we're not going on a cruise. We need to figure out treatment options," Uncle Billy says.

"There are no good treatment options. I'm not sitting around some hospital room with fluorescent lighting, stuck to a chemo drip for the last few months of my life. I've booked the cruise. It's done."

"What makes you think we can drop everything and take a cruise?" Aunt Mary raises her flinty voice. "You are not thinking clearly."

"Well, let's see. Aaron's a teacher, you and Trish are homemakers, a term I use loosely, and the kids have summer break. Wessy and Bill can turn over the business to the staff for a while. I'm thinking very clearly, dear."

The air is trying to get into my lungs, but it can't get past the growing lump.

"Ralph has a few confidentiality documents for you to sign before I continue. Titi, I need a little nibble of a macaroon, dear."

"Mom, this is absurd. What documents?" Aunt Mary is shouting now. "Don't you think we should talk to your doctors?"

"Mary, when have you ever known me to involve you in my medical affairs?" Gram's voice stays calm, but she's getting annoyed. She crosses her arms and watches Crusty Head pass out the documents.

I stare down at the stapled stack of papers with glazed eyes. My stomach quakes violently. I've never known how to process horrible news. When I was seven, I watched my Jack Russell terrier, Bub, get squished by my own school bus when he was running to greet me. That one required therapy with a woman who used puppets to talk about death. Dad's mother died a few months later, but it didn't bother me, for some reason. She was kind of mean and hard-edged, and she smelled like grease. The puppet lady said I probably couldn't grieve her death properly because I was still grieving Bub. Then when I was thirteen, Grandpa Martin had a heart attack and died in his golf cart twenty minutes after he and I had shared a tuna sandwich. I was so traumatized, I refused to go to his funeral.

All of that was awful. But this is my gram. She's supposed to get me settled at NYU and take me to brunch and have my future college friends over for dinner parties. She is supposed to walk me down the aisle when I get married and plan my exotic honeymoon.

I feel like puking, but I just start sobbing. I can't help it. It hurts so much. The stupid document gets blurry, and tears drip shamelessly onto the paper. I hang my head, and my hair covers my face, the paper, everything.

"Oh, my dear Maddie girl." Gram comes over. Janie starts bawling, too. "Oh, my babies." Gram kneels down on the floor in front of us. I focus on her hand, her blue veins popping out of waxy skin, her nails, still perfectly painted red. Her beloved sapphire, big as a bird's egg, seems silly now on a hand that's about to be dead.

Across the room, Mom makes a terrifying huffing sound.

"Oh, lord, Trish is hyperventilating." Gram stands up. "Titi, please bring my children some cocktails. I am old, guys. Death happens."

It takes twenty minutes for Janie and me to gain control of ourselves. As usual, my stomach is a mess. Mom has a drink. Uncle Billy has a drink. Wes holds Uncle Billy's hand and reads the document. Sour-faced Aunt Mary and Brit sit with their arms crossed. Aunt Rose asks Dad if he knows her husband, Karl. Jeb stares straight ahead. Crusty Head eats a macaroon.

My phone vibrates on my lap. **OMG Abby peed on my foot. Ethan wandering. Sooooo many hot college boys. Where the fffff are u?** I cannot deal with Remy's text right now.

Gram returns to her spot behind the desk and clears her throat. "Okay, where was I?" she says. "Oh, yes: I'm dying. And I want to take you on a cruise. Don't worry, it's not one of those tacky, all-you-can-eat buffet ships. It's a lovely ship, state of the art. And all the passengers are dying, or accompanying someone who is dying."

"Well, that's terrible, Astrid," Aunt Rose says.

"No, Rose. It's not terrible at all. We, the dying, get to plan the entire voyage. We get to customize it to satisfy our final wishes. Maybe we'll tie up some loose ends around the globe or add a few items to our bucket lists." Gram winks at me. I fake smile back. "The best part is while we're at sea, and when I'm ready, I will go to my private cabin where a trained physician will inject me with potassium and a sedative. Then I will go to sleep, and you charming people will see me off."

"Oh my God, Gram. You're freaking me out." Janie buries her face in her hands.

"There's nothing to freak out about," Gram says. I clutch Janie's sweaty hand. "They will bag me and release me into the sea, my last wishes fulfilled. No invasive, silly, life-prolonging meddling. No pain. It's death with dignity, the way it should be."

"Mom, there is no such thing as a death-with-dignity cruise ship. You're goddamn delusional. Aaron, do you have psychiatrist friends at Sloan Kettering, too?" Uncle Billy is turning red.

"Ralph, will you tell these jackasses the truth? I'm exhausted."

Everyone looks at Crusty Head. He steps forward. "Don't kill the messenger, folks. Astrid has indeed booked you all on a ship that caters to the dying. It *is* technically a death-with-dignity ship, part of a kind of underground movement. Trust me, this is all recent news to me, too." Ralph pauses and neatens the stack of papers. "The nondisclosure agreement also protects Astrid, since she has been a benefactor of the movement for a few years now, and she would prefer to keep her involvement confidential."

"What are you even talking about?" Aunt Mary says. "Speak English, Ralph. Are you saying there are ships where they kill people and throw them overboard? And Mom has been bankrolling this?"

"Not overboard, Mary. There's a cute little door they slide you through. You're so melodramatic." Gram walks around the desk and stands next to Ralph. "I had the privilege of joining my friend Ruth on her ship. We took quite a ride around the Horn of Africa."

"You said Ruth had a heart attack at the McDonald's drive-thru," Mom says.

"That was her alibi. Mine will be more nuanced. So that's it. I have a fantastic 'Astrid's Last Hurrah Mystery Tour' planned for us, kids. Are you in or out? I need to know tonight."

"How much is this going to cost?" Aunt Mary says.

"Oh, of course Mary brings up the money," Uncle Billy says, throwing his arms up in the air.

Aunt Mary glares at Uncle Billy. "It's a valid—"

"I don't know." Gram cuts Aunt Mary off. "It's a lot. Don't worry, there's plenty more for you to squander when I'm gone. Now, if you'll excuse me, I need a minute." Gram leaves through the secret passageway.

"Nice going, Mary," Mom says. "You know what? Maybe this isn't about you. Maybe Mother is serious about all of this."

"Oh, shut up, Trish. I still don't believe she's dying. She's a drama queen. I can tell you I will not be going on a death-with-dignity cruise. I just can't believe she's doing this."

Mom shakes her head back and forth violently. "No!" she shouts. "Mary, you will not do this. It's always about you and your life and your issues and what's going to inconvenience Mary. So, for once, just stop. She may or may not be dying, but we're going to do what she wants." Dad puts his arms around Mom and plants kisses all over her face.

"Gag." Janie turns away from them.

"Tell me about it," I whisper. "But good for Mom, though, standing up to her." I nod toward Aunt Mary, who sits staring straight ahead.

"What are we going to do with the business?" Uncle Billy's face is still flushed.

"We'll figure it out. Donna can take over," Wes says. "And we'll find a temporary chef. Whatever, Billy. We need to do what Assy wants to do." Only Wes is allowed to call Gram Assy.

Brit sits hunched in her chair, texting furiously, with an ugly scowl on her face.

"Brit, come sit with us," I try.

"No thanks, Maddie. Don't you have a party to attend?" asks the cyberstalker.

"Did you not hear anything Gram said? She's dying, Brit. Gram is *dying*." Janie's eye makeup is smeared all over her face. I grab a tissue from the desk and dab around her eyes. Janie has always been the prettiest cousin. She looks like her dad, blond and cute and Scandinavian. Brit got all the ugly Aunt Mary troll genes.

I used to be so jealous that the twins lived two blocks away from Gram. She kept snacks for them in her pantry and had Titi fix them dinner on school nights. *Please let me live with you,* I begged her. *I won't be difficult like the twins.* She always responded the same way: *Your parents wouldn't like that very much.*

The room buzzes with all kinds of tones and salty language. Nobody's crying anymore. There's too much to complain about.

It feels like we've been sitting in these folding chairs for hours. Janie pulls me toward her and whispers, "How the hell are you going to do this cruise? You can't even be in the same room with Grandpa's ashes."

They burned Grandpa Martin's body like he was a marshmallow. I went back to the puppet lady because I couldn't handle knowing his ashes were in Gram's apartment. I was terrified somebody would knock them over and my quiet, red-faced grandfather who loved golf and whisky and Irish music would spill out onto the floor.

"We don't have a choice, Janie. Right? I mean, do we?" The throat lump has migrated to my stomach. The anxiety is almost unbearable.

"Why does Gram have to be so over-the-top about every single thing?" Janie says.

"You sound like your mother."

"Never say that again."

The main library door slides open. It's Titi with a man I've never seen before.

"That is definitely not Titi's husband." Wes elbows me in the ribs.

"No. I don't know who that is," I whisper. I've met Titi's husband. Joe is a male version of Titi, short and squat with glasses and orthopedic shoes. This guy is tall and broad, and older, maybe early eighties, and he has the longest salt-and-pepper dreads I've ever seen. He's wearing a fitted white T-shirt and army-green cargo pants with leather sandals, and turquoise rings that somehow suit him, a rare exception to the guys-look-stupid-in-jewelry rule.

Dread Guy gives us all a nod and sits on the desk next to where Crusty Head is standing. I can't imagine Gram would want a random stranger sitting on her imported mahogany desk with gold etchings.

Gram comes back in, probably from standing in the secret passageway with her ear against the wall. She's still so normal looking in her tailored jeans and cropped leather jacket with the double strand of pearls. How can she have cancer?

"What's the plan?" she says. "Who's in, who's out? I have a lot to do, so let's get this settled."

"Who's the black man?" Aunt Rose blurts.

Wes looks at me and, with a smirk, mouths, *Oh. My. God.*

"You don't recognize him? It's been a long time, I suppose. It's Bob Johns, Rose."

Aunt Rose squints as if squinting will help her remember this person. "Is that you, Bob? My goodness, you're as handsome as ever," she says. "What on earth is Bob Johns doing here?"

Dread Guy jumps off the desk, pulls Aunt Rose to her feet, and picks her up into a big bear hug. Aunt Rose giggles and gives the guy an awkward kiss on the chin.

"Who the hell is Bob Johns?" Wes and Janie whisper at the same time.

I shrug.

"Everyone, this is Mr. Robert Amos Johns, the love of my life." Gram extends her arm toward the guy like a magician's assistant and looks up at his dread-framed face.

"Funny, Astrid. The jokes keep coming," Dad says.

"Nope. Not a joke. Bob is the love of my life." Gram takes a sip of Uncle Billy's drink.

Janie pinches my leg.

"Mom, stop. We're having a tough enough time here," Aunt Mary says through clenched teeth.

"Hi, folks," Bob Johns says. "I'm thinking this might not have been a good night to meet you all." He has some sort of an accent and a deep baritone voice.

"Bob's coming with us," Gram announces, slapping Bob on the back.

"I'm done," Aunt Mary says as she grabs Brit by the arm. "Not happening, Mom. This is ridiculous. Dad was the love of your life. *Dad*. Remember him?" She pauses for a moment as if her body wants to stay, but she won't let it. "Come on, Jane."

Gram walks over to Aunt Mary and faces her. She puts her hands on her shoulders and looks up at her miserable face. "My funny little Mary Mae. It's okay if you don't approve," Gram says as if she anticipated Aunt Mary's reaction and practiced her response a hundred times. "I love you just the same. Always have. Always will."

Gram turns to Brit, who looks like she's going to hurl. I can't tell if she's sad or mad. "I love you, too, my sweet baby girl." Gram tucks a strand of hair behind Brit's ear and smiles. Brit can't bring herself to look Gram in the eye.

Aunt Mary's lip trembles furiously. She motions for Janie to get up.

"I'm going on the cruise," Janie announces, as she stands to follow Brit.

"Enough, Jane," Aunt Mary snarls.

Aunt Mary and Brit storm out. Janie hugs Gram and follows them. "See you on the water," she says.

"Keep it real," I yell. Whatever that means.

We're all tired. Gram tells us about how she met Bob at a jazz club where he was playing trumpet and they had to keep their relationship a secret from her uptight parents and the rest of the backwards-ass world of the 1940s. I watch her lips move and wonder what the

23

cancer looks like inside her. It is a dream. I will wake up and she will be fine.

—&o&—

It's nine o'clock, but it feels like midnight.

"Good to meet you, dude." Jeb gives Bob Johns a fist pump and grabs his bag of groceries. "Gram, email the plan." I realize Jeb hasn't said a thing the entire time, which isn't unusual. Mom always says to leave him alone, that he's an introvert and he needs to get his energy from a quiet place inside himself and that she can relate. I think he gets his energy from paint fumes and really good weed.

Our exit is full of awkward hugs and misplaced kisses and small talk. How do you leave an evening like this in any normal way? I look back as the elevator opens. Gram is standing there, her arm around Bob Johns, his arm around her. They grin and wave, as if they have been doing it this way every day for sixty years.

—ᣜ∘ THREE ∘ᣝ—

I DRIVE THE minivan to Connecticut while my parents snuggle in the back. Mom is talking in her baby voice about how she's in shock while Dad rubs her neck and goes on and on about his friend at Sloan Kettering. I decide to dump them off at home and go to the party.

By the time I get there, everybody is in the pool.

Remy runs up and tackles me. She's soaked, and it feels cold and awful, but it wakes me up. It's good to be back to my normal state of being.

Yesterday everything was perfect. I took my CPR class for lifeguarding with Lizzie and got my nails done. I helped Ethan with his math homework, we made out a little and ate pizza, and I organized my summer clothes. I wish I had appreciated yesterday more.

I could use a hug.

I get a text from Janie. Mom and Brit are def not going on that cruise. FYI. Thank you, God!

I scan the crowd of bobbing wet heads for Ethan. I don't know when or how I'm going to tell him that I'm leaving for the entire summer.

I spot his yellow baseball hat moving back and forth. At first it looks like he's dancing. Then I see the misshapen head of Ellie-the-sophomore, who pushes her way into every party. She is not cute. Her head is shaped like a pineapple. My boyfriend is making out with Ellie-the-sophomore in the unmistakable way Ethan always makes out, with his head ramming back and forth. My brain can't begin to wrap itself around this little surprise.

I back into the shadows of the pool shed and gather my thoughts. If this were any other night, I would have ripped that girl off my boyfriend and yelled *Ethan is a premature ejaculator* for everyone to hear. But this isn't any other night. It's the worst night of my life.

Why did I leave? I should have stayed with my gram.

I peek around the shed and see Ethan and Pineapple sitting on a lounge chair chugging from red cups. Remy and Abby run right past them, holding hands, probably about to pee on each other's feet again. Then it hits me. Ethan needs this girl to boost his pathetic ego.

I sneak over to the other side of the pool and pull Lizzie off Kyle. She's confused, but I give her the look we give in emergencies and she follows me. I point out Ethan and Pineapple. Lizzie looks ready to dig their eyes out. In a split second, she's processed what this means:

No more meeting up at Starbucks. No more four of us going to the movies and sitting by the lake with leftover popcorn. No more four-way texts to discuss the next plan. Lizzie's life is about to turn upside down.

"I'm done, Lizzie."

"You need to kick that ugly girl's ass. How dare she mess with us?" I grab Lizzie and pull her toward them, as Pineapple tosses her stringy hair and laughs, oblivious to our approach. I'm right behind her when I spot Abby and Remy running in our direction.

I tap Ethan on the shoulder. He turns. His face looks like he just walked into a surprise party, but the ones shouting surprise are maggot-covered demons. I should say something to ruin him, but I don't like him or hate him enough.

"Hey, Eth." I smile. "Hi, Ellie," I say with unwavering lightness. They don't move. "I see you two are getting to know each other. That's really special. I wish you both the very best. I'm sure you'll be so happy together."

I turn and walk away before Ethan has a chance to grovel, and I essentially spend the next twenty minutes in a headlock until I promise, double promise, and swear on my family's life that I won't kill myself over Ethan. The E's finally let me go.

I send a quick Please pick up the E's text to the Sober Sisters, our school's designated driver club—the Sober Sisters' summer just got a lot busier. I have three missed texts from Rachel. What's the news? What's the news? and Hellllloooo? What's the news? I text back: Tonight was a star imploding after a nuclear meltdown on the night before the SATs and pull away to the strangely soothing noise of my hundred closest friends as the clamor blends with the beat of the music.

When I get to my driveway, I see ever-dependable Rachel sitting on her front step.

"What happened?" She unwraps the cinnamon scone tray and hands me a bottle of water as I plop down next to her.

I don't even know how to begin, so I defy the stupid nondisclosure document and tell her everything. Unlike my other friends, Rachel never judges. She's the only one who doesn't make fun of my chronic stomach problems, or irritable bowel syndrome, as Mom likes to call it. She knows all my issues, like how I'm revolted by slurping sounds and people who lick their fingers. She knows I'm freaked out by death, and the possibility of death, and the way hospitals smell. She gets that I don't drink because I hate watching Mom slur her words and laugh like a fool.

Rachel is my secret keeper.

"And to top it all off, I ruined another thong because of my stupid irritable bowel syndrome," I finish.

"I don't get why you torture yourself with thongs" is all she says about that.

Rachel reacts to the news about Gram the way I hoped she would. She shares my grief. The E's will be sad for me, sort of, but they don't know Gram the way Rachel does. They will go directly from telling me they're sorry my grandma is sick and they're sure she'll be fine, to their own place of sadness that I'll be gone during that critical stretch of human development known as the summer between high school and college.

"What are you going to tell everybody?"

"I guess that I'm taking a spontaneous family cruise," I say. "People are used to me jetting off to Bermuda."

"Remember when we were ten and Gram invited me to Bermuda?" Rachel says. "We went down to those underground caves, and she surprised me for my birthday with a candlelit table and chocolate cake on the beach."

"That was a good birthday."

"I always wished I had a grandmother like her. My grandma was diabetic with face warts and an amputated foot. She scared the hell out of me, and I was glad when she died. I'm sorry, that's terrible, but it's true," Rachel says.

"I know. She scared me, too."

"What about when we went down to Gram's apartment in the city and she invited that guy who actually knew some of the original *Star Trek* cast members? Titi made us dinner, and the guy sat there all night while I grilled him."

"Yeah, you said you'd marry that guy someday," I say.

"That's right." Rachel laughs. "I should look him up."

I'm glad I trusted Rachel with my secret.

We tap our water bottles together and toast to Gram, the most amazing person we have ever known.

-ξ∘ჳ-

I barely sleep. Ethan drunk-texts apologies all night long. I eventually text back Stop bothering me. It's over, but he doesn't get the hint. I just want him to go away.

It's not even seven when I go down to the kitchen and find Dad drafting an email to the principal at his school, telling her he can't teach the summer robotics camp due to a family "situation."

I catch a train to Grand Central. I'm in no shape to drive. It's weird to be on the train early on a Saturday morning with the deli workers and nurses going about their normal routines. People are reading newspapers and sipping coffee, laughing and making small talk, and I kind of hate them for not feeling the same anxiety I'm feeling right now.

The elevator opens to Bob Johns sleeping on the sectional with my favorite blanket. I try to sneak past him and go straight to Gram's room, but he opens his eyes.

"Hey there, Maddie." He knows my name.

"Hi." I have no idea what to say to this guy.

"You here to check on your gram?"

"Yeah."

"Janie's in there with her. She came late last night with all her luggage. She says she's moving in until the cruise."

Janie beat me here again.

I sit on the edge of the ottoman and take a yoga breath. I need to get my shit together before I go in there.

"Do you live here now?" I ask Bob Johns.

"No, no. I wanted to make sure Astrid was okay. She was nervous about telling you all the news." I'm pretty sure the accent is Jamaican.

"I'm sorry my family acted like a bunch of idiots last night. Gram kept you a secret. We had no idea."

"Yeah, my kids were pretty surprised when I told them I was going on a cruise with an old girlfriend," Bob says. "And then when I told them she was a white Park Avenue debutante, they nearly fell to the floor laughing."

"That's better than my aunt Mary's reaction. Trust me, she's mean to everyone."

"She wasn't mean. She was just being protective of her mother."

I don't even know what to say to that, so I blurt out the first thing that comes to my mind. "How long did you and Gram date?"

"About three years."

"Wow. That's a long time."

"Yes, but nobody was going to be okay with Astrid North and Bob Johns living happily ever after. We had a good run, though, with our wild jazz club friends."

"My grandpa Martin preferred Irish music."

"Would you believe I knew your grandfather?" Bob smiles. "He wanted to meet me, so we got together for a beer one night and joked about your gram."

I try to picture this big dreadlocked guy with quiet, balding Grandpa Martin.

"He was a good guy. I'm thinking he and my wife are smiling down on us from heaven."

"Do you think Gram's as sick as she says?"

His eyes fill with pity, and I know the answer before he says it. "Yes, kiddo. I do."

We sit for a minute in silence. All I can think about is what cancer looks like on the inside. Does it have a color?

"How about we have one of Titi's gigantic chocolate chip muffins?" Bob says.

"Not hungry. I think I'll go get into bed with them."

The room is dark. Gram loves her remote-control blackout shades. I feel my way over to the bed and crawl between Janie and Gram, who is snoring softly, making *p-p-p* sounds.

I can't believe this is happening.

–꿈o꿈–

We spend the day going through stuff in Gram's apartment. She's planning to have a farewell open house weekend for all her friends and neighbors before she leaves for the cruise. She'll tell them about the cancer, but leave out the part about the death-with-dignity ship.

"Look, girlies," Gram says. She holds up a photo of Janie, Brit, Jeb, and me on the sprawling porch of Aunt Rose's Charleston house. We're all under the age of five and completely naked. "I think I'll post this one online."

"Why are we naked?" I say.

"You were always naked," Gram says. "Luckily the sun wasn't as strong back then, although your neurotic father was obsessed with sunscreen." She stares back down at the photo. "Oh, those were the days."

Every picture and random relic holds memories. There's the pink sand in crystal vases from Gram's Bermuda house and the shadow box with our locks of baby hair and the collage of our traditional Christmas Day photos, always taken in Central Park.

"What happened to Bob Johns?" I ask, realizing he left the apartment at some point.

"You know, you can call him Bob," Gram says.

"I like Bob Johns. It has a nice ring to it."

"Are you girls okay with Bob coming along on the trip?"

"As long as he knows we're your favorites," Janie says.

I honestly don't know what to think of my grandmother's long-lost boyfriend. He seems nice, but he's showing up at kind of a bad time.

"Look how hideous I was," I say to Gram as I hold up a picture of me with blue-banded braces and choppy hair.

"You come here," Gram says. I get up from the floor and sit facing Gram on the edge of her bed.

I look into her blue eyes. They're the very same eyes as my own.

"You are gorgeous and smart and full of life. You always have been. Now you need to work on finally getting out of your high school comfort zone. I want you to savor every minute of our adventure."

"I've been out of my comfort zone. Lots of times."

"Honey, skiing in Switzerland and swimming in Bermuda are about as comfortable as you can get. We're going to see the world. And I want you to do it without your scrunch face."

"What scrunch face?"

"The one you put on when I try to take you for dim sum in Chinatown."

"That place is gross."

"That's my point. If you view the world as gross, you'll never be able to enjoy it. Lose the scrunch face."

"Tell that to Jeb."

"No, he's not scrunch face, he's downer face."

"I'm glad you have face nicknames for all of us. What about Janie?"

"Janie's clueless face."

"Oh my God, Gram. That's so mean." Janie looks up from her stack of pictures.

"You need to get a clue, Jane Margaret, or the world will eat you up," Gram says.

"Okay, wrinkle face." Janie leans over and squeezes Gram's cheek.

"Hey, these wrinkles are the badge of a life well lived, missy. Watch it, or I'll kick your little behind to the streets. Or even worse, back to your mother's apartment."

—Ɛ∘ FOUR ∘Ȝ—

WE'RE ON THE plane to Gram's Bermuda house, and Janie and Jeb and I are scattered about coach, the plane version of the kids' table at Thanksgiving. The rest of them get first class, compliments of Gram, who is already in Bermuda with Titi, Titi's husband, and Bob Johns.

The past three weeks are a blur. I muddled through school, distracted by the Gram news and the Ethan drama. I refused to answer his texts, which made him text me more. Thanks to the E's, Ellie-the-sophomore will forever be known as Pineapple, even if she never knows why. The E's had a hard time with me leaving at first, but they used my departure as an excuse to celebrate. Lizzie threw a crazy graduation party the weekend after finals. The night ended with my friends piled on top of me chanting *don't go* over and over again until

I couldn't wait to go. The pressure of bodies must have been too much for Abby, who puked all over me. That was the grand finale.

Gram's open house was epic. According to Titi, Gram invited people to take something from her apartment to remember her by. There was a steady stream of Gram's beloved groupies, from Saks lunch counter workers and limo drivers to socialites and famous jazz singers. People lingered and told funny stories, and Gram gave everyone souvenirs from her vast collections. It was as if having an object that belonged to Astrid North O'Neill would infuse a little bit of fabulous into their lives.

Janie sticks her boobs out and flirts with the guy next to me until he agrees to swap seats with her. I'm not sure why she bothered, since she might as well be sitting by herself. She obsessively picks at her split ends and is barely talking to me. I'm thinking it's because her horrible mother and sister abandoned her and haven't even opened the DVD Wes made of Gram saying her good-byes after they refused to answer Gram's calls.

"What is it?" I say, hoping she'll stop the annoying picking.

"Why can't Gram just have a regular funeral at the Episcopal church with a pretty casket and those round flower arrangements like everyone else?" She looks at me.

"Because she's Gram."

Janie sighs.

"Maddie?" she says a few minutes later.

"Yeah."

"Do you think I'm clueless?"

"No, not at all." She's so pitiful looking. I can't stand to see her like this. I grab her calf and yank on her shoe. "You're only clueless when it comes to wearing good plane shoes. Why are you wearing heels? You'll burst the raft if we crash."

"I'll take my chances," Janie says before she brushes a pile of split ends onto my tray table and I smack her.

—ξο3—

The cliff-side Bermuda mansion feels like home. It belongs to the North family estate, passed down by generations of people with loads of money—"old money." Nobody seems to know where it came from in the first place, whether it was shady money or hard-earned. It's just there now, in trusts and offshore accounts, feeding off itself and swelling ever greater.

I'm so tired; I leave the dinner table during Wes and Uncle Billy's argument over whether they should cancel their cable service while we're gone. I make a beeline for the guesthouse, lie on the daybed under the ceiling fan, and fall asleep immediately. I wake to Gram standing over me, an angel in her white nightgown, holding a bowl of applesauce with raisins and a tiny silver spoon. It's just the two of us in the guesthouse as twilight drapes Bermuda in dusky pink.

"Hi, Maddie girl." Gram sits on the edge of the daybed and hands me the applesauce. "I wanted to come talk a little before we go. I dropped a big bomb on you, and it's been quite a whirlwind."

"I thought you were going to outlive us all." I sit up and eat a spoonful of applesauce.

"Well, you know I'll always be with you, nagging you in your ear to stand up straighter and smile more and worry less." She covers me with a blue blanket. "Who knows, maybe I'll come back to life as something adorable, like a little chipmunk, and I'll pop up when you least expect it to make you smile."

"Now you know every time I see a chipmunk, I'll think it's you."

"Good. I'll be sure to scurry over next time you're with that hunky boyfriend of yours."

I set the applesauce bowl on the floor and turn toward Gram. "Okay, first of all, nobody uses the word *hunky*. And second of all, we broke up. It was so unimportant; I didn't even bother to tell you. Oh, and in case you were wondering, I'm still a virgin."

"Still a virgin, huh? I thought you people were doing it at thirteen these days."

"No. That's just Janie."

"I've always said, if girls don't get attention from their fathers, they'll find it in all kinds of sordid ways. I sure did." Gram gives me her naughty schoolgirl grin. "So why would anyone break up with my darling girl?"

"I broke up with him. I caught him kissing a sophomore at a party. He was lame anyway."

"Bastard. I hope he was a bad kisser." Gram pulls herself closer and rests her head on my shoulder.

"Let's put it this way: He kissed like a jackhammer dipped in cheap beer."

"The next one will be better," Gram says. "I have a good feeling."

I look out over the sea and the famous pink sands of Bermuda. On the horizon, all shades of violet and orange stretch up and fade together. The sky rounds over the ocean, and I feel like I'm in a snow globe, like our house on the cliff is alone in a tiny, fragile, glass-domed world.

"Snow globe moment?" I say to Gram. Our family of stargazers says that a lot.

"It's funny, Jebby just said that a little while ago. But I always feel like I'm in a snow globe here. It's my happy place, always has been."

"So why are we leaving? Why wouldn't you stay here in your bed and get nurses?" I flop back on a pile of pillows and Gram slides next to me.

"Because I have things on my Loose Ends list, silly, and time is ticking. And I suppose I'm a little afraid to die. It brings me comfort knowing I can go on my terms."

"This is so hard, Gram."

"I know, Maddie girl. But I've lost a lot of people in my life. I've seen how people can go on and on, long past their expiration dates. Your mom and Aunt Mary and Uncle Billy had to watch my mother suffer for years." She shakes her head slowly. "The woman was too damn stubborn to go to a nursing home, so she festered in her apartment, and I was forced to take care of her. I'm not going to put you or myself through that hell."

We're quiet for a minute. Gram rolls onto her side and faces me.

"We had the opposite with your poor grandfather. He went so

quick he didn't have time to say good-bye. See? I'm the lucky one." She shifts a little, and her protruding hipbone stabs my thigh.

"Wow, your breasts are perky." She squeezes my boob. "Poor Janie inherited my big bosom."

"Ow, that hurts, you old pervert."

"Hey, Mads, one more thing. I want to make sure you understand that this trip is not about poor, dying Gram." She looks at me, her face serious. "That is not what I want from all this. I want to have some laughs, and get you people out of your boring little lives. This is not about dying. It's about living. Do you understand?"

"Yes. I get it. But I'm offended. Drinking chai at Starbucks and watching my friends argue over who gets the front seat is *not* boring."

But the truth is, I don't know if I get it. I don't know if I get any of this.

The darkness gathers around Gram and me. We snuggle on the daybed and stretch out our snow globe moment as long as we can before we both fall asleep.

❧ FIVE ☙

WE'RE THE ONLY ones standing on the departure platform, and Dad won't stop talking about how big the ship is. Gram had told us that they repurposed a former big-name cruise ship for these death-with-dignity trips and there's a huge wait list, but they only choose a few people for each sailing.

"I can't even imagine the square footage of this baby," Dad says. "Although I could probably figure it out. Let me think."

"Nobody cares," Jeb says. Jeb's always been weird, but I don't remember him being this irritable all the time.

A nervous little man with a thick mustache and black plastic glasses scurries out to greet us. "Welcome to the Wishwell, everybody. Where is our guest of honor?"

Gram is still in the limo saying good-bye to Titi and her husband. How do you say good-bye to someone you've known for decades and are never going to see again? Titi was more than a housekeeper. She was Gram's best friend. I don't know how they're finding the strength to do this.

"She'll be here in a minute," Uncle Billy says. He and Wes prop up Aunt Rose, who seems to be having a hard time with the trip so far. She's more frail and confused than ever.

"Rose never should have come. This is too much for her," Dad whispers to Mom and me.

"She wanted to be here, Aaron," Mom says. "They're joined at the hip. She's not going to leave my mother now." Uncle Billy gives Aunt Rose a sip of his coffee and wipes the dribbles from her chin with his sleeve. "It's just the stress of traveling is hard on a ninety-three-year-old woman. She'll be okay once she's settled in her cabin."

Gram climbs out of the limo and wipes her eyes with a handkerchief. Titi sticks her arm out the window to wave.

"What are Titi and Joe going to do now that Titi's not her housekeeper?" Janie asks Wes. We watch Gram blow kisses at the limo as it disappears down the deserted street.

"She's sending them to Hawaii. That's Titi's prize for putting up with Assy all those years. The woman's a saint."

"Titi loves Gram," I say.

"Assy loves Titi more," Wes says.

Mustache Guy introduces himself as Eddie and steps forward with an announcement.

"Okay, listen up, everybody. As confidentiality is of utmost importance to the Wishwell guests and crew, we ask that you relinquish all electronic devices, including phones." We literally gasp. "Don't worry, you will get them back. We promise to keep your equipment in a safe until you've completed your journey. If you need to make a call or text, you have fifteen minutes to do so now. Sorry for the inconvenience."

Wes and Uncle Billy nearly drop Aunt Rose into the crack between the landing and the sludgy water. "What the hell?" Uncle Billy throws up his hands. "How can they do this?"

Wes runs to the end of the dock and back like a lost ostrich and frantically starts texting and tweeting. Uncle Billy calls their catering assistant, Donna, and yells at her to wake the hell up, it's an emergency.

Nobody takes the time to argue with Eddie. We all realize that would be wasting the last precious moments of our contact with the civilized world.

Mom calls Aunt Mary, because Janie refuses to waste time on her mother. Dad calls Bev. Janie and Jeb sit on the cold walkway and text furiously. It's a symphony of words silent and spoken propelling into cyberspace: No signal. Won't be able to talk. Text me so I get your texts as soon as I get back. Going to exotic places. Just found out no cell service.

"Don't worry, Mary, we'll take good care of her." Mom pauses and hands the phone to Gram. She talks in whispers to her firstborn daughter. I only hope Aunt Mary is being nice.

It's the middle of the night, although my family doesn't seem to mind waking up the entire East Coast. I lose time trying to figure out which of the E's to call so I decide to group text them all. Urgent. We just found out the cruise doesn't have cell service OR an Internet café. I won't be able to contact you until I get back. I love you all so so so much. Please don't forget about me. This is so hard. OMG. I LOVE YOU. Don't do anything I wouldn't do. Ha Ha. XOXO

I pull up my various accounts and post a simple sentence: Going on a world cruise with the fam. No service. Have a good summer, suckers. ☺ I immediately regret using the word *suckers,* but it's not worth changing at this point.

Bob Johns is on the phone with one of his kids. "I love you, too, sweetheart. Give the little ones kisses. I'll see you in LA."

The only ones not irritated by the device abandonment order are Gram, because she clearly already knew and didn't tell us, and Aunt Rose, who just keeps saying, "Somebody call my doorman and tell him to feed Weebles."

"Rose, Weebles died in 1973. He's fine," Gram insists.

I get instant replies. Love you too. Life will come to a halt until you get back. (Remy) I've already done everything you wouldn't do and plan to do more. Love you so much. (Lizzie) Try to make out with a waiter so we can be even. (Abby, who never misses a chance to bring up her hookup with a waiter on her cruise.)

Rachel's text comes at the last minute. "I have been, and always shall be, your friend."—Spock (fitting Star Trek quote)

And then it's over, like a ripped-off Band-Aid that pulls hairy patches of skin with it. One by one, Eddie collects our most prized possessions.

"Don't worry, we have thousands of books and DVDs on board," he says, as if books and DVDs will make up for our collective loss. Stupid, stupid Eddie the mustache guy.

-&o3-

Two men hoist our embarrassing volume of luggage onto the ship.

Eddie leads us through security down a long hallway. I've been on a few cruises with my parents. I'm expecting the typical glitz and over-the-top gold-plated everything. But the ship's lobby isn't like that at all. It's a tropical paradise, all fresh and clean and vibrant. There's a tranquil waterfall, surrounded by trees and flowers and clusters of bamboo swings. Looking up, I can see all the way through the curved glass ceiling to the sky.

I want to sit on a swing and take in the cool mist of the waterfall, but Gram tells Eddie to show us around. "We'll rest when we're dead," she says.

Eddie leads us into a ballroom with lush red velvet drapes and a handful of tables covered in off-white tablecloths. A mural showing a row of conga line dancers dressed in vintage clothing spans the entire length of the inside wall. Eddie sees me staring at the words above the mural. AND STILL WE DANCE. "It's our motto," he says. "Nice, huh?"

"It's beautiful," I say, studying the happy faces of the conga line dancers.

Uncle Billy makes a beeline to the grand piano sitting between the side of a stage and an expanse of windows overlooking the sea.

"Play 'Heaven,' because that's where we are," Wes says. "Check out the chandeliers. They're modern and vintage at the same time. Look how they've hung them at different heights. Genius."

"Can we get something to eat?" Jeb says.

"In a minute, Jebby. Come on." Gram motions us to follow her. She's full of energy and excitement like an elf taking us through Santa's workshop.

"This is the café, our most popular hangout spot, other than poolside," Eddie says. The café is filled with patchwork chairs and rustic tables and a thousand books on floor-to-ceiling shelves.

A family sits in the corner eating waffles. I'm surprised to see a baby in a high chair.

The family turns and waves. There's a very cute couple, obviously the parents of the baby, and then an older man and lady who both look haggard and sick. The baby slams her hands on the tray and Cheerios go flying all over the place. The cute mom with the blond pixie cut leans down to clean up.

Mustache Guy leads us over to the counter and opens a cabinet. He pulls out small tablets in yellow cases and gives one to Jeb. "I know we've asked a lot of you, especially the young people here, by confiscating your electronic devices." The mom gives the baby a bottle, and she bangs it on the tray. "We call these bees because they're yellow and they buzz."

He hands each of us a bee and keeps talking. "Each bee has been programmed for you individually. This is your upgraded smartphone."

My bee's MADDIE O'NEILL LEVINE screensaver is obnox-iously flashing my high school yearbook picture. I hit the SHIP icon. *Arcade. Art Studio. Bingo. Café. Chapel. Chemotherapy Lounge.*

"Every guest is programmed in. Crew goes by title, for example, waitstaff, concierge, emergency nurse, cabin attendant."

Dance Instruction. Grief Room. Ice Cream Parlor.

"Of course, there's no outside contact, but we make things very easy on board."

Massage. Memorial Planning. Movie Theater. Patients-Only Floor. Pool Deck. Radiation. Side Excursions. Yoga.

"This is so cool." Janie scrolls down the music list.

"Where's the casino?" Dad calls out in his abnormally loud tour-ist voice.

"We ended up replacing it with the patients-only floor, but we have an arcade and a nice card room." Dad scowls. In addition to science and useless trivia, Dad loves the craps table.

Aunt Rose looks a little dazed. She's sitting in an oversized chair with her head drooped to one side.

"Hey, Janie," I whisper. "Do you want to hit the pool deck or the chemotherapy lounge first?"

"How about we meet in the middle and go to bingo?" she says.

We continue touring the main floor of the ship. The old-school arcade will be fun. The good news is there are lots of places to hide from my family if they annoy me.

Our eyes move from our bees to the view from inside the glass elevators.

"I cannot wait for you kids to see your cabins. I've been working on this for a long time," Gram says.

"Astrid, you just found out you were sick. How have you been working on this for a long time?" Dad says.

"I found out I was sick last month. I've known I'm old for a while now. I started planning my trip as soon as I got home from seeing Ruth off. I just kept hoping not to get hit by a bus or murdered before I could do this."

"You've always been a planner, Mother," Mom says as the door opens.

"Here we are, babies." Gram steps out first. "Bobby and I need some alone time. Don't bother us until tonight."

Our cabin is straight out of the best episode of a home decorating show, only with better linens. Gram stocked the room with our favorite toiletries and candy and issues of *Vogue* stacked next to issues of *Scientific American*.

"Look, Janie, we can figure out obscure patterns in the universe by analyzing changing fashion trends," I say.

She stares at me. "Or not," she says blankly.

I pick up the silver framed picture on my nightstand of Gram and me watching fireworks in Bermuda when I was three years old. Gram's pressing her face into my mess of curls, and I'm laughing up at the sky. That is how I will always remember us.

Janie and I sit on the bamboo swing on our very own balcony and watch the newest arrivals learn they won't be able to use cell phones.

This family is huge. There must be more than twenty of them. They are all dark-haired and stubby, running around and making sweeping arm movements.

We watch the stubby family follow Eddie onto the ship, and decide to unpack while we're still running on adrenaline. I fling open the closet and find a treasure trove, a bounty fit for a *Vogue* editor. The colors and textures blend like a bouquet in size four for Janie, size eight for me.

"Of course Gram has to label the outfits," Janie says, pointing out the tags looped around each hanger. "Can you say control freak?"

"Ooh. This one's for the Latin night. That could be fun." I pull out a flouncy electric-blue dress.

Somebody pounds on the door. We both jump.

Jeb is standing outside with a dumb-ass grin on his face.

"Come see my room."

"No, Jeb. We're busy," I say, closing the door.

He pushes the door open. "Just come, assholes."

We follow him next door. I figured Jeb would use this trip as an opportunity to sit in a chair and masturbate to his crazy music while playing with his piercings and thinking about how dark and gloomy life is. He opens the door, and we discover a Jeb oasis.

Jeb's room is an instrument, freshly tuned and ready to make art. There's a blank canvas stretched from floor to ceiling on every wall and tables filled with art supplies. I'm hoping this will cheer up my bummer-faced brother, who gets irritable and kicks us out after Janie tries to mess with the easel on his balcony.

We're suddenly exhausted. We nap for hours in our cozy little nest and wake to the jarring sensation of the ship's engines gearing up to leave port. My bee wakes me with a welcome text from Francesca, the Wishwell's founder, inviting us to a forties-themed opening dinner.

Then Gram texts, We're off! Join us for hors d'oeuvres at six in Trish and Aaron's cabin. Come dressed for dinner.

We try to maintain our footing as the ship lurches clumsily. The crew is shouting outside, pulling up the ramps, and getting ready to set sail.

"It looks like they've finally loaded all the people and supplies," I say.

"Great," Janie says, chugging a bottle of water. "There's no backing out now."

"At least we're in it together."

I put on the designated Forties Night outfit, a vintage lavender dress and stunning T-strap heels. Janie comes out of the bathroom in a red dress with matching lips. I pin one side of my hair with a jeweled clip and work on creating Janie's updo. At six o'clock sharp, we find my parents' cabin at the end of the hallway.

Mom answers the door, smiling in blue polka dots.

My parents' cabin is peaceful and elegant, with a collage of black-and-white family photos above a sitting area facing a jumbo-screen TV hooked up to a computer.

"Your dad is so excited he actually kissed Gram on the lips," Mom says, gesturing to a massive telescope out on the balcony. "And come see my closet."

Mom shows us her own treasure trove. "Mother even set up a cookbook library, you know, because she wants me to cultivate my baking gift." Mom chokes on those words a little. She always wanted to be a professional baker, but our school activities and house stuff and sipping gin with Bev got in the way.

Gram and Dad are on the massive balcony in front of the telescope. He's pointing out something on shore. She looks through the lens and punches him. "They're not humping, you fool," Gram says. Dad laughs.

"Girlies, come out. Hey, Jebby." Jeb is behind us in high-waisted pants and suspenders. "So, do you like?" Gram says.

"Yes, yes, yes." Janie hugs Gram. Even tiny Janie makes Gram look like a hobbit.

"We love it all. You are the best grandma in the entire universe," I say.

"The art stuff is cool, but I really don't want to wear this shit," Jeb says, snapping a suspender.

"Oh, come on. Just humor your gram and wear the suit. You look sharp. You are very handsome under all that metal and ink, Jebby." Jeb got two neck tattoos before the trip. He snuck them in while Mom and Dad were distracted and distraught.

I'm ravenous. I go back to the sitting area and stuff three mini quesadillas into my mouth, chasing the hardened globs of tortilla and cheese with alternating mouthfuls of guacamole and salsa.

"Astrid, I saw a documentary about abuse of cruise ship workers, and—"

"Aaron, stop." Gram holds up her hand. "You and your documentaries."

"Well, it's a valid point. These people are paid something like sixteen dollars a month," Dad says.

"This isn't a regular cruise ship, Aaron." Gram puts her hands on her hips.

"Every single crewmember is an intern, and their hearts and minds are with the movement. Some are doctors or nurses. Many have been on the ship with a loved one, and all are well educated and informed, even the damn dishwashers and galley hands."

"Well, that's good to know." Dad turns back toward the telescope.

"Francesca pays well, trust me," Gram says. Dad's already looking for distant planets, even though the summer sun has not yet set.

I sink into a lounge chair and stare at Gram in her teal swing dress and pearls as she does all her normal Gram things, like berating Dad and eating canapés and criticizing Mom's lipstick color. She doesn't seem like she's reaching her expiration date. It's not as if her expiration date is stamped on her bottom like a metal can.

A horn blows. "We're off," Gram yells. "Come on, everybody."

Wes and Uncle Billy escort Aunt Rose, aptly wearing a rose-colored drop-waist dress and her diamond earrings. Dad pops open a bottle of champagne. I pour myself a seltzer on ice. Bob Johns rushes out to the balcony and grabs a glass. His hair is tied back, and he's sporting a burgundy zoot suit and a cane.

"Just in time for our bon voyage toast, Bobby," Gram says. "I'm not going to get mushy. I just want to say thank you all for dropping everything to join me on this journey. It means the world to me. This is going to be a hoot. Now, let's go make some friends." We stand in a circle and hold our glasses together for a brief moment. "Cheers, dears, and farewell, my beloved Bermuda, land of a million memories."

As we glide toward the open sea, Bermuda is a smudge on the horizon. I focus on the guacamole. It's the best I've ever had.

❧ SIX ❧

THE PARTY IS about to start. When we get there, I'm going to see them: the disfigured, the dying. How will I be able to eat around them? How will I make it through a whole summer of this?

Gram slaps my arm, hard. "Get rid of scrunch face."

Mom pulls me aside just as we're leaving. I assume she's about to give me a pep talk.

"Honey, that's an adorable dress, but it's a bit clingy. Why don't you try this?" She opens a drawer and pulls out nude Spanx.

"Really, Mom? You want me to squeeze my body into Spanx to hang out with old people?"

"It'll smooth you out. Come on, do it for your wacky mom." She gives me her pout face.

"Fine, Mom. But you are ridiculous, you know that?"

"Thank you, honey. I'll see you down there."

I kick off the shoes and pull the Spanx up. I can barely get them on. My mother never lets me leave the house without tweaking me in some absurd way. I can't get air, but I head to the elevator anyway, dreading what lies ahead.

I'm reaching up under my dress to yank at the Spanx just as the doors open. A guy is standing in the elevator, staring at his bee. I quickly remove my hands from deep under my lavender dress and walk into the elevator as he looks up. My God. He's gorgeous.

He nods hello, and the doors close. They open again two floors down, and he nods again before he gets off. I barely smile. It all happens so fast.

I take a minute to collect myself. Clearly the guy isn't going to the reception. I can't tell if the tightness in my throat is from the two-second encounter with the ridiculously hot guy or the party I'm about to attend. I try to take a yoga breath, but my torso circulation has been cut off.

People are gathered in the ballroom bar. I recognize the stubby family. Even close up, they all look alike.

I make a beeline for Wes just as Gram rushes over to hug an old man with tubes in his nose lugging around an oxygen tank. "Vito," she gushes.

"She knows people?" I say to Wes.

"She met some of them in New York."

"Can you stay with me? This isn't my thing." I follow Wes to the bar.

"Is this anybody's thing, Maddie? Seriously?"

We stand awkwardly and watch the people file in. A very pale elderly woman, completely bald, with purple lipstick, chats with a broad, dark-skinned middle-aged man in a striped suit and Harry Potter glasses. He has a hand on the shoulder of a woman in a wheelchair. From the way she's kind of slumped over, I don't think the woman can move at all.

"What's wrong, Mads? You creeped out?" Wes says.

"A little. I don't even know what to say to these people."

"The key to small talk"—Wes sips his bourbon—"is to find something in common with the person. It can be anything. Come on, I'll show you how it's done." Wes takes my hand and pulls me toward the bar. "Shirley Temple, Mads?"

"No. Just get me a Coke."

Wes turns toward a huge pasty guy with a pockmarked face wearing a Batman T-shirt under a blazer. He's holding a straw to the mouth of a smiling guy in a wheelchair.

"Hi, I'm Wes. This is my niece Maddie," Wes says to the big guy.

"Oh, dude, for a minute there, I thought you were a couple. I was, like, jailbait alert!" The guy laughs like a buffoon.

"Nope. I'm with him." Wes points to Uncle Billy, who is talking to Janie and the Harry Potter glasses guy.

"Oh, you two are gay? I mean, that's cool. We have a gay cousin. Or technically a lesbian cousin, because she's a girl."

Wes glances at me, clearly also aware this person is a buffoon. He looks down at the guy in the wheelchair, who is actually good-looking and in no way resembles the oaf. "So then are you two related?" Wes asks.

"Yeah, this is my brother, Mark. I'm Burt. We're from California."

"Where in California?"

"LA," the guy in the wheelchair says.

"No way. I lived in LA for almost ten years." And there's the thing in common. Wes is a genius at this. Meanwhile, all I can think about is the fact that this guy is here to die and his brother is here to watch.

I try to make my way to the bathroom, but Gram chases me down and introduces me to Vito from Queens. He's dying of lung cancer. He says he never smoked a day in his life, but the warehouse where he worked for forty years was contaminated with chemicals.

It's my biggest nightmare—a dinner party where people intro-duce themselves by telling you how they're dying. I would do any-thing to be at the lake club right now, where my friends are probably building a campfire and choosing make-out gum flavors. I'm sure Lizzie and Kyle are fighting and Remy is wearing her hoodie and Abby is telling her she looks like a man. It's probably really buggy, and I'm sure the boys are whining that they can't find alcohol. I'd be bored already, but I don't care. I want to be there right now. This is fucking depressing.

My family sits together at a table in the dining room. I slide in next to Janie, who also has scrunch face.

"I just met a woman who can't move at all. Like, she can't even talk. Her husband talks for her. She has ALS. I mean, look at her. She can't be older than thirty-five," Janie says. I glance quickly at the woman. She's the one with Harry Potter glasses guy. She's propped up at her table in a wheelchair.

"This is awful, Janie."

She nods.

I move salad around on the plate and watch my family inhale steak with truffle butter.

Eddie stands up with a microphone.

"Hello, passengers and crew," Eddie says, pushing up his praying mantis glasses. "We are honored to have you on board the Wishwell. As many of you know, our founder, Dr. Francesca Ivanhoe, lost her husband and her father to long, debilitating diseases. Since then, she's made it her lifelong mission to ease the pain and suffering of good people across the globe, teaming up with others at the Wishwell Research Facilities to launch our ship."

A blond, very tan guy, probably just out of college, walks in through the side entrance. I elbow Janie. "Three o'clock," I whisper. He's dressed in a white suit, more seventies chic than forties, but somehow he pulls it off.

"And I'm happy to announce by this time next year, we'll have two more ships on the water."

People clap and cheer.

Janie whips her head around. "Oh my God. He's mine," she says.

I quickly scan the room for Elevator Guy, but he's not here.

"Francesca is a truly beautiful woman, inside and out. You would never know from her gentle demeanor that she is a revolutionary, a world changer, and we are so lucky to have her. It is my great pleasure to introduce Francesca Ivanhoe."

The clapping and cheering erupts again. A striking woman walks to the front of the room wearing a ruby-colored mermaid dress and killer heels. She tosses her long black hair and smiles. Her presence makes the room feel lighter.

"Oh, you amazing people, I love you all so much. Welcome to this ship that is close to my heart for many reasons," she says with a thick Italian accent. "Something ugly brought us together. But something amazing will connect our souls forever."

I don't know whether to crawl under the table or join in the cheers. I lean over to Janie. "She's a death cheerleader."

"Shh. I like her. She's fun."

"As you begin your journey, I ask that you open yourselves up to those around you. Search inward, search outward, challenge the depths of your being, and of course, do it with a spring in your step or, Holly and Mark, your wheels. Now let's party."

The wall separating the dining room and the ballroom slides open to reveal the deep glow of the room at sunset. We make our way toward the ballroom. Janie keeps her eye on Mr. Three O'Clock, who is talking to Eddie. Janie's going to get him. She'll toss her blond hair, wrinkle her little nose, and stick out her huge edible boobs, and he'll need help sopping up the bodily fluids. Don't be embarrassed when it happens, Three O'Clock. It's a perfectly normal reaction when falling under the spell of Janie O'Neill Peters.

"I'm so excited. I never thought I'd be hooking up on this trip. We need to give him a good nickname." Janie catches Three O'Clock's eye and holds his gaze for a full three seconds, then looks away. He keeps looking.

"How about Captain Do Me?" I say.

"Captain Do Me is perfect. Come on, I need to dance."

Janie walks toward Gram. She's holding hands with Bob Johns, who is carrying a trumpet case like a purse. I love the way Bob looks at Gram. She's his princess.

"Might I request a prayer?" the bald purple lipstick lady's husband calls out. Somebody starts a chant: "Prayer, prayer!"

"Oh, God, this is annoying," Janie whines.

"Come on, you heathens, a little praying is good for us," Gram says.

We assemble in two layers of circles. I know there are seven patients, and with all the families, and some of the crew, there are at least forty, maybe fifty of us.

Jeb's standing awkwardly next to Wheelchair Lady.

"That's so sad," I whisper to Bob Johns. "The lady in the wheelchair."

"Wouldn't wish it on my worst enemy," Bob says.

"Please take your neighbor's hand. Don't worry, I'm a retired minister. I know what I'm doing." The tiny man is as bald as his wife and only slightly taller. Jeb crouches down and holds one of Wheelchair Lady's hands. I look around at the little old people and the two wheelchairs and the pained faces. For some reason I have the urge to laugh my ass off. I hold my breath.

"Lord, thank you for giving us the gift of life and for allowing the Wishwell patients the chance to enter your kingdom in peace and comfort. Thank you for giving your humble servants the opportunity to join our loved ones as we sanctify and celebrate the gift of life. May every last breath we share be joyful. Amen."

"Amen," they all say. I feel my face turning scarlet as the circles start disbanding, and I cover my mouth with my hands to muffle my laughter.

"What the hell is wrong with you?" Uncle Billy is on the other side of me.

"I don't know." Tears stream down my face. I can't stop laughing.

"How is this funny?" Uncle Billy is not amused.

"Just go." I shoo him away and dab my eyes with a cocktail napkin, pretending the prayer made me emotional.

I gain my composure as the band starts. This is our kind of music. Gram forced us all to endure dance lessons, so I've been dancing since I was three. *I won't have a knucklehead with two left feet at one of my affairs,* she always said. Janie and I are probably the only teenagers who can dance the Lindy.

Wes and Uncle Billy grab Janie and me and pull us out to the dance floor. Wes throws his back against mine and flips me over his head, giving the crowd a great Spanx shot. The people line the dance floor and watch as Uncle Billy pulls Janie through his legs then throws her into a cartwheel. We jitterbug to the moon and back. All those days practicing routines with my uncles on Gram's lawn in Bermuda were worth this moment. I think I see Wheelchair Lady dancing with her eyes.

The song fades to "In a Sentimental Mood," and Uncle Billy ditches me for Wes. Couples flood the dance floor, and I go in search of water. "That's my Maddie girl. You were brilliant, honey," Gram says when I pass her slow dancing cheek to cheek with Aunt Rose.

The ceiling retracts above us, revealing a sky full of clustered constellations. I sit on a bar stool and catch my breath. The blond pixie haircut lady we saw with the baby walks over. "Did they hire you guys to get the dancing started?" she asks. "It worked." She orders a chardonnay. She has amber eyes, the kind that are marbled with specks of gold, and is probably ten years older than me, and decades younger than most of the passengers.

"Ha! No. My grandmother trained us all to dance."

"You're so good. I just plant my feet on the ground, wiggle my ass, and hope for the best." She sips her wine and waves to her parents on the dance floor.

I don't want to ask her which of her parents is dying, so I decide to try the Wes approach and find something in common.

"Where are you guys from?" I ask.

"Chicago. My parents live in Florida now, but they've been back and forth a lot."

"One of my friends is going to Northwestern in the fall," I say.

"College," she practically shouts. "Oh, I loved college. Where are you going?"

"NYU."

"No way! I got my master's in education at NYU. I loved every minute of it."

"Oh! Where did you live?"

"In student housing near Union Square. I don't even know how I passed my classes. I went out every night. Beware. That's a bit of a problem in New York." She reaches over the bar and takes a handful of maraschino cherries. "Want one?"

"Sure." I suck the cherry off the stem.

"Oh, I'm so jealous of you. I mean, I have the husband and the baby and everything, but sometimes I think I'm a twenty-year-old stuck inside a thirty-two-year-old body."

"My cousin and I are as close to twenty as you're going to get on this ship," I say. "You can hang out with us and pretend you're still in college."

She smiles and arranges the cherry stems in a circle.

"Okay, you can be my little sister. I was a Delta Gamma in undergrad."

"I'll totally be your little sister." I'm guessing she was in the pretty girl sorority.

Pixie Hair's husband walks up behind her and kisses her neck. "I'm hoping this is my husband, but at this point anything goes." She turns and hugs him, then looks back at me. "What's your name?"

"Maddie."

"Lane, this is Maddie. She's going to NYU in the fall. Small world, right? Maddie, this is Lane, and I'm Paige."

"It's nice to meet you, Lane and Paige."

They go out for a dance and leave me trying to tie the cherry stem with my tongue. Lane hugs her close to him, and they sway slowly, foreheads touching. I hope I find somebody to dance that close to someday.

I turn toward the bar and notice a man and woman sitting in the dimly lit corner of the room. The man's so skinny it looks like he came from a prison camp. The woman is old and obese, like the people who hang out all day at the Chinese buffet. They sit silently, staring at the dancers, pathetic and unkempt, not even wearing forties clothes. They don't react to Bob Johns's trumpet solo. They don't tap their feet or snap their fingers. I don't know why I can't stop looking at them. Skinny Guy catches me staring, and I wave. He waves back with two fingers. Which one is the patient? I'm not even going to guess.

I hear Mom's cackling laugh before I see her stumble through the middle of the dance floor, practically plowing down Paige's parents. Gram makes her disapproving face and waves her hand at Dad, her signal for *get Trish out of here before she causes a scene.* I've seen that signal at Wes and Uncle Billy's wedding, Jeb's graduation trip to Montreal, and lots of other places. Dad puts his arm around Mom and pulls her through the ballroom door.

$$-\text{\textsection}o\text{\textsection}-$$

"Why are you naked?" Janie is doing nude yoga on our balcony.

"Come try it. Nobody can see us. It's open sea. It's liberating."

"I'll pass," I say. I climb onto the bed and watch my cousin's perfect little body mold into downward dog position in the glow of the moon.

I'm actually kind of proud of myself for making it through the first night. Dying people are slightly more normal than I expected.

"What was up with Aunt Trish tonight? She's not usually that bad," Janie yells over the wave sounds.

"I don't know. Open bar mixed with a new diet? She's never liked parties anyway. She'll probably be mortified in the morning."

Janie finally comes in from naked stretching and gets into bed.

"I used to think dying was the worst thing that could happen to someone," I say, getting under the covers, "but the misery some of these people have to deal with...death might be better."

"Duh, Maddie. Everyone knows that."

"We need to take better care of ourselves."

"You're such an old lady."

I go to sleep with a dull ache in my back. It's probably from flipping around on the dance floor, but I can't help wondering where my pancreas is.

—&° SEVEN °ζ—

GRAM GATHERED US all in the café for breakfast this morning. She told us we're not sleeping this trip away and she wants us doing some activities. Janie and I made searching for Captain Do Me an activity. We recruited Aunt Rose to make it look less suspicious. She couldn't really keep up, so we made her wear Mom's tennis shoes, and when she was still too slow, we pushed her around the ship in a wheelchair from the infirmary. We took a break from searching to sit with Mark the wheelchair guy and his brother, Burt, in the café and found out that Mark has a really bad kind of multiple sclerosis.

"Is it strange that I'm also slightly attracted to a forty-year-old in a wheelchair?" Janie says.

"Yes," Aunt Rose shouts.

"He's really hot," Janie says. "It's hard to believe those two are brothers. The hot guy got the disease genes, and the ugly guy got the healthy genes."

"Hot guy used to be a world-class surfer. His brother told me he has erectile dysfunction and has to wear a diaper," I say.

"Why would he tell you that?" Janie asks.

"Payback for being the not-hot brother?" I can see Janie is trying to process that thought. "I don't know, he acted like it was funny. He's a buffoon."

–ε○�‑

Vito's family doesn't seem to know that baby oil isn't sunscreen. They're all splayed out on deck chairs frying their leathery bodies while Janie and I hide in the corner, reading *Vogue* in our bikinis. The pool area has a little hot tub oasis with waterfalls. We've named it "the Grotto." The bald lady with the purple lipstick and Gram are in there right now, drinking champagne and sexually harassing the poor waiter.

Wes cannonballs into the pool, and Vito's daughters shriek at him.

"What? Don't sit by the pool, then," he snaps. Uncle Billy and Wes have been fighting since we got to Bermuda. They're barely talking to each other, and they're both cranky.

"Hi, Maddie," Paige says, wheeling the baby in her stroller.

She plops down next to us in her skirted mom bathing suit and giant sun hat.

"Paige! Hi. This is my cousin Janie."

"Who is this? Can I pick her up?" Janie reaches for the baby. "Oh, my gosh, she's so cute. Can I take her in the pool?"

"Her name is Grace. And by all means, go for it." We watch Janie ease into the pool and dip baby Grace's toes. She screeches with joy.

"I was hoping I would see you up here, little sister," Paige says.

I turn on my side and prop my head on the fluffy towel. "Shouldn't there be some sort of an initiation if I'm pledging your sorority?"

"We can just skip to talking about boys and eating frozen yogurt," she says. "I have to say, I could not stop thinking about college last night."

Janie bounces Grace in the water. Every time Wes goes under and pops up, she laughs hysterically. All babies love Wes.

"Look at her, she loves it," Paige says.

I tell Paige about the E's and the boyfriend sagas and Ethan and the "accident." She tells me she had a stoner boyfriend with the opposite problem. I didn't even know that was a thing.

Jeb runs past us and flips into the choppy pool. Burt comes from the other side of the pool and yanks down his shorts.

"Full moon tonight," he yells.

"Full hairy moon," Paige jokes.

"Fro yo?" She gets up and pulls her maxidress over her suit.

"Totally. Swirl with sprinkles, please."

Paige makes her way across the deck to the frozen yogurt bar. I turn over on my stomach and see someone walking in the shadows toward the stairwell.

It's the guy from the elevator.

He's tall and lacrosse-body lean with brown hair and a strong jaw. He's shirtless and sweaty and wearing running shorts, chugging a bottle of water and swinging a towel. He rounds the corner and disappears. I think I'll keep Mystery Guy to myself. I don't need Janie getting her grubby little paws on him. This one's mine.

-8o3-

I'm trying hard not to have scrunch face at the first Mix-and-Mingle dinner, otherwise known as the awkward sit-with-two-strangers-and-talk-about-random-nonsense dinner. They deliberately make us sit four to a table so we can get to know one another better. Wes and I are sitting with Obese Lady and Skinny Guy. Thank God Wes can talk to anyone.

Skinny Guy is the patient. His name is Dave, and he's an alcoholic. He's only forty-seven but has end-stage liver disease, and he says he's tired of fighting his demons.

"This one seems to be a stretch," I say to Wes as we watch them make their way back from the buffet. "How is alcoholism as bad as these other diseases?"

"Honey, I'd take the cancer card over those kinds of demons any day." Wes has a point.

Skinny Dave stinks a little like a homeless person and sips clear liquid from a tall glass. His mom's name is Barb. They live together and probably sit in front of the TV every night with a bottle of vodka and a vat of ice cream. Oh my God. They're Mom and Bev.

"So what kinds of takeout do you guys like to order?" I'm employing the Wes "find something in common" technique.

"Chinese, sometimes Italian," the mom says.

Skinny Dave perks up. "Thai food is my favorite. I love pad Thai with the peanuts. I squeeze in two or three limes. Damn, that's good."

"We have great Thai places in New York." Wes nods. I almost tell them they should come visit us sometime, but I stop myself. I have a tendency to say things I regret. It's the Astrid North O'Neill blurt gene. Except Gram doesn't regret anything she blurts.

The conversation shifts to freak waves.

Skinny Dave says he hasn't been able to sleep with the constant rocking. His mom says she has a fear of a giant freak wave engulfing the ship.

I think a giant freak wave has already engulfed the ship.

—ঃ০৪—

I'm in my bed scrolling through songs on my bee.

Somebody knocks on the door, and I jump. I'm edgier than usual these days.

Janie answers with a face full of zit cream.

"Girls night in?" It's Paige, carrying a vat of jelly beans, and our room attendant, Camilla, holding a bucket of ice and a six-pack of beer.

"Paige!" I yell. "Give me some jelly beans."

"Nope. They're for the game. We're going to play Never Have I Ever. We'll get you all geared up for college."

Janie slides open the balcony door, and a warm breeze sweeps into our little sorority den.

"I want to start it," Janie says. "Camilla, are you staying or dropping off our pillow chocolates?"

"She's staying," Paige says. "I recruited her. She's never played Never Have I Ever."

"In my college, we just drank vodka and fucked. We didn't need the games."

"See, girls? I found a live one," Paige says.

Janie opens a beer. "How's Maddie going to play? She doesn't drink."

"That's what the jelly beans are for. We're playing jelly bean Never Have I Ever."

Janie gets up. "Wait, I have to get one more player."

"No boys allowed," Paige says.

"It's not a boy."

Janie runs out of the cabin. Camilla tells me she's a graduate student from Panama who took time off to do the Wishwell for her doctoral dissertation research, but she actually likes cleaning cabins. She says it's therapeutic.

"We're back." Janie walks in with Gram in her nightgown and slippers. This should be interesting.

"Okay, Astrid, it's simple," Paige says, handing her a beer and a paper towel full of jelly beans. "Someone says a sentence beginning with 'never have I ever.' If you have done whatever the person says, you eat a jelly bean."

"Have or haven't?" Gram pops a jelly bean into her mouth.

"Have," we all say.

"Never have I ever kissed two guys in one night," Paige says. Camilla and Janie eat jelly beans.

"Never have I ever had sex in a car," Janie says. Camilla, Paige, and Gram eat jelly beans.

Gram takes pity on me. "Never have I ever dumped a bad kisser," she says.

We all eat a jelly bean.

Gram belches loudly. "God, I hate beer."

"Maddie, you need to get out more," Camilla says in her annoyingly sexy Spanish accent.

"Hey, leave her alone. She's my little sister," Paige says.

Janie comes up with a series of over-the-top Never Have I Evers to mess with Gram.

"What the hell is ass play?" Gram says. "In my day, ass play was when your husband goosed you in the elevator." Paige is in hysterics.

By the end of the game, they're all sick and I've had two jelly beans.

"You'll catch up someday," Janie says, patting me on the head.

We stay up late, tossing jelly beans to the fish and talking about boys and men and all the deadbeats (Gram's word) in between.

—ξο჻—

Vito and his family are crisping their stubby bodies again and Wheelchair Mark and Burt are sitting in the shade listening to music on their bees.

Gram and Janie and I are hanging out in the Grotto. Gram claims she's on her unmarried honeymoon, so now I can't escape the horrifying visual of Gram's bony body getting slammed by old Bob Johns.

"How are you feeling, Gram?" I ask.

"I'm tired. I have a nagging pain all around my pelvis and lower back like I've started my period again. It's so aggravating. But the doctors are fabulous. They're giving me meds and keeping me happy."

Janie digs her nails into my leg so hard flesh-eating bacteria are probably invading the wound. "Ow! What are you doing?"

"It's him. Captain Do Me." Janie peeks through the grove of trees rising above the Grotto. "My heart is beating out of my chest," she says, ducking a little.

"Who, him?" Gram says loudly. "Oh, that's Ty. He's one of my doctors."

"How is he a doctor?" I ask. "He looks more like a fugitive from one of our lake parties."

"He just finished Duke medical school. He's an intern here, and very passionate about the movement. He's seen your gram in the buff, girlies. Lucky boy." Gram waves Do Me over.

"Hello, Ty. Come meet my granddaughters. They've been calling you Captain Do Me. Isn't that darling?"

Janie's face is a deep shade of mortification.

"Oh, yeah?"

He grins and stares right at Janie.

"She's nineteen, Ty, so she's perfect for you. And these girls can beat the best of them in science."

"Gram, please. Not the science. Leave something to the imagination," I joke, trying to deflect. I can feel Janie's humiliation travel through the depths of the Grotto like an electric current.

"It's nice to meet you," Ty says. He gives Janie one more smile and walks away.

"Gram, I can't believe you," Janie says. Gram can still trigger the tween in Janie.

"I broke the ice, didn't I? Now, don't put out too quickly with this one. It would be nice to die knowing one grandchild is spoken for."

Janie gets up and wraps herself in a towel. "I'm in college, Gram. Stop trying to marry me off."

I can't stop thinking about Mystery Guy. I dragged Aunt Rose around in the wheelchair again this morning, hoping to see him. But no luck. Aunt Rose has become like one of those puppies single guys take to Central Park when they're trying to pick up women. We ended up sidetracked, talking to Dad, Bob Johns, and Uncle Billy, who were playing poker with Vito. Then we got tied up in the arcade with an old-school game called Whac-A-Mole, where little mole heads pop up and we hit them over the head with a hammer.

"Okay, honey, time to hoist my shriveled bum out of the tub. I have to go to group."

"Oh, please pull your suit down, Gram. Your tattoo is showing."

"So what? I'm not ashamed of it."

"What's group?" I slap a towel around Gram's waist.

"It's on the patients-only floor. We get together and talk about doomsday, and bitch and moan about what pains in the ass our families are, and so on and so forth."

"Nice. Have fun with that."

-ε﮿o﮿ᶾ-

Mom and I find Aunt Rose on her balcony tossing popcorn to a flock of seabirds trailing the ship. She flings a handful, and one of the birds head-butts another, then dives into the whitecaps.

"Ride, Aunt Rose?"

We take the elevator down to the lobby and push Aunt Rose through the tropical maze of flowering plants and down the windowed corridor to the ballroom. We pause to study the conga line mural and weave through the café. We stop at the chapel where big buffoon Burt is sitting alone in a pew. He sees us and gives an awkward salute.

"Hey there, ladies," he says. "Just taking a minute to get my prayer on."

"Where's Mark?" I push Aunt Rose into the chapel. It's a beautiful room. A stained-glass window spans the outside wall and lets in trickles of light that streak the pews with color.

"He went to group with Paige."

"Wait, I thought group was patients only."

"Yeah, it is." Burt looks at me funny.

"So she dropped him off?"

"No. She went with him. Oh—" Burt's face drops when he realizes he's breaking bad news. "Paige is a patient. Brain tumor."

"Oh my God. That's terrible," Mom says. "Poor thing. I assumed her dad was the patient. Well, I'm just sick about this."

Somebody had stuck a wad of gum behind one of the pews. I wonder how many pieces the person had to chew to get such a wad. And what would make a person stick it here, in this beautiful room?

"Mads? You okay, hon?"

I'm not. I'm not okay.

"Yeah."

"I'd like to pray," Aunt Rose says.

"How about we give Burt some privacy?" Mom turns the chair toward the door.

"No, that's okay. Wheel her over. I'll bring her back up in a little while."

We leave Burt and Aunt Rose in the chapel, and I drop Mom off in the café. I can't listen to her crap about how fatty the fish is on the ship or how her seasickness patches aren't working. My big sister is dying.

—ε₀ҙ—

Sunsets are big on the Wishwell. Today they're playing a song on our bees, to remind us that the sunset will peak in fifteen minutes. Eddie invites us to meet at the pool for cocktails and photos.

I'm under the covers when the song comes on. Beethoven or Bach. Who the hell knows?

Camilla buzzes three times. She wants to get in to do turndown. I decide I'm just going to talk to Paige. I can't avoid her.

Everyone is on the deck, clean and shiny, dressed for dinner and poker and other stupid things. Gram and Bob are laughing over cocktails with Gloria, the bald woman with the purple lipstick, and her husband, the minister. I find Paige sitting cross-legged on the Grotto steps with Grace on her lap.

"Little sister, come sit with us." She pats the step next to her. "Gracie and I are guessing what colors we'll see tonight."

"Paige, why didn't you tell me about you?"

Her smile never changes. "What do you want me to say?"

"I feel like you should have told me."

"Why? So you could feel sorry for me and treat me like a fragile little paper puppet?"

"What's a fragile little paper puppet?"

"Ha-ha. Maddie. What do you want to know?" She kisses Gracie's head.

"I don't know, like, what? How?"

"Who? Why?" she says. "All the newspaper reporter questions?"

"Ba." Grace reaches toward her bottle. Paige sticks it in her mouth and cradles Grace in her arms.

"I had a bad seizure in the middle of the night, and they found a tumor deep inside my head. I refused treatment because I was pregnant." She moves her lips from side to side like she's trying to stifle a cry.

"Could they have treated it?"

"No, not really. I started chemo right after Gracie was born, which broke my heart because I wasn't able to breastfeed her." She looks at me. "You would not believe how bitchy other women can be. They judged me mercilessly for not breastfeeding."

"That's stupid."

"Yeah, it is. So anyway, the tumor keeps growing, and the symptoms are getting worse. I heard about the Wishwell from a cancer friend at Cleveland Clinic. And here we are."

"I'm sorry, Paige."

"Can't we just be sorority sisters and not get all deep and depressed?"

"I don't know the right thing to say right now." I give her a weak smile. "Like a month ago, my big drama was cleaning my friend's puke off my minivan floor."

"So then don't say anything. Just be normal. I give you permission to completely ignore reality." She pats my leg. "It'll be good practice for college."

The Beethoven or Bach song fills the deck as deep purples and a narrow shock of orange spread low across the sky.

"Fine, Paige. I'll completely ignore reality. But only because I'm your pledge and I have to do as I'm told."

I force a smile, wanting so badly to completely ignore reality.

Baby Grace pushes her bottle away, leans over, and plants her slimy mouth on my kneecap. She sucks my stubbly knee as Paige and I send Dad to get frozen yogurts with sprinkles. He marches toward the yogurt stand, his conductor's arms flailing to the climax of Beethoven (or Bach).

-ξo⅗-

I skip the pizza party under the stars and curl up in a ball on our balcony.

"What's wrong?" Janie squeezes onto my lounge chair.

I tell her about Paige.

"I want to be her friend and just be normal. But it's so, so sad." I think of Paige laughing with baby Grace, dancing with Lane, tossing jelly beans off the balcony. "She's just like us."

"We have to be what she needs us to be right now, Maddie. However much it sucks for us, imagine how Paige is feeling." I turn over, and she spoons me. We stay like that for a long time, two cousins getting way too big to share a lounge chair, listening to the surf smash against the ship. At some point I must fall asleep, because I wake with a wicked cramp in my neck. Janie's singing in the shower, and there's a worry doll on my pillow.

Janie hated her parents' divorce more than most people hate divorces. She was in middle school at the time and went ballistic. She did shots and stole Aunt Rose's back pain pills. She slept with three guys in one weekend and texted pictures of herself smoking weed to Aunt Mary. Nobody knew what to do, so Gram took us to Aunt Rose's Charleston house. Gram hoped Janie would sip iced tea, read Faulkner, and heal. But she didn't. She crashed on the daybed in the den and barely got up for a month.

When she finally agreed to take a shower, Brit and I brushed her hair, doused her with perfume, and half carried her to a Mexican restaurant. The kind Guatemalan lady who delivered our homemade tortillas gave Janie a tiny patchwork bag of worry dolls. There were seven or eight of them, each the size of a pinkie toe. The lady told Janie to put them under her pillow and tell them her worries, and everything would be just fine.

Janie is not the type to listen to random restaurant workers, and she's definitely not the type to talk to miniature dolls. But I guess she was desperate, because every night she would take out the dolls, carefully line them up under her pillow, and close her eyes tight. I swear those dolls saved my cousin.

"Thank you for my worry doll. I have lots to tell her," I say when Janie gets out of the shower.

"You're welcome." She stops toweling off her hair and looks at me with a very serious expression. "Her name is Esperanza."

—ε∘ȝ—

I'm still awake at two AM, so I decide to go for a run. It's cool on the track, and the sky is thick with stars.

Uncle Billy comes full speed around the bend and nearly takes me down.

"Mads, why are you still up?" he pants.

"Couldn't sleep. Why are you still up? Don't you go to bed at nine?"

"Nah, my circadian rhythms are way off." He gulps from his water bottle. "Come on, you promised you'd train with me for the marathon one of these days."

"Okay, but you know I can't run and talk at the same time."

Uncle Billy stays with me, even though I can't keep his usual pace. We stretch a little, and suddenly I'm really tired.

"We should do this every night," I say.

"Or on the nights Wes doesn't get me drunk. He's telling me he can only tolerate me after we've both had a few cocktails."

"That sounds healthy."

We lie on our stomachs and dunk our heads in the pool.

"Hey," Uncle Billy calls out.

"What's up?" I hear a guy's voice as I'm pulling my face out of the water.

It's him. Uncle Billy just said hi to Mystery Guy, who is on the other side of the deck. He looks back and gets into the elevator.

"Who is that?" I say.

"I have no idea. Crew, maybe?"

I'm hoping he didn't notice me lying on the deck with my face in the pool.

When I get back to the room, I scroll through the crew photos on my bee. He's not there. If Paige is a patient, he could be, too. But he's not on the guest list either.

Mystery Guy is somewhere near me right now. Above me. Below me. So close, and yet so far.

—ᘒ∘ EIGHT ∘ᘓ—

THE SHIP JERKS back and forth about a million times and stops in the middle of a bay not far from Jamaica, our first official stop. Aunt Rose and I are waiting for everyone in the lobby.

"Aunt Rose, how are you doing?" I talk to her like she's a deaf immigrant.

"Oh, I feel pretty good in the mornings. This is a great adventure, huh, Maddie?"

"Yeah, it is. Do you think Gram made the right choice, you know, doing this?" I don't know if Aunt Rose even fully understands what "this" is. I realize I've never noticed Aunt Rose's eyes. They're milky gray and kind of pretty.

"I had my friends Alice, Maude, and Bitsy. My plumbing didn't work, you know. The girls were my family."

I'm not sure where this is going.

"Karl and I played bridge every Saturday with the girls and the husbands. Then all of a sudden, we got old. We started dropping like flies, only we weren't flies. We were friends. And now I'm the only one left. And that's hard, to sit with the memories." She pauses. "I could never have children, you know. My plumbing didn't work."

I take her hand. "Can you teach me how to play bridge, Aunt Rose?"

She smiles. "Yes, dear. I would love to."

Uncle Billy swoops in, grabs Aunt Rose's face, and leans in for a big kiss. As gruff as Uncle Billy can be, with his reading glasses and his newspaper and his snobby attitude, he's always had a soft spot for Aunt Rose.

"Can you stop stealing my damn sister?" Gram's wearing her safari clothes. "Somebody text Bob. He's looking all over the ship for her."

Mom and Dad show up holding hands. Now that they're about to be empty nesters, maybe they should take up cruising as a hobby.

We line up behind Eddie and pile into the dinghy boats bound for Jamaica.

"Okay, Astrid, enough with the cryptic clues." Dad clings to the dinghy pole. "Are we going to Jamaica to see Rasta Bob's homeland?"

"I'm actually not Rasta," Bob chimes in. "I'm Catholic."

"Rasta is a religion?" Janie says.

Gram ignores the conversation. "Aaron, after my diagnosis, I came to Jamaica for a week with Bobby when you all thought I was in the Hamptons with Denny." The dinghy hits a wave, and we all leap off our seats. "Whoa," Gram says, holding on to Bob. "I spent time with Bob's big, wonderful family on the other side of the island. So no, we're not going for Bob. We're going for ganja."

"Weed?" Jeb perks up.

"Yes, Jebby, weed. It's for the sick people. They're going to stock the ship with cannabis oil, which is the only thing keeping some of these people going, and the rest of us get a day in Jamaica. Francesca's local contacts are putting together a big Wishwell dinner on the beach."

"Well, there's a win-win," Wes says.

"Mother, isn't going on a marijuana run with the kids just a little inappropriate?" Mom says.

"Yes, it's better to get wasted on gin and make an ass out of yourself in front of the kids." Jeb inserts dagger.

"Jebby, don't talk to your mother that way," Gram snaps. "She's been handed down the damn O'Neill drinking gene—it's the Irish curse."

"I thought the Irish curse was a small penis," Wes says.

"Oh, boy, can we stop? Please. This family is over-the-top." Dad's still holding the dinghy pole.

Mom looks down, totally unable to defend herself. Jeb glares at her. He's such an asshole lately.

"Karl and I smoked marijuana," Aunt Rose announces.

"Trish, I'm not planning to smoke with the children, although I'm sure you've all tried it." Gram looks at me.

"No, never." Janie elbows Jeb.

"I've never smoked anything," I say. I don't add that it's because of the movie I watched in seventh grade where they showed a guy trying to smoke a cigarette through the hole in his throat. I think I had a contact high once, in a tent, when Lizzie and Remy blew it in my face.

"That's not a surprise. Trish, did you know our Maddie is a virgin?" Gram announces.

"Really, honey? That's terrific," Dad says. "I'm so proud of you."

"The prom queen is a virgin?" Jeb snorts. "You can't make this shit up."

"Shut up, Jeb. You don't even know me. I was homecoming queen. Not that you cared. Lizzie was prom queen, idiot. And at least I could have sex if I wanted to. What's your excuse, freak?" I hate that I'm letting Jeb get to me.

"We're all glad you made it through high school without putting out, Mads." Uncle Billy puts up his hand to high-five.

"Oh my God, you're all so annoying. I'm going to have sex with someone today just to shut everyone up."

"Me too," Janie says.

"Me too," Aunt Rose says.

$$-\mathcal{E}\circ\mathcal{F}-$$

We finally escape the dinghy hellhole and find ourselves in a beachside cove. The other Wishwell people are already there. I want to run up and hug Paige and show her I'm prepared to completely avoid reality, but she's wrestling with a raging Grace tantrum.

A tall, lanky man with missing teeth greets us. He calls himself

Tits. It's clear how he got his name: He's a skinny man with moobs. He's at least a C cup.

I notice Skinny Dave and his mom didn't come, and I feel kind of bad. Wes texted them last night to see if they were looking forward to Jamaica. They didn't text back.

A grinning woman in a pale yellow dress walks out of a building that says JAMAICA MAMA on a faded Coca-Cola sign. Tits introduces her as his wife, Mama. She hugs everybody. Mama's massive, flabby arms engulf Gram. She turns to me and squishes me in a hearty embrace. Her armpit smells like dead food, but I instantly love this gorgeous woman.

"Welcome to Jamaica, everyone," Mama bellows. "This is your home today. You go sit on the beach. Get comfortable. There's a shady special spot for you wheelchair folk. We'll cook you a feast on the beach later. Now, if you're going on the secret cave tour, go over to the bus with Tits."

"What's the secret cave tour?" Dad yells.

"Jamaica is full of tourist caves, but we're going to a secret cave where the runaway slaves hid out back in slave days," Tits says. "They say it's a mystical spot, with healing properties."

"Cool," Dad says. "Let's do it."

The sun is torturing me. This is why people don't venture to the Caribbean in the summer. I look up the stretch of road. The white-washed buildings with pink and blue and yellow shutters stand in various states of disrepair. A group of old men sits at a picnic table drinking Red Stripe beer. They wave to a hand sticking out of a car puttering up the one road in town. There are a couple of bars, a town hall, and a fruit stand. I decide to take the secret cave tour.

Paige's parents push an overloaded stroller to the beach line with Wheelchair Lady, also known as Holly, and her nurses and most of Vito's family. Paige and Lane join the rest of us in the secret cave line.

My family occupies the back half of the rickety bus. The duct-taped seats smell like pee. I settle in next to Dad and behind Gram, who is swapping New York stories with Gloria. It takes Tits; Holly's husband, Marshall; and three other guys to help Burt carry Mark onto the bus and dump him in the front seat, but he's determined to come.

Tits lurches down a bumpy dirt road along the beach, then into a thick forest, where the road gets even bumpier. Dad and I clutch the seat in front of us, while Janie flips through a *Vogue,* completely unfazed.

"My goodness, people are living in those shacks," the minister says to Dad, who nods as he cranes his neck to get a better glimpse of the tiny houses lining the roadside. "One of our sumptuous Wishwell feasts could pay for food for a year out here. The inequality of wealth is staggering," the minister continues.

Gram turns around. "We're supporting these people with marijuana tourism, Minister. Think about it. The Wishwell is boosting the local economy. Buy some pot if you want to help these people."

"Astrid, the minister is entitled to share his concerns without being encouraged to buy pot." Dad gives Gram a dirty look. I wonder if that's what my scrunch face looks like.

After an hour, we enter a clearing and the bus stops because there is no more road. We get out and stand on the edge of a steep cliff overlooking a lush valley.

"Hey, Janie, remember when we used to play land of gnomes and fairies?" I say.

"Of course."

"I think we're there."

Mark basically has no use of his arms or legs. He can move his head, but his body is soft and floppy.

"No worries," Tits says after they drag Mark off the bus. "He can ride in here." Tits points to a donkey that is waiting impatiently for the guys to load Mark into his cart.

"Oh, this is classic," Burt says.

"Get pictures, bro," Mark says, laughing hysterically, as Burt and Marshall lower his limp body into the donkey cart.

We walk in a pack through a patch of lush forest. I feel creatures staring at me from hidden places. The minister holds on to Gloria, but she still can't keep up, so Uncle Billy lifts her onto his back. We reach another clearing, shrouded in mist. I hear Jeb say, "Oh, shit, the mother lode." It's a field of marijuana as tall as I am. The reddish-brown soil sticks to my sandals as we pass the giant plants. Now I know why they call it weed.

We arrive at a cluster of green tin shacks, and a white woman with a blond rat's nest of furry sausage dreads walks over. She's bra-less, and her saggy boobs flop around as she pulls Cokes out of an outdoor cooler. She's Tits Number Two.

"Hey, everybody, welcome to the caves." Tits Number Two is

American. "Grab a Coke or water if you want, and Tits will take you in." She points to the cart. "The cart won't fit in the cave. Do you mind riding in a wheelbarrow?"

Mark laughs. "Hell, no. Bring it."

Gram hobbles along, holding on to Bob and me. Wes and Uncle Billy half carry Aunt Rose until we get to a rock formation jutting out in the middle of the forest. Tits leads us to a narrow opening about eight feet high and covered with hanging moss.

"This is neat!" Mom shouts. She's the first one in. I can't believe my mother is waltzing into a cave in kitten heels.

We squeeze through the crack into a dark cavern.

"Generations of ancient peoples made this their home," Tits says, "and then groups of escaped slaves built thriving communities in these caves."

"It's an actual underground railroad," Janie says.

"Yeah, except there's no railroad, genius," Jeb shoots back.

We weave through the rocks, and Jeb and Burt point out every formation that can possibly pass as penis-shaped. Lane wraps his leg around one of them for a picture as Burt wheels Mark over for a wheelbarrow photo bomb.

We shuffle single file to the entrance of another creepy fissure in the wall.

"We need to be quiet when we go into the bat city," Tits says softly. "It's home to millions of bats. Shh. No loud noises or fast movements. It's very nice to see them asleep, but they will panic if they're disturbed. Sometimes they even drop their babies."

The group pushes through the fissure before I can turn around and run out the entrance. I can't stand bats. My stomach starts cramping, and I'm trapped.

I wade through a thick layer of bat droppings in my flip-flops while Tits Number Two shines a light toward the ceiling. Paige grabs my head and nearly drags me to the ground. Janie is trying to bury her head in my armpit while Wes clutches my arm from the other side. Do they think I'll protect them when this bat colony attacks us?

"Holy bat cave, Robin," Burt whispers really loudly.

"Shh," we all hiss.

"Asshole," Paige says.

"Look up," Tits whispers way too loudly. "Tonight they'll wake and eat the bugs. If you look closely, you can see some of the babies sleeping on their mommies."

I want to hit Tits for the way he says "mommies." Dad and Jeb are staring up with their mouths open.

"Incredible," Dad says.

I keep my mouth shut tightly and look up for a second. It's revolting and amazing at the same time. These things are heavy breathing as they fidget in their sleep. There are so many it looks like a dense, fungus-covered stalagmite or stalactite, whichever one grows downward.

I finally exhale when we exit toward the sound of running water into a massive cavern with light streaming through. The cavern is damp and misty, and when my eyes adjust to the light, I'm looking down at a pool of water under a baby waterfall. It feels like we are inside the earth's nostril, with the moss-covered walls and dribbles of water. Somehow standing inside a nostril feels strangely calming.

"Let's get a group picture," Burt says. Burt is really into taking pictures.

We assemble in front of the waterfall and behind Mark's wheel-barrow. Wes pulls Tits in next to Gram while Tits Number Two positions Burt's bee.

"Say penis cave," Burt yells.

"Penis cave!" We all humor him.

We walk out the mouth of the cave and into a clearing and slowly make our way down a path and back to the green shack.

"That was one of the coolest things I've ever done," Paige says. "It was such an adrenaline rush."

Uncle Billy and Wes carry Aunt Rose and Gloria on their backs. We pass a makeshift sign nailed to a tree that says HERB IS THE UNIFICATION OF MANKIND—BOB MARLEY.

I'm thinking the true unification of mankind is actually fear, or death, or penis jokes, or all of the above.

$$-\xi\circ\xi-$$

We survive the ride back to town, probably because Dad sits in front and nags Tits to slow down. As our mutant tribe disperses, Janie and I decide to explore.

We wander until we find a tin-roofed restaurant in front of a shady cove. Ceiling fans whir above a circular bar, and reggae music welcomes us like an old friend.

We order delicious meat-stuffed fried patties and dipping sauce from the scrawny, gold-toothed bartender. Within minutes, Janie is drunk on rum and rambling about Captain Do Me. The bartender tells her there are too many fish in the sea to fret over one. We pull our bar stools over to a growing group of locals, men and women of various ages. I feel like I'm back at the lake club, talking about random things with half-drunk people.

"What do you think Brit is doing right now?" Janie says.

"Probably calling the cops on some party she didn't get invited to," I say. "God, remember when we were kids and she was more normal? What happened to her?"

"Gram says Brit will get better when she has something for herself and can stop wallowing in jealousy."

"We never did anything to make her jealous."

"She's miserable with herself, and we're not. That's all it takes with Brit." Janie motions to the bartender for another drink.

Somebody comes in through the side entrance. The room erupts in greetings. I assume it's another regular, since they seem to greet everyone with this kind of enthusiasm. Then I spot him from the corner of my eye.

"Holy shit. Oh my God." I duck between the bar stools and pretend I lost an earring.

"Are you even wearing earrings? What earring?" Janie is making it worse.

"I have to go to the bathroom." I dart around the bar to the utterly disgusting unisex bathroom and close the door. I need to breathe, but

I can't because I'm inside a shit tank. Why is Mystery Guy here? I look horrible. And after trudging through a foot of bat excrement, I smell like dirt and donkey.

I squint to look at myself in the credit-card-sized distorted mirror. I have a vision of Mom telling me I should always carry a lip color and a compact because *you never know when you'll need to look presentable.* I should have listened to her.

Somebody pounds on the door.

"Maddie, what the hell? Are you having an irritable bowel syndrome attack?" Sloppy Janie yells at the top of her lungs.

I open the door a crack and yank her in. "Shut up. Get in here." She squeezes in and pushes me against the moldy wall.

"What is your problem?" She blows her hot rum breath in my face.

"You know the guy who just walked in?"

"Yeah. His name is Enzo. I just met him." Janie pushes me out of the way and squats to pee.

"Okay, well, he's mine."

"Fine, maniac. You can have dibs on random Jamaican bar guy."

"Listen, he's on the Wishwell."

"No he's not." She washes her hands in the grubby sink and wipes them on my shirt.

"Yes he is. I saw him a few times. You need to pretend you're not wasted and help me here."

"Maddie, you have a blotchy rash all over your chest. Get ahold of yourself. It's just a guy. Remember the thing we always say, 'They're just boys'?"

"I know. I have to get out of this shithole bathroom. I need air. Do you think I could fit through the window?"

"You're acting like a loser girl. Come on."

Janie flings open the door and yanks me out into the open.

I stand up straight and walk back to my seat as nonchalantly as I can. I take a sip of my warm ginger beer. *You should have done something with your hair,* the Mom voice says.

"Enzo, come meet my cousin Maddie."

All of a sudden he's standing in front of me.

"It's you." He smiles.

"Hi." I smile back.

He tilts his head slightly to the right. His eyes are gray-green, with freakishly long lashes. He's even more beautiful close up.

"So why weren't you on the cave tour?" Janie says.

"Did Tits take you to see the bats? I haven't done that in a long time," he says.

"You've done the Wishwell before?" I say. After being blindsided by Paige, I can't assume he's not a patient. Maybe the first trip didn't take.

"It's a long, not very exciting story. Drinks?" He squeezes in next to me and flags down the bartender. He's so close that his arm brushes against mine, and I can smell him, clean and soapy and slightly spicy. It's intoxicating.

"Are you British?" Janie asks, studying his face as if his expression will give her the answer.

"Guess the accent is hard to hide. I grew up in England, well, half grew up in England."

"I knew it. I'm really good with accents. What kind of name is Enzo, anyway?" She's carrying the entire conversation.

"It's Italian, short for Vincenzo. How about Maddie? Is that a nickname?" He's looking at me again. Not Janie. Me.

"Yeah. It's short for Madeline."

The bartender comes over.

"What are you having?" He looks at me again.

"I'll have rum and Coke," Janie says.

"How about you, Maddie? Rum and Coke?" He eyes my ginger beer.

"Um. Whatever you're having is good," I say.

"Two Red Stripes." He drops Jamaican money on the counter and leans toward me. Our hands are so close, if I move my finger the width of a straw tip, we'll be touching.

I take a sip of beer. It tastes like rotten bread crust.

"I have to admit I've been calling you something else." He smiles.

"Oh, yeah? What?"

"The Girl in the Purple Dress." He remembers me from the elevator. I will not reveal I've been calling him Mystery Guy.

A loud song comes on. He leans even closer, and I feel his warm breath on my cheek. "So, how's the Wishwell?"

"It's growing on me," I say. I shift in my seat. "I feel like somebody's new cat. You know how they hide under the bed for a while, but then they're good?" I don't know why I just blurted that out. It was getting too intense, with his breath and his eyes.

He laughs. "I know what you mean. We've had a lot of house cats. They all do the same thing."

Janie pulls her bee out of her bag and tosses it like a hot potato. She looks down. "Oh shit, Gram's pissed. She wants us at the beach. They're waiting for us."

I don't want to leave.

"That's okay. I need to get to the beach to meet some university mates here on holiday."

Janie pulls me toward the door. "Bye, Jamaican buddies. You guys are super cool," she yells.

I shake my head, look back at Enzo, and go for the nonchalant wave.

"Bye, Maddie," he shouts over the music.

"Oh my God. Janie. Why was I so nervous?"

"Maybe because he's painfully hot and has a British accent?" She stumbles over the curb and nearly runs into a man on a moped.

"Janie! You have to sober up. Gram is not going to be happy. Come on. Think sober thoughts."

I grab Janie's hand and pull her up the street. All I want is to turn around and grab Enzo's perfectly tanned hands instead. I'd pull him away with me to the secret Jamaican caves, even if they are infested with bats.

—౩o౩—

Gram's standing with her hands on her hips as we approach the crowd of misfits gathered around a line of tables down the beach from Mama's restaurant. Waiters rush back and forth with giant platters of food.

"Where were you? Astrid's furious," Dad says.

"We told you we were going exploring," I say. I'm hoping Janie doesn't open her mouth.

"That was hours ago. Come on, girls. Tits and Mama went through all this trouble to make a nice evening. Get over there and be charming." Dad pushes us toward the tables.

"Glad you could make it." Gram is not happy. "You missed the cocktail hour."

"We're sorry. We got lost," Janie says.

"You got lost in a one-street town? Are you drunk, Jane Margaret? There are no words." She walks away, leaving us feeling like terrible people. Gram does not like anyone missing her planned events.

"Everyone, come eat," Mama calls. "We have a feast set up for you." Mama must have timed the dinner to start at the beginning of the long Jamaican sunset. Reds and purples fan out over the scarlet expanse of sun disappearing on the horizon.

I don't know where to sit. There's a spot next to Holly, but I don't think I can eat next to someone in a wheelchair. Holly is scary to look at. It's as if she's been blown by a warping mechanism that twisted her body into a distorted shape. She can't eat, so liquid nutrition tubes feed into her stomach. I talk to her like she's Abby's mentally challenged dog and hate myself for it, but I can't stop. I say stupid things like "Marshall tells me you were a dancer. Isn't that nice?" I get tongue-tied.

Mom and Jeb are taking turns holding a seashell to their ears. I guess she's gotten over the alcoholic remark and he's managed to smoke some grade-A Pineapple Skunk. Bob Johns waves me over.

"Maddie, I want to introduce my old friend Delly and her son, Joseph."

A woman wearing a coral-colored headscarf and piles of beaded jewelry smiles up at me. Gram always talks about people's energy. This lady's energy calms me down right away.

"Come pull up a chair here." Delly makes room for me. I squeeze in between her and Joseph and end up directly across from Holly. Janie plops down next to her. Poor Holly is probably getting a massive dose of rum breath, and she can't even move away.

I'm suddenly ravenous. Mama was right. It is a feast. Bob's friends give me a play-by-play of all the dishes: the fruity rice, the meat, the fried patties. It's so good I want to lick the drippings out of the barbecue pit. Delly and Joseph are getting a kick out of the skinny girl throwing back a massive amount of food.

"Wait, let me ask something else and see if I understand you." Janie is talking to Holly like they're old friends. Janie is asking questions, and Holly is blinking answers with her eyes.

"Do you miss eating food?" Janie asks. Ridiculous question.

Holly blinks twice. "Yes? That's yes, right?" Janie cranes her neck around the rigid, twisted body of this poor crumpled woman with big brown eyes and hair cropped close to her head. It's hard to figure out what she might have looked like once.

Her husband laughs. "That's yes. I'm thinking she would love some of this food right now."

"Do you want us to turn your chair around so you can see the sunset? It's breathtaking." Janie studies Holly's eyes. "Yes. She blinked twice. Turn her around."

Marshall and Janie turn the wheelchair around just as the sunset is taking over the entire Jamaican sky. We all seem to pause to see what she's seeing. Thank God she still has her eyes.

I've never thought about how brief a sunset is. It's so brief, it's almost cruel.

I tell Bob's friends about New York and NYU, and we talk about education in Jamaica as we all suck the last of the barbecue off our fingers. I look down the long table to see Burt feeding Mark soft food with a spoon. Paige's mom watches her laugh at Gram's long-winded story, as if she's trying to memorize her laughing daughter's face. It feels like we're gathering for a holiday, only the holiday is death.

My stomach, full of meat and fried deliciousness, hangs over my shorts. Two guys play guitar and bongos near the bonfire. Bob steps up with his trumpet. Gram and Aunt Rose hold hands and wiggle their hips like groupies. We all dance with Tits and Mama and their friends, swaying to the music as tiki torches throw bursts of light on the faces of my grandmother, parents, brother, cousin, uncles, and great-aunt—all the people who mean the most to me.

I pull out my bee and text Jeb. He feels around his pocket and looks down to read Snow globe moment ☺. He gives me a thumbs-up and a goofy grin. It's been a snow globe kind of day.

—೮∘ NINE ∘ঽ—

I CAN'T SLEEP. I try to wake up Janie, but she slaps me. I curl
up with my blanket on the balcony. Everything's black: the sea,
the sky.

My bee buzzes under my leg.

Hey Maddie. Any chance you're up? I'm by the pool if
you want to talk. Enzo (from the Jamaican pub earlier)

Oh my God. It's him. It's a photo on the bee of Enzo's face with
his adorable side grin looking up at me. I can't believe he feels the need
to remind me of where we met. I have to calm down. Janie would tell
me to recite our favorite line, *They're just boys.* He's just a boy.

Actually, I'm on my balcony reading Scientific American.
Delete.

We're in the middle of a movie, but maybe tomorrow?? Delete.

Sure! I'll be there in a few minutes. Send.

I throw on clothes and brush my hair and teeth, moving just slowly enough that he won't think I'm too eager. I put on a little makeup so I don't look like a pasty vampire chick and walk calmly toward the elevator. For a second I worry again that he is a patient. Maybe he wants one last fling before he goes. I don't know what to think.

Wes and Uncle Billy's TV is blaring through their door, but otherwise, everything is quiet. I take the elevator up to pool level. I walk toward the Grotto looking for Enzo and nearly trip over something hanging half off a lounge chair. My heart sinks. It's Skinny Dave. He's facedown, half on the chair with his legs sprawled on the floor. I can't tell if he's alive or dead. He reeks. I know Janie would probably shake him or check his pulse to see if he's alive, but I cannot do this. I race around looking for someone to help me.

Enzo is sitting on the Grotto steps with his baseball cap and his seashell necklace and his smile. For a second, I forget Skinny Dave.

"Hi, uh, we have to help this guy. He's passed out," I say, flustered.

"Where? Show me." I lead him to Skinny Dave. He immediately kneels next to him and feels for a pulse. I stand awkwardly, not knowing if I should hit the red emergency button on my bee.

"I think he's just hammered, poor guy." Enzo shakes him a little. "People tend to do that on the Wishwell."

"He's actually an alcoholic. Like, that's his disease."

"Yeah, well, he's definitely drunk. Go and grab some towels.

We'll get him straightened out." I grab a stack of towels from the bin and lay them out on a chair. Enzo hoists Dave up and gently lays his greasy head on a folded towel. I cover him so his head is the only thing peeking out. He's a sad, smelly little boy, curled up and snoring.

We leave him to sleep and go back to the Grotto steps.

"That was awkward," I say.

"That was nothing. I've seen it all on this ship."

"What do you do here?"

"Me? I'm visiting. Francesca's my mum. I come every summer and sail around for a few weeks, visit friends in Jamaica or Brazil. Believe it or not, this is my holiday, so I try to avoid getting involved in the scene here."

"Wow. I guess I'm relieved to hear you're not a patient."

"That wouldn't be fun, would it?" He pulls his chair closer so we're facing each other. "How about you? Your cousin said your gran is the patient?"

"Yeah. Pancreatic cancer. She told us about the cancer and the trip all in the same night. Oh, and she also introduced us to her long-lost Jamaican boyfriend. It was a lot of news to process."

He laughs. "Well, that's one way to get it over with."

"True. But I think it would have been better to know about the cancer first. Even now, I hear about all the treatments these people have been through before they got to this point, with years of chemo or experimental drugs or whatever." I stop talking, afraid for a second I might break down. "I just—I'm wondering if it's too soon. Like she had it in her mind to do this, and she's not even willing to try to live."

He nods, and I get the feeling he's heard this before. "It's hard for people to know when to do the whole Wishwell thing. If it's any help, I've seen the pancreatic people. It's usually pretty quick."

"So you've been around this stuff a lot."

He nods again. "I'm sort of immune to it all. I mean, it's sad, but the suffering is worse. I watched that part with my dad. We had heard about the Wishwell Research Facilities in the Pacific, where they experiment with revolutionary medical trials."

"I just found out about the research facilities. I had thought the Wishwell was just a ship."

"Oh, no. Just wait until Wishwell Island. You'll see it soon enough."

It's a little unsettling to be reminded that I have no idea what is on the itinerary.

He takes a drink from a plastic cup and holds it out to me. "Thirsty?" I drink from the same side he just sipped. I can taste the Enzo germs in the root beer.

"We went to the island when Dad was really sick, as kind of a last-ditch effort. But it was too late to save him. That's when my mum had the ship idea. She wanted to create a place where people who were beyond repair could find relief."

"I'm sorry. About your dad."

"Thanks. It was a long time ago now." He gets up and grabs a bunch of towels. He lays two down over me and covers himself. "So let's talk about Maddie."

We talk for hours. I tell him about my friends and Connecticut and the lake club summer I was supposed to have. I talk about Gram and all the amazing things we've done over the years. I show him constellations, because there are millions of stars painting the sky above us. I tell him how I wish I could be close with my brother like we were before he got weird and angry.

He tells me how he half grew up in Italy and that now he's in university in London, where his dad was born and raised. He loves soccer and surfing and has had a lot of girlfriends but none of them stuck. He brushes my hair out of my face and looks into my eyes and smiles as he talks. He tells stories about his crazy drunken friends, and I tell him they would get along swimmingly with my E's.

"I have a million questions," I say, sliding closer as the chill of early morning sets in.

But my questions can't compete with Enzo's hands pulling me toward him or his warm lips or his arms wrapping us together in beach towels. *Never have I ever had the best kiss of my life with a ridiculously hot guy on a secret ship beneath a dense band of stars.* There aren't enough jelly beans for this one.

The screech of a deck chair wakes me up. We actually fell asleep making out. The pool maintenance guys are escorting Skinny Dave past the Grotto. He's disoriented and having a hard time standing.

Enzo sits up and rubs his eyes. He looks at me and smiles.

"Welcome to the Wishwell," he says. "It's always an adventure."

He walks with me to the elevator and kisses me good-bye when the doors open on my floor. "Bye, Girl in the Purple Dress," he calls. The doors shut before I can answer.

—ʒ∘ʒ—

We get Lane's invite just as Janie is grilling me about Enzo. **Friends, please join us in the ballroom at 8 pm sharp for a pajama party to celebrate Paige's birthday with her two favorite things: a campfire sing-along and chocolate. Shh. It's a surprise. Wear your PJs.**

"This is so cute," Janie says. "Lane is adorable, the way he carries Grace around in that pouch thing." She jumps on my bed. "So did you fool around? Like fool around, fool around?"

"We made out."

"That's it?"

"I mean, like, for hours. I have chafe from his stubble."

Gram texts, **Vito invited us to his cabin to see his Christmas village. Meet me in ten.**

"Gram is the bossiest cruise director," Janie says. "I'm hungover. I'm really not in the mood to see Vito's Christmas village."

We meet Gram and Wes in front of Vito's wing.

"Where's everybody?" I say.

"Who knows?" Gram says. "It's like herding cats."

The hallway blinks with colored lights. We knock softly. Vito's daughter Karen lets us into the cabin where Vito is in an oversized recliner (or maybe it appears to be oversized because he's undersized), covered with a red-and-green blanket.

A Christmas village, piled with fake snow, snakes around the cabin. I'm mesmerized by the lights, and tiny people ice-skating, and elves in moving sleds, and gumdrops, and candy cane trees, and miniature stacks of presents.

Vito is an elf peeking in on Christmas.

"Vito, your cabin is magical," Wes says. "This is fantastic."

I sit on a chair next to a fully decked tree. The glowing angel tree topper's skirts change color every few seconds. Bing Crosby's "White Christmas" comes on, and suddenly I'm back in Gram's apartment, drinking hot chocolate and playing with her Austrian advent calendar with the moving reindeer.

"Welcome to my fantasy." Vito lifts his arms and pulls at his tinsel-wrapped oxygen tank. "I've always thought, wouldn't it be nice if it were Christmas all year long? And now it is."

Janie and I sit on the floor, and Gram and Wes sit on either side of Vito as this old, withered man shows us decades of family Christmas photos. "...And this is Rockefeller Center—we always took a trip to see the tree. Oh, we got all the kids on Santa's lap for this one," Vito says in his Queens accent. He holds a picture to his chest. Karen and his other daughter, Roberta, come over with plates of Christmas cookies.

"It's our grandmother's recipe," Roberta says. "Would you believe Francesca has them deliver these wonderful cookies every morning?"

We eat cookies, and Wes tells the story of the time when he was four and decided to yank off Santa's boot while Santa was doing story time at the library. He ran down the street in the snow, his mother chasing behind, and threw Santa's boot in the river.

"That's disturbing," Gram says. "Crave attention much, Wessy?"

"I probably thought it was funny."

"You would have gotten the belt if you were my kid," Vito says.

"That's a festive thing to say, Father Christmas," Wes says. Vito laughs until he starts hacking and can't stop.

Karen and Roberta walk us out. "Thank you for humoring Dad," Roberta says. "He always loves a fresh audience."

It's ninety degrees out, and I can't stop humming "White Christmas."

-ૐ૦ૐ-

Gram has the biggest balcony of all of us. I'm barely functional now that the exhaustion from my Enzo night has caught up with me. But I'm massaging Gram's knotty, raptor-like feet while she lies on the lounge chair telling me about Gloria's cabin.

"She and the minister have been married sixty-two years. Their family gave them a bon voyage party, all excited that the minister and Gloria were treating themselves to a cruise. They never told their family *what* kind of cruise this is. To each his own."

I squeeze lotion on the top of Gram's foot. "Wait, the family thinks they're on a regular cruise?"

"Yep. I can't imagine getting on the ship without at least saying an honest good-bye. But people are funny that way."

"So, what about the cabin?"

"Oh, the minister loves old cars and proposed to Gloria in a 1930s Ford. So they have a refurbished 1930s Ford bolted to their balcony. Every day, they sit in the front seat, holding hands and watching the sea."

"Wow. Francesca Ivanhoe hooks people up, huh, Gram?"

"Don't you mean your boyfriend's mother?" Gram raises her eyebrows.

"He's not my boyfriend. You'd better not say anything embarrassing like you did with Ty."

"Oh, stop. You girls are too easily embarrassed. If Enzo's anything like his mother, we'll get along just fine. I adore Francesca. That woman is an incredible force. She understands what I've been trying to say to you kids. She took all that pain in her life and grew something beautiful." She waves her hand. "Come here."

I wipe my hands on a towel and sit on the edge of Gram's chair.

"That's what you should always do, Mads. Take the pain and grow beauty." She sits up and faces me. "You know I've always loved volcanoes. I love how they spew searing, deadly lava that goes on to nurture the most beautiful landscapes on earth. It's from searing pain that the deepest beauty can sprout."

I know she's right. I just don't see much beauty coming from the things I've seen on this ship.

"You're a wise old lady, Astrid North O'Neill." I lean over and kiss her cheek.

"Who's calling me old, you little shit? Anyway, back to Gloria and the minister, bald as billiard balls and sailing along in their little car. That's great love."

"Do you wish you'd had sixty-two years with Bob?"

"Hell, no. Then I wouldn't have my precious babies." She points her finger at me. "Martin was an angel, and he's still my angel. But when I'm next to Bobby, my heart flutters." She holds her hand on her heart. "It's electric."

"Gram, you're blushing."

"Am I? Great love does that, honey."

—&o&—

I can't stop thinking about Enzo. I take Paige for a birthday manicure, and she makes me tell her every detail of my night. "If Ethan kissed like a jackhammer dipped in beer, then Enzo kisses like the moon dipped in music," I tell her.

"What a beautiful kissing metaphor," she says. "I need to kiss Lane more."

Paige tells me her first kiss was with a kid a foot shorter than her who gave her a hickey on her face. I almost blow the whole surprise party by telling her how I want to invite Enzo but he doesn't socialize much with guests. I'm so glad I catch myself before the destructive blurt. Lane would be pissed.

—&o&—

On the way to the party, Janie and I run into Skinny Dave walking out of the infirmary. His hair is greasy, and he smells like stale urine. He stops and says hello, and that he won't be able to make the party because he's not feeling well.

"Feel better," I say.

I stop for a split second and look him in the eye, remembering how I covered him in towels and helped him get comfortable last night. It was a bizarrely intimate moment between three strangers, and he has no clue it even happened.

"Thanks, Maddie," he says as the elevator opens.

Janie adjusts her pink bathrobe. "He stunk," she says.

"Stop. He's sick."

"With what?" I don't want to get into it, so I change the subject.

"Did I mention how good Enzo smells?"

"Okay, enough with the Enzo talk. It's wearing on me already."

The ballroom ceiling is open, and there's a bonfire in a fire pit in the middle of the room. This would never happen on a normal cruise ship. The comfy sofas and chairs from the café are set up around the fire, and there's a box of long sticks on a table stacked with marshmallows, graham crackers, and chocolate bars. Mom's gabbing with Vito's daughter Roberta on one of the sofas. This trip is turning both my parents into social butterflies. Jeb appears to be flirting with Camilla, who is very cute, but she's missing the obligatory eyebrow rings, tattoos, and cat-eye glasses of Jeb's usual type.

Dad looks like a balding toddler in his fuzzy slippers. Embarrassing father aside, it's funny to see all these people in sleepwear. The room vibrates with laughter and excitement. Wes and Uncle Billy escort Aunt Rose in her floral nightgown to a chair next to Gram and Bob. Paige's parents come in with baby Grace. Wes reaches up to take her, and she goes right to him.

Our bees buzz at the same time. Shh. We're on our way! Eddie fiddles around with the karaoke machine, and the two screens on either side of our giant circle light up with the lyrics to "Brown-Eyed Girl."

The music starts and we all sing. Mark is behind me, belting it out. He has a really good voice. I guess multiple sclerosis doesn't affect that. When the doors open, we're on the *sha-la-la* part. Paige stands in yellow pajamas with her face frozen in an expression of total disbelief.

Lane whispers something in her ear. She blows kisses at everyone and starts to twirl around the room.

I wonder if she would have done that before she was dying.

We serenade her as she spins around the room with Lane. Her mom and dad jump up and circle around Paige. Wes bounces baby Grace on his knee. She laughs with her two bottom teeth sticking out. Lane swoops down to pick her up, and he and Paige dance close with Grace between them. *Sha la la la la la la la la la dee dah.*

The song ends, and Paige sits between Janie and me. The campfire karaoke continues with Vito belting out a Frank Sinatra song, despite the tubes hanging out of his nose.

The whole crowd sings Bob Marley's "Three Little Birds" as a tribute to Tits and Mama, brandishing our marshmallow sticks at the chorus. We're a loop of pajama-clad karaoke fools, hell-bent on making this Paige's very best birthday.

"I didn't realize we had a group of professional singers on the Wishwell," Eddie says into the mike. He takes Paige by the hand and pulls her up.

"Paige, we understand you are a great fan of all things chocolate." Paige nods enthusiastically. "Well, I hope you haven't had too many s'mores, because the crew has prepared a special birthday surprise."

The panel slides open. Behind it, the entire crew—nurses, doctors, everyone—is smiling in their pajamas. They've formed a semicircle around an enormous chocolate cake topped with sparklers in the shape of a thirty-three. As we sing "Happy Birthday," tears stream down Paige's face.

Janie pulls me into the crowd of people ogling the chocolate buffet, and I don't even know where to begin. There's a chocolate fountain, a donut tree, chocolate animal sculptures, and shot glasses of mousse. I'm thinking I might need to cut back on the endless calorie consumption now that I have the potential to be naked with a very hot guy in the very near future.

Tonight, I eat for Paige. Tomorrow, I run for Enzo.

Janie flicks me a few times. Do Me is coming toward us. I pretend I don't see him and make a beeline for the strawberries. I set my heaping plate next to my brother's and look for a tall glass of milk. I run into Vito near the bar.

"Vito, it's like a chocolate Christmas, isn't it?"

"It's a dream. Now if only I had a lady to share all this good stuff."

"What about your wife?" I look over at Vito's wife by the chocolate fountain.

"Marie? God forbid. She's my *ex*-wife. The woman is a nut."

"So why is she here, then?" I blurt out.

"Good question." He laughs. "We're a family. She's the mother of my children, and nana to my grandchildren. She needs to be here for them, you know, when I depart."

"Wow. And I thought she was your wife all this time."

Vito laughs. "We fight like husband and wife. Between you and me, I still love her. I know it's sick. I guess I can't live with her, can't live without her. She is a nice-looking lady, isn't she?" We look over at Marie, with her inflated hips and ten inches of teased black hair.

"Yes, Vito. She is," I say. He stares at his ex-wife a few seconds, then pulls his oxygen tank to the coffee bar.

The chocolate hit the spot for the first twenty mouthfuls. Now I'm nauseated. Janie and Captain Do Me have gone missing. The rest of us are in sugar comas, lying on pillows and sofas around the smoldering bonfire. The stars form a blur of light as I squint my eyes the way I used to on Gram's lap in front of the Christmas tree. Paige is lying on a blanket between Lane and me. She leans over and kisses Lane on the tip of his nose and rests her head next to Grace, who is asleep on his chest.

"Happy Birthday, P," I whisper as I get up.

"Thank you, little sister," she whispers back. "It's been a really good day."

—ε₀ξ—

I've been waiting all night to see Enzo. My stomach immediately reacts with nervous excitement when I get to his cabin. I take a deep breath and knock.

"Donut?" I hand him a chocolate-glazed in a napkin.

"Hey." He looks groggy, like he's been asleep for hours. He's wearing a worn red T-shirt and plaid boxers.

"Are you tired? Do you want to hang out tomorrow?"

"No, no way. Come in." The TV is on, and two empty Red Stripe beer bottles wobble a little when the ship hits a bump. He shuts the door, and within five seconds, we're kissing. I pull away. I'm obviously not going to admit that the massive quantities of chocolate are not digesting quietly. I need a little digestion space.

"Can we talk for a while? I don't know why, I just feel like talking."

"Let's talk, then." His hair is adorably messy. He takes my hand and pulls me out to the balcony, and we stretch out on matching lounge chairs.

I tell him about Paige's party and how cute it was that Lane's theme was "Paige's favorite things."

"So tell me your favorite things," Enzo says, pulling a beer out of a bucket on the table between our chairs.

"You mean the real things or the things I'll invent to impress you?"

"Real things only. You've already impressed me." He pries the cap off his beer with a bottle opener.

"Let's see. . . . I love fashion, it's kind of my hobby. And my family has an astronomy fetish."

"That explains my constellation lessons last night. Very handy talent, I might add."

"You go next. What are your favorite things?"

He unwraps the donut, takes a big bite, and chases it with beer. "Hmm. Okay. Football. I've been kicking a ball around since I could walk." His voice gets animated. "My friends and I played the Jamaican kids on the beach when we were there. They killed us. Anyway, your turn." He holds the donut up to my mouth and, despite my already-distended stomach, I bite.

"I love to dance. My grandmother taught us all the old dances. I'll dance pretty much anywhere."

He laughs. "I'm a pretty good dancer, if I do say so myself. My sister makes fun of me. But for my next thing, I'm going to go with Egypt. The country. The artifacts. It's all fascinating."

"Have you been there?"

"Yes. It was amazing. I couldn't get over the pyramids, how massive they were; and the mummies, real people preserved all those centuries, sharing themselves with us. I'm going there for a study abroad program this year. That's why I've been trying to get all the surfing out of my system."

"You're spending a whole year in Egypt? That's brave of you."

"Yes, we'll see. I'm kind of scared of dust storms." He licks the last of the donut off his fingers. "And I'll miss surfing. That's been one good thing about this whole Wishwell life."

"This is random," I say, "but I love starfish. I can't believe nature managed to create a living thing shaped like a star. And even when they die, they stay perfectly intact."

He looks at me funny. I'm wondering if the starfish thing is making him think I'm a huge loser. But he brushes the hair away from my face and looks at me with those eyes.

I lean toward him, and we kiss. It tastes like chocolate donut. He pulls me over to his chair and then on top of him. I press into him, and my body wants me to press harder. He's intense and gentle all at the same time. He pulls at my shirt, and I stop his hand.

"Not yet. Not yet." I have to say it twice to believe it myself.

"Okay. Sorry." I get up and sit on the edge of the chair. "I am obviously incredibly attracted to you," he says apologetically.

"Me too. It's just—I better go. To be continued?"

"Will you come back tomorrow?" he says as he turns on his side and lays his hand on my back.

"Yes. Assuming I can get away from the planned events. At this point, my annoying family knows you're here, and they're bugging me to bring you around."

"I know. I've already had a dozen texts from your grandmother inviting me to dinner. I'd forgotten how much the Wishwell intensifies family closeness."

"Have you done this? I mean, before?"

"Kissed a patient's family member?" He shakes his head. "No. This is a first. But I've hung out with a lot of families. When I saw you at the bar, I didn't think, 'This is a stunning girl, but I should leave her alone due to her fragile family situation.' I thought, 'Hot girl, go find on ship.'"

"So you talk to yourself in caveman language?"

"Yes, as a matter of fact, I do. How about tomorrow caveman and hot girl have proper date?"

I laugh. "I know just the place to take you. But you need to come to dinner after. For my relentless grandmother."

"Deal. And you need to kiss me one more time. 'Hot girl, kiss now,' says the caveman."

I do as he says.

—&o&—

It's two in the morning, and Janie's not here. I'm sure she's topless and slobbering all over Dr. Do Me in some starlit deck corner. I shower and snuggle under my cozy comforter, tired and happy. I'm drifting, drifting, thinking about Enzo, and then a text comes in. The bee's going crazy. OMG. Do Me is in the bathroom. We've been fooling around for hours. His penis is minuscule. I don't want to have sex with this pickle thing. HELP! What do I do?

Come back to the room, stupid. Tell him you're not that kind of girl and you need to leave.

Okay.

I guess college doesn't teach people how to get out of a pickle.

—&° TEN °&—

"OKAY, I HAVE one thing on the con list and seven on the pro."
We've been lying in bed talking about Do Me, now nicknamed
Pickle, for two hours.

I read the list. "The pros are: doctor, really cute, funny, nice, car-
ing, smart, and likes our family."

"I know," Janie says, "those are all good qualities. I get it."

"The con is the pickle. Janie, think. Is it a breakfast sausage link?"

"No, not really."

"A crayon?"

"No, Maddie. It's exactly the size and shape of one of those gher-
kin pickles. It's awful."

"He's a doctor, right? Maybe he'll find creative ways to use it."

"I don't care if he's a gynecologist with a PhD in sex ed. There's nothing to work with. God, why do I care? Why? Why? Why?" Janie buries her head in a pillow.

My bee vibrates. Maddie, come to our cabin. I need to tell you something important. —Wes.

Now what? I'm curious, and a little tired of analyzing Pickle. I leave Janie drowning in a vast sea of *whys* and walk over to Uncle Billy and Wes's cabin. Wes opens the door. He looks stressed as he leads me out to their balcony.

"Mads, I'm just going to tell you straight up: Dave died last night."

"Oh my God," I say. "Wait, who is Dave?"

"The alcoholic guy from our table."

The familiar lump rises from my chest to my throat. Skinny Dave is dead.

"What? How did he die? I just saw him yesterday. What happened?" I grab the railing. Wes must see the shock on my face.

"Aww. Come here, Mads." He hugs me, and I press my face against his chest.

"He was ready. He wanted to go, you know, the way he came to go."

"Oh." I picture the pathetic figure slumped over the lounge chair. "But he didn't live out any of his last wishes. He didn't *do* anything."

"I know. He couldn't. He was too far gone. He wrote us a note."

"Why?" Wes doesn't answer. He pulls a note out of his pocket and hands it to me. It's written on a yellow piece of paper in neat handwriting.

Dear Maddie and Wes,

I want you both to know how much it meant to me that you treated me like a man. Most of my life, I've been the drunk good-for-nothing to everyone around me. You talked to me like a normal person, and Mom and I appreciate it more than you will ever know. I thought this would be good for us, but I feel like garbage. I'm ready now.

Be good.

Dave

I sit on the deck chair, stunned. Wes tells me he spoke to Dave's mom. She said Dave had tried rehab and AA dozens of times, and it just didn't work for him. He suffered so long he just couldn't pull himself out of the abyss, not even for this trip. She told Wes she held his hand as the doctor gave him medicine to go to sleep. He was tucked in with his favorite blanket and hugging his childhood zebra. She kissed him, and he drifted off. She swore she had never seen him so peaceful.

Dave's mom said she had felt Dave's soul leave his body a long time ago. She wants to be alone with her grief, and she's going to fly back home when we get to Rio.

I think about last night, when I stopped to talk to him. I had no idea he was about to die, but I'm glad I stopped, even if it was only for a minute. Wes reminds me that Dave loved Thai food, so I order us vegetable pad Thais. We sit on the balcony as morning makes the subtle shift to afternoon. Wes touches his pad Thai lime to mine, and we toast to Dave.

"Do you think Mom will ever get as bad as Dave?" I say.

"Dear God, I hope not," Wes says.

We sit on that for a while.

"Wes, deep question. Do you think Uncle Billy is your great love?"

"You sound like Assy." He throws his lime overboard. "She's been harping on the great love thing. It's easy to have a forbidden romance, leave the guy for sixty years, reconnect during the high-adrenaline act of dying, and then call it a great love. Billy and I are in the thick of things. He's pissing me off royally right now. He's such a prick."

"Yeah, why is he so pissy?"

"Oh, he doesn't know how to deal with Assy being sick. He holds everything in, and then he walks around with a stick up his ass."

"So I guess he's not your great love," I say.

"Billy? Oh, he's my love. I don't know about *great love*. I had some 'great' loves in my day. They were great, but they weren't love."

"Wow. That's depressing."

"You're such a teenager. Hey, can I trust you to keep a secret?" Wes has that devilish look in his eye.

"Actually, despite the fact that I'm a teenager, I can keep secrets. I'm keeping one for Janie as we speak."

"You mean about the pickle? She already texted us. I say dump him. It's not worth another notch in her notched-up bedpost." He has a point. "Anyway, you know how Billy has always wanted a baby and I've always said no because I'm terrified of parenthood?"

"Yes. Didn't he dump you once because of it?"

"Who told you that?"

"Gram."

"Of course she did. Anyway, after we got married, I agreed to put our names on an adoption wait list, figuring it would take years and by then Billy would be too old to care."

"So it worked. You're both way too old now, right?"

"We're not that old, Maddie. Actually we got a call right before Assy gave us her news. A pregnant woman chose us to love her baby."

"What are you going to do?"

"At first I went bonkers. I panicked. But then all this happened, and everything feels different. I get it now. I want it to be more than two of us. I want to be a family."

"You're going to do it? I'm going to have a baby cousin?" I jump up and study Wes's face, trying to assess if he's serious or bullshitting.

"Yep. We're taking the plunge. But don't say anything to anyone. We want to make sure it's official before we tell people."

"I'm going to have a baby cousin!" I jump on top of Wes. "We're going to have a baby with tiny fingers and toes and drool and poopy diapers."

"Get off," he says. "Your breath stinks like the nation of Thailand died in your mouth."

"Thanks for the complex."

"Trust me, I'm doing you a favor."

Wes won't let me leave until I pinkie swear I won't tell anyone about the baby. I do it, but I don't know how I'm going to keep a secret this juicy for long.

I text Enzo on my way to meet Mom and Aunt Rose for lunch. The drunk guy from the lounge chair died. (The Wishwell way.)

He texts back right away. He's at peace now.

$$-\xi\circ\xi-$$

It's even hot in the shade. Mom and Aunt Rose are wearing matching sun hats to combat the tropical rays. The deck is pretty empty because the patients are all at group. Nobody really knows what group is. Not even Paige or my blurting grandmother will talk. I doubt Gram is sitting in a circle talking about how to cope with death. But they all go down, even Holly with the nurses, and have their secret dying-people club with their special food for the chemo palate and cannabis oil.

"Karl loved kielbasa. I couldn't stomach it," Aunt Rose says.

"We know," Mom and I say at the same time.

"Gave you gas," Mom says.

"It sure did. Or maybe it was the—"

"Sauerkraut," Mom and I finish.

I leave them after Aunt Rose's second helping of peach pie and before Mom can suggest a more appropriate outfit for my date, and wander around killing time until I'm supposed to meet Enzo in the arcade. I'm getting that feeling again, the sinking-stomach feeling. I spent all those years dating boys I could barely have a conversation with because they were the best I could muster up. I hope that's not how Enzo sees me. I've never felt this way about anyone. I've never wanted anyone to like me this much.

The nauseating smell of cigar smoke drifts down the hall from the rowdy card room. The Rat Pack is playing poker again. Nobody even bothers looking for Dad, Uncle Billy, Bob Johns, Vito, or Paige's dad anymore. If we need them, we slap at the thick smoke seeping though the cracks in the door and choke our way into their little man cave. Isn't there enough cancer on this ship?

Enzo is in the arcade playing Whac-A-Mole.

"Want to play pool?" he says.

"Sure, I'll play some billiards, old chap."

If it weren't for his distracting kisses every time I get a ball into a pocket, I'm pretty sure I could have beaten his ass in pool. There's nothing more cliché than the guy-presses-against-girl-and-makes-out-on-pool-table-as-cues-drop-to-ground routine.

This is so different.

His mouth is warm and firm, and hungrier than the other boys I've kissed. His hands pull me toward him by the base of my back, and it's the smell of his soap and the slight stubble on his face and the little guttural sounds coming from somewhere deep inside me. One word repeats in my head, over and over again.

More.

⫸ ELEVEN ⫷

WHEN I GET to the Mix-and-Mingle dinner, Janie is sitting in a
chair facing Holly's wheelchair and staring into Holly's eyes.

"So should I stay with him despite the pickle, or not?"

Holly blinks twice.

"Wait—does that mean yes, I should stay, or no, I shouldn't?"

Marshall is laughing and shaking his head. I follow him to
the bar.

"I am so sorry. My cousin has no boundaries. I'm mortified
right now."

"Are you kidding? Holly loves this," Marshall says. "I wheel her
around all day getting pissed off because people look at her like she's
a freak. Or they throw a pity party with their faces and walk the

other way. Nobody gets that there's a complete mind inside that paralyzed body." We watch Janie whisper something in Holly's ear. "Janie doesn't even seem to notice Holly's disabled. Holly loves that girl."

"Okay, as long as she's not being too inappropriate. Holly could be a total prude. How does Janie know?"

"Trust me, Holly's not a prude. She was the life of the party, the one leading the conga lines." He points up at the conga line mural. "Drink?"

"No, thanks. I have to find my mingle table."

Janie's still grilling Holly's eyes, so I look for my place card. I'm seated at table eleven with Janie, Mark, and Burt. I scan the other place cards. Great. Enzo's with Gram. God only knows what embarrassments she's going to blurt out tonight.

Janie arrives at our table just in time to hear Burt and Mark's nicknames for everyone on the ship.

They accuse us of being entirely void of creativity when we tell them we were calling them Wheelchair Guy and Wheelchair Guy's Brother.

Mark calls Janie Barbie, because she looks like a Barbie doll. I'm Queen Bee because they say I strut around like a snobby teenager. I guess between that and scrunch face, I should get the hint and smile more. Mark and Burt call Vito's kids Ornaments because of the Christmas theme and how they all look alike. I'm stealing that one.

"Can I have your attention, everyone?" Francesca quiets the room right away. "I hope you're enjoying tonight's Mix-and-Mingle. I'm learning so much about you all. I wanted to introduce my wonderful son, Vincenzo." Heads swivel to see where she's pointing. Enzo shrinks in his seat. "Enzo is a university student in London and a star football player. He's usually very shy about these events, but it seems one of Astrid's lovely granddaughters has pulled him out of his cabin."

The noise level in the room rises. Enzo half stands and waves, shaking his head.

"Which of Astrid's lovely granddaughters is banging the boss's son?" Burt says.

Gross.

"Her." Janie points to me. "I'm seeing Ty the intern."

"Doctor Ty? No way. We have a nickname for him, too," Mark says.

"Oh, yeah?" Janie says.

"Ken Doll," Burt says, laughing.

Enzo texts. Now you know why I avoid these things. By the way, your gram is fucking hilarious.

Janie chugs three out of Burt's four pomegranate martinis and tells Mark and Burt about Pickle. She says she scoured the ship for other prospects. She even asked Eddie for a tour of the kitchen, pretending she was interested in culinary arts, so she could see if there was a cook or dishwasher worthy of a hookup. Nobody. It's Pickle or celibacy. Meanwhile, Pickle thinks she's playing hard to get, which makes him even more obsessed with her.

"I say go for it. It seems like Barbie and Ken Doll should be together," Burt says. "Plus, it makes sense, right? Ken dolls don't have man parts." Mark and I laugh out loud.

Janie dips her fingers in the half-full glass and flicks martini at Burt. "I feel bad. I shouldn't have told you guys. He's such a nice person. Please don't say anything."

"How about this: I'll confess to you that Mark had a pickle even before his erectile dysfunction," Burt says. "There. Now we're even. Now you have our biggest secret."

"Nice," Mark says. "Way to have my back in front of the chicks."

These guys are high school kids in old bodies.

After dinner, we migrate to the ballroom. The ceiling is open, and the crowd flocks to drink cappuccinos. Enzo actually seems to be enjoying his physics conversation with Dad.

"Hey, Enzo, come meet Mark. He used to be a professional surfer," I say.

"Hi, Enzo. Mark Hill. I'd shake your hand, but I can't move, so I hope you're man enough to let me wink hello."

"Wait a second. Mark Hill from California?" Enzo studies Mark's face.

"Yes. That would be me."

"You are a surfing legend. I can't believe you're here. I mean, shit." Enzo can't stop staring at Mark.

"You can't believe it because I'm all deformed in a wheelchair or because you love surfing?"

"Both. No. That came out wrong." Enzo pulls a chair up to Mark's wheelchair. "My roommates have made a job out of smoking weed and watching your YouTube videos. You were unbelievable."

I leave Enzo talking to Mark about surfing and look for Gram.

Our bees buzz in unison. Thirty minutes until we cross the equator. All hands on deck. You won't be disappointed.

The whole dining room empties toward the elevators. I make my way up to the Grotto with Gram and set up equator-viewing chairs for her and Aunt Rose. I'm picturing the line I've seen on maps all my life and wondering what, exactly, an equator looks like.

Dad and Jeb come up behind me.

"Look, kids." Dad points to the horizon. "The sky's different than in Connecticut, isn't it? We're about to enter a whole new hemisphere. We'll be able to see another set of constellations, like the Southern Cross and the Centaur. We need to get on that telescope later."

"I'll do the telescope tonight," Jeb says.

"Mads?" Dad looks at me with his you-never-pay-attention-to-your-dear-old-dad-and-it-hurts expression.

"Yeah, I'd love to," I say, trying to sound like doing the telescope is as enticing as lying on top of Enzo Ivanhoe.

I don't know if the sky is different yet, but it feels as if we're catapulting through space on a rocket, soaring toward the next galaxy or another dimension. It's as oddly comforting as Dad's arms around Jeb and me. The deck lights shut off. People feel around for the railings. Then a loud noise explodes from the distance. Fireworks. Everybody cheers.

More fireworks light the sky, and I can't tell if they're a mile or a hundred miles away. I'm guessing a bigger ship has crossed the equator.

Enzo comes toward us. "There he is!" Dad says. He slaps Enzo on the back. I guess Dad approves. I rarely invite boyfriends to my house months into a relationship, and here I am subjecting my crush to my family before he even knows me.

"Ladies and gentlemen, welcome to the Southern Hemisphere." Eddie's voice blasts through the sound system and cuts Dad off. "I hope you're feeling hot, because it's time for our favorite Wishwell tradition."

Ole, ole, ole, ole, feeling hot, hot, hot.

The conga line begins. Eddie runs over and yanks Enzo and me toward the crowd. Wes and Uncle Billy carry Gram and Gloria on their backs. I end up behind Dad, who has no rhythm, and Vito is holding my waist for dear life while one of the Ornaments drags his oxygen tank. Paige and Lane push Mark in the front of the line.

We circle the deck five times until people drop out, one by one, and the group disperses for bingo and baby bedtime, leaving behind the "kids," as we are now called.

"So, you want to get high?" Jeb says to Enzo.

"Sure. Come on, Maddie."

I feel scrunch face coming on. "Uh...that's not my thing."

"Oh, come on, you prudish imp," Jeb says to me. He is so weird.

"Jeb, we promised Dad we'd do the telescope."

"We'll go down in a while."

Janie and I run down to change. We get back to find Ty already soaking in the Grotto. Jeb sinks into the water in his grubby boxers. I jump into the steaming cauldron of bacteria and stray Pickle germs

130

before Enzo has a chance to compare my boobs to Janie's massive cleavage.

Ty pops the cork off a bottle of champagne and takes a long swig before passing it to Janie. Jeb leans on the rough deck with his elbows and rolls a joint from a plastic bag full of weed. Ty takes a hit. I'm next.

"Go ahead, Mads. You need to pop your weed cherry at some point," Jeb pressures me.

But do I? Do I really need to pop my weed cherry at some point? There are millions, maybe billions of people who make it through life without ever smoking weed. Besides, it's my brand. *I'm Maddie O'Neill Levine and I'm popular even though I don't drink, do drugs, or sleep around.*

Overthinking. Probably with scrunch face. That's what I do. I'm on a ship in international waters where even the ninety-year-olds are getting high. It's weed. It's not crack. Or meth. Or heroin.

I grab the joint from Ty and almost drop it into the depths of the Grotto. I suck on it. It's disgusting. The tip is all flat and soggy from multiple mouths. Nothing comes out.

"Suck harder, Maddie." I hear Janie's voice as I stare cross-eyed at the joint, waiting for the tip to light up. I suck as hard as I can and feel the harsh smoke singe my throat. My mouth fills with a nasty taste. I blow the smoke out. My lungs are charred, but I go back for more because at this point, why not? I keep going back. Each time, my lungs fill up and I choke a little. It's all very unpleasant, and I'm not even feeling anything.

"Save some for me," Enzo says, moving so close our legs touch. I pass him the joint and watch him suck. God, he's hot. Janie is on top of Ty, straddling him and giggling in his ear. It's slightly fascinating watching Barbie and Ken about to rub their parts together.

Jeb swirls the water in front of him and stares at the foam as it rises and falls. I look up at the curve of the palm tree hanging over us. It's as if tiny tree nymphs work all day making perfectly ridged circles on palm tree trunks. I want to invite them to a party with ladybugs and dewdrop drinks. I want ice cream. And potato chips.

"What is that annoying ringing?" Janie says.

"Somebody's getting a call on their bee," Enzo says. His hand is fully on my leg.

"Oh, shit. Come on, Jeb. We can't be assholes to Dad."

I kiss Enzo just long enough to let him know I'm sorry I have to go do the telescope with my parents.

Jeb and I find Dad and Mom snuggled under a blanket on their balcony. I'm worried they'll be able to tell I just smoked weed. I feel so strange, like I'm a hungry bug walking inside a lantern.

"You kids finally ready for some stargazing?" Dad's obviously thrilled to have us here.

We take turns at the telescope. The sky is almost too cluttered to see the constellations. It's like the palm tree nymph took two handfuls of glittery fairy dust and thrust them up toward the heavens, and then the fairy dust stuck to a universe-sized piece of flypaper. Dad can barely control his excitement. What would Dad be like if he smoked weed? I'm pretty sure Dad still has his weed cherry.

"That, right there, is Ptolemy's Argo Navis, the ship of Jason and the Argonauts." I don't see it, but I pretend I do, just to make Dad happy. "And see that, right there? Can you make out the shape of the Peacock? That's Pavo." I actually do see the outline of a peacock. It's spectacular. "There's Eridanus, the River. If you hold the scope just right, you can see it perfectly."

"That's awesome," Jeb says. I can't figure him out. Is he only into this because he's high, or does he need to get high to show his feelings? I try to remember if he ever talked more when we were little. I'm pretty sure he was always the kid in the background, chewing on his pencil and hiding his deranged sketchbook from us. But he was nicer. And we were closer.

I text Jeb: Have you noticed Mom hasn't been drinking as much since that one night?

He looks down at his bee and texts back: Not really. Don't hold your breath. I'm sure she'll be falling down and pathetic again real soon.

I write: Can you just be nicer to her? Her mother is dying, douchebag.

Jeb marches over to Mom and plants a kiss on her cheek. "You look pretty tonight, Mom."

"Thanks, Jebby," she says. "I had my hair blown out up at the salon." She smiles like the kid who got an A on the test everybody else failed.

I text: Was that so hard?

He gives me the finger.

We order pizza and potato chip sundaes. I'm sharing a spoon with my mother, and I don't even care because I'm ravenous. Janie sends me a whole series of texts: We did it. It was amazing. I like him a lot. We can't call him Pickle anymore. I'm sleeping in his cabin. Time for round two.

I'm delighted for her, but I will still call him Pickle.

–{o}–

The cabin feels lonely without Janie, and I'm lying here with a stale weed taste in my mouth. I'm not sorry I smoked weed, but I won't be making a habit of it. I've also decided I will never say "pop my cherry" again because I despise the way it sounds.

I've been thinking about Skinny Dave. I wonder if he's in heaven, up past the glittery constellations, in some paradise-shaped other dimension. I want him to be there, far away from the demons that betrayed him.

I don't ever want to get addicted to anything. Not even Enzo Ivanhoe.

‑ℰ⚬ TWELVE ⚬ℰ‑

I FOUND OUT this morning that the reason Gram keeps disappearing isn't to bang Bob Johns five times a day, like she claims. And she's not walking funny because she's having too much sex, also like she claims. Pickle has been giving Gram chemo in her cabin since we boarded the ship. She's tired and wobbly because she's trying to keep herself alive long enough to get through this trip. I know I have to maintain Gram's charade and pretend she's the picture of great health and freakish geriatric sexuality. But she's getting sicker, and it's happening faster than I thought.

The woman who always tells me to stand up straight walks with a bend in her back now. The woman who yelled at us for being tired after nine games of Scrabble excuses herself after one. The woman whose favorite line was *you can sleep when you're dead* naps almost every day. I see now that the cancer is devouring her insides while she delivers witty lines and struts around the ship wearing her bravest face.

"So what's the plan, Gram? I know we're going to Rio at some point, but can you at least give me hints about the rest?"

I'm drinking a smoothie with Gram and Bob on their balcony while Bob rubs Gram's bunioned feet with lavender lotion and jazz music plays on an old record player.

"No," she says. "All right, fine. It involves planes, trains, and automobiles."

"Interesting. I hope we're not going on one of those propeller planes. Dad will throw a fit."

"We'll see, won't we?" Gram says. "Changing the subject, you need to tell me more about Enzo. Stop being coy. How's the kissing?"

"Incredible."

"See, remember I told you back in Bermuda that the next one would be better?"

"He seems like a nice kid," Bob says. "I had criteria when my children started dating. I didn't want to be the judgmental overprotective type, but I definitely had my criteria."

"Do tell," Gram says.

"I wanted to see that the young man or lady looked me in the eye when we talked, didn't shy away from personal questions. Not too personal, of course, but things like, what's your passion in life? I also wanted to see that they bothered to ask me something, anything, about myself. Even 'How long was your car ride here?' was good enough."

"Those are fair things to ask," Gram says. "Although Wessy was so nervous when we met. He would have failed miserably."

I can't imagine Wes being nervous.

"My daughter's ex-husband failed all three. He looked good on paper—bigwig lawyer, good education—but he refused to look me in the eye. He evaded all my questions and never once asked me anything about myself." Bob shakes his head slowly. "That creep was bad news."

"Come on, Bobby, fess up: Did Enzo pass? Maddie's kissed a lot of frogs, and you talked to him for a long time last night. We need to know."

"Flying colors," Bob says. He pats my arm.

"Eww. Not with your bunion lotion hand."

Bob laughs, and Gram hits me with a pillow.

"Hey, Gram, what happens at the mysterious group you patients are always sneaking off to?"

"Nothing exciting, Mads. We talk about death. Would you like me to elaborate? I know you love the topic."

"That's okay. I plan to think about you alive and well until you're not."

"Good girl. Oh, speaking of alive and well, Rose is not doing so well. She was always sharp as a tack. I was the airhead of the duo. Now I have to hear the damn Karl-proposing-in-Central-Park story over and over, and about how she can't eat kielbasa."

"And how the plumbing doesn't work," Bob says.

"Exactly. Listen, Mads. I don't trust your mother. She's too self-absorbed, with her rigid little suburban routine. Billy loves to be too busy, and Mary's a wash." She pulls me toward her and grabs my shoulders. "I need you girls to take care of Rose. Make sure they don't stick her in a goddamn institution. We have plenty of money to get her the best help at home. Don't you let them take her out of that apartment. You'll be in New York now. Treat her to the Saks lunch counter from time to time."

"Of course, Gram." I see the worry in her eyes.

"Good. And make sure to—"

"I'll keep her far away from kielbasa and sauerkraut."

"Thank you, my dear."

-ξoζ-

I meet Enzo for a run. He laps me. I run harder and faster than I have, probably ever. I'm on the verge of barfing, but I want to impress him. I want him to look at me and think, *Oh my God, I get to be with that girl.*

It's sweltering in the Southern Hemisphere. We jump into the pool in our running clothes. The Ornaments are on their lunch break, and it's just Enzo and me and a swimming pool where the waves mimic the choppy ocean.

"Come here, hold on to me," Enzo says. I doggy-paddle over and wrap my legs around him. We bob up and down. The waves pull us, and I hold him tighter.

"You look beautiful with wet hair," he says, staring right into me.

"Really?"

"You're a mermaid."

He kisses me. We're moving in sync with the waves, and I feel his whole body tense. I'm a mermaid suspended in the sea, wrapped around Enzo Ivanhoe.

"Get a room." Awesome. It's Burt and Mark.

"Or better yet, keep going and we'll watch." Burt needs a life.

"Don't you guys eat lunch?" Enzo says. I climb out behind him.

"Enzo, you want to come hang out and have some beers?" Mark says.

"What do you think?" Enzo raises his eyebrows and flashes the side smile as we walk away.

We spend the afternoon at Enzo's, getting as close to the edge as we can without jumping in.

$$-\text{\textghog}\circ\text{\textghoz}-$$

My bee is going crazy. I read Janie's text in the elevator. Come to Gram's. Uncle Billy thinks we're picking up a Nazi.

The whole family is abuzz on Gram's balcony. The Wishwell is sailing down the coast of Brazil to some random town to pick up another patient.

"Why do you think it's going to be a Nazi?" I ask Uncle Billy. Uncle Babysitter Wes is holding baby Grace by her fingers and helping her tiptoe around.

"We're picking up an elderly guy named Heinz from a German town in Brazil."

"Stop it. There are no German towns in Brazil," Janie says.

Uncle Billy shakes his head at her. "Haven't you heard of the German enclaves in South America? They're full of escaped Nazis and their neo-Nazi offspring. I heard the guy we're picking up is ancient. It makes sense that he'd be a Nazi."

"I think you're the only one binge-watching the History Channel, Bill," Wes says.

"I watch the History Channel," Jeb says. He's sketching the birds that trail the ship. "I'm going with Nazi."

"Is this a replacement for the alcoholic guy?" Janie says. "I don't think they should have let him come."

"His name was Dave, and he was sick, Janie. What's wrong with you?" Wes snaps.

"Sorry. Sensitive much?"

"Enough, people. You'd do damn well to respect these patients, whoever they are. It's not your place to judge the dying." Gram's pissed.

"Come on, I can't imagine Francesca would allow a Nazi on the ship," Dad says. "That's all a little far-fetched, Billy. Aren't most of them dead by now anyway?"

"We shall see," Mom says in her singsongy I-don't-have-anything-to-add-about-this-topic way.

"They won't send Karl, will they? Oh, I couldn't bear that. He's not a good soldier." And now Aunt Rose thinks it's World War II.

I text Enzo: Ask your mom if we're picking up a Nazi.

He texts back: ????? to which I reply, Just humor me.

We've been hugging the coast for a while, watching the landforms of never-ending Brazil rise up from the Atlantic.

"How about we talk about the feast we're going to have in Brazil? My taste buds are damn near dead. I need some flavor," Gram says.

"This is creeping me out," I say. "What if the Nazi gassed our long-lost relatives?"

"Oh, come on, Maddie. You didn't even have family in the Holocaust," Gram says.

"As a matter of fact, my grandfather's sister's husband and his family were killed in Bergen-Belsen," Dad says. "She had come to New York to try to get them visas. Talk about guilt."

"What? How have you never told me that?" I say. Did Dad have his head in his ass during my whole Holocaust obsession phase?

"He didn't want you to get even more mentally disturbed, maybe?" Jeb says, not even looking up from his sketchpad.

"Oh, okay, Jeb. Why don't you sketch more birds so you don't have to learn how to talk to people?" I'm getting annoyed.

People used to make a big deal about me being half Jewish, even though we didn't do anything Jewish, other than latkes and the menorah once a year at Dad's mother's house. When I was nine, I went in search of Judaism and stumbled upon the Holocaust section of the public library. Everybody made fun of Maddie's Holocaust obsession. Nobody knew how terrified I was of being taken away at night by scary soldiers and pushed inside an oven or that I lived it all again when they burned Grandpa Martin.

It didn't matter that he was already dead.

"Can we just have a nice cocktail on my balcony for once without drama? I should have brought Ruth's family on this trip, too. They were angels." Gram has scrunch face.

"Anybody want to head down to the theater?" Bob is the best tension diffuser for this family. "They're showing *The Shawshank Redemption*."

"I'll go," Dad says. "Great flick."

Enzo texts.

"Oh my God, Enzo says Francesca refuses to answer him about whether the patient is a Nazi. She told him to mind his business."

"Definitely a Nazi," Wes says.

"Definitely," Billy says.

"That does it. Everybody out." Gram ushers us out of her cabin as the ship creeps to port.

$$-\xi\circ\xi-$$

The sun has nearly set, casting dim shadows over the approaching landforms. Janie and I get out the binoculars we borrowed from Eddie's bird-watching kit. When we get close enough to the port, we notice a group of people standing near the dock area.

Uncle Billy rushes down the gangway and past them to find an Internet cafe. Now that Wes has confided in me about the baby, I hear whispered blow-by-blows about the adoption process ten times a day. We watch Vito's kids, otherwise known as the Ornaments, scatter for twenty minutes of port shopping. From here, the town looks more like Switzerland than Brazil, with gingerbread buildings and a massive German beer sign hanging from a lamppost.

The crowd grows, and we realize the people are surrounding a man. They're hugging him and hanging on him. A few young women sob uncontrollably as children stand around looking confused and scared.

"Those are definitely a lot of blond people, for Brazil," Janie says.

The ship horn blows a warning that we'll soon be disembarking from this strange little alleged Nazi port. We take turns with the binoculars. The moaning and sobbing grows to a crescendo when Eddie walks out to escort the patient onto the ship. He's hunched over, almost skeletal. At first I can't figure out who he looks like. Then the bright light of the ramp shines on him and it hits me. He's Gollum from *Lord of the Rings*. I watched that trilogy with Rachel a hundred times. I know a Gollum when I see one. I can almost picture him uttering *precious* as he turns to wave a craggy hand at the crowd. A woman lunges at the ship as the crew pulls in the ramp. I guess alleged Nazis have loved ones, too.

Gollum has come to die all by himself.

It's dark now. The lights from the little German town sitting precariously on the edge of Brazil twinkle like a fairy village.

-&o&-

Paige comes over with leftover pizza after she puts Grace to bed in her parents' cabin. We tell her about the town and the alleged Nazi.

"I'm sure he's not a Nazi, you guys. The poor old man is coming on the ship all by himself. Let's give him the benefit of the doubt." Paige is so nice that it makes me feel bad. She's lucky she's not part of my judgy family.

Paige tries on a bunch of my clothes for tomorrow night's Latin dance party and settles on a black sequined dress that fits like a glove. It feels like a sleepover with the E's.

"Let me do your makeup," Janie says.

"Don't make me look like a ho," Paige says. "Or you can. Why not? I'll surprise Lane when he gets back from poker. I've never been a ho. It could be fun."

By the time Janie's finished, Paige is the prettiest mom I've ever seen.

"I'm going down to Holly's to help her sort pictures." Janie leaves Paige and me to eat gummy bears and read magazines.

"This is heaven," she says. "I haven't done this since long before Grace. Enjoy these little things. When you have a baby, it all goes away." She gets up and reaches for a bottle of water. She stops and tilts her head and stares at me.

"What? Why are you looking at me funny?" I say.

Paige's arm curls in and goes stiff. Her body starts shaking, and she falls to the floor. She looks up, dazed, and her arm shoots out violently.

"Paige!" I yell. "Oh my God."

Her eyes roll back, and she makes a grunting sound. I freeze.

There's a weak voice inside me. It tells me to get help. I rush past Paige. Her arm doesn't stop punching at air. I run out to the hall and scream, "Help! Help me."

Jeb comes running out in his boxer shorts. "What? What, Maddie?"

Camilla comes out after him in underwear and a tank top. She follows me into the cabin. Paige's entire rigid body has moved across the floor.

"She's having a seizure. It's okay. It's just a seizure. Jeb, move those shoes and the stuff away from her." Camilla presses the EMERGENCY button on my wall. She kneels down and firmly pushes Paige onto her side.

The nurses arrive within a minute or two. Paige is still thrashing. Her eyes are open and stare straight ahead. They're dead eyes. "Go on out, honey," a nurse with a Southern accent says. "We'll get her comfortable. Go on. Give us a little space to work."

Jeb holds my arm gently and guides me toward the elevators. "I need to tell Lane." I feel my lips moving, but everything is happening in slow motion.

"Come on. We'll find him. Let's go down to the poker room." Camilla runs out of Jeb's room, fully dressed.

I walk slowly with a stitch in my side.

"That was intense," Jeb says. "I feel so bad for her."

I can't breathe.

There's laughter coming from the poker room. Why is everything funny? None of this is funny. It's awful. I stand in the doorway. Mom sees me first.

"Maddie, what's wrong?"

"Paige had a bad seizure. Maddie was with her," Jeb says.

I walk like a zombie toward Lane. He's at the back table wearing a baseball hat backward, pointing at Bob and yelling something with a smile.

His face changes when he sees me.

"Paige had a seizure. The nurses are with her in my room."

"Oh, shit. I knew I shouldn't have left her." He gets up, but pauses next to me. "I'm so sorry. That is not easy to witness. But it's okay. It happens all the time."

Mom and Gloria sit me down and give me water. Enzo comes over and hugs me. I don't want to see any of them right now. I want my gram.

"I want to sleep with Gram tonight," the weak voice says. "I just need to be near her."

Bob takes me up to Gram's cabin. He tells me Aunt Rose is with her, that they sleep together most nights. It's dark with her blackout shades. Bob turns on the bathroom light. Aunt Rose stirs.

Gram sits up, disoriented. "What happened?"

"Gram." I climb into bed between Gram and Aunt Rose and tell Gram about Paige. I get as close to her as I can and smell the lavender cream on her skin and the faint chemical smell of hairspray in her hair. She holds my hand, and I lie sandwiched between two snoring old ladies. I can't sleep because of the snoring and the image of Paige and the dull pain in my back where I think my pancreas resides.

Rachel told me never to Google health stuff. That was after I Googled sweating and decided I had lymphoma. If I hadn't Googled pancreatic cancer, I would never know there's a strong family predisposition. If I hadn't Googled pancreatic cancer, I might be asleep right now.

I woke up in the middle of the night and went back to my cabin, where I discovered I had my period. I'm sure cramps are misdiagnosed as pancreatic cancer all the time.

Mom's buzzed me this morning with pedicures? That's her way of saying *I'm so sorry you had to see Paige's seizure. Let's make it all better by painting our toenails.*

I stop for a smoothie on the way to the salon. The deck is empty. I pass the Skinny Dave chair and think of him. I still can't believe he's gone.

Mom is soaking her feet and sipping a latte.

"I have a new job," she announces as soon as I sit down.

"What do you mean, a new job?"

"Gloria and I have been hanging out a little in the kitchen, baking treats for the crew."

"That's cool, Mom. You have a baking buddy."

"It's a lot of fun. Anyway, Gloria loves to cook, but she does everything from her head. She's asked me to write down the recipes and deliver them in book form to her grandchildren. Won't that be a nice gift?"

"That's a perfect gift. Is she going to let you have a copy?"

"Absolutely. She's paying me in recipes. Roberta is helping, too—you know, Vito's daughter." She leans forward to check the nail lady's work.

"So, to change the subject," she says, "I'm sure last night wasn't easy for you, honey."

"No. It was not." I look out at the whitecaps swelling under the cloudy sky.

"Doesn't this whole trip make you nervous, Mom? Like about the *D* word? I just feel like it's in my face all the time."

"Can you cut them a little more?" Mom is notorious for scrutinizing her pedicures. "Um, oh, nervous? No. I'm going to miss Gram, like we all will. But death doesn't make me nervous. Put me in front of a bunch of people and make me give a speech, okay, then I'll pee in my pants."

"Did you just say you're more afraid of public speaking than dying?"

"Oh, yeah. Petrified."

"Wow. You're more peculiar than I thought."

"What's peculiar is your choice of nail color. Seriously, Maddie? It's, like, chartreuse."

"Okay, Mom. I'm going to close my eyes and relax."

"You do that, honey. Then you won't have to see your green toes."

-ε○З-

Paige texted Come visit! so I'm getting her cupcakes from the café.

Janie is sitting with Holly, who now has a poster hanging from the back of her wheelchair.

"Mads, come see the poster Eddie and I made for Holly. These are all her favorite pictures." Janie holds up the poster. The woman in the pictures dances and smiles and hugs Marshall and holds a puppy. She sits on a sled on a mountaintop and wears an evening gown the color of raspberries and poses in a black leotard with her arms stretched up toward the sky.

I feel like throwing up all over the poster. It's just so sad.

"These are great pictures." I'm careful not to say how pretty she *was*. "Is that your puppy? It's so cute."

Holly blinks once.

"No, it's her brother's. He lives in Texas. He's pretty hot. The brother, not the puppy," Janie says.

"What are you doing now?" I ask.

"Wes is bringing baby Grace down to hang out. Holly loves when we hold Grace close so she can observe her cuteness."

Holly blinks twice.

As soon as I'm in the elevator, I take a yoga breath and exhale the poison. I don't understand why that Nazi Gollum gets to be hobbling around in his nineties while Holly and Paige and Mark are dying so long before their expiration dates. I rest my head against the wall, slamming it a little too hard on the glass. Fuck this. This is worse than the worst thing I had imagined. I don't know how much longer I can do this.

$$-\xi o \xi-$$

I'm not sure what to expect when I enter Paige's room. The last time I saw her, she was frothing at the mouth with her eyes rolled back in her head.

It's a relief to see she's sitting out on the balcony playing with her bee while Lane sits next to her, reading the *New York Times*.

"Paige!"

"Ooooh. What did you bring me?"

Lane takes a cupcake. "Do you mind if I go in for a shower?"

Of course I mind. I will be grabbing you by your naked ass if she has another seizure. "No. Go ahead," I say.

I look over the railing as he heads inside, making room for me on the balcony. The ocean is angrier than I've seen it in a while. It's not helping my stomach.

"Yum. Bring that tray over here." Paige looks pale and tired.

"How are you?" I say.

"I'm okay. Just exhausted. I feel like I did a triathlon—my whole body aches. I'm sorry you had to be there. Lane said you were really upset."

She sounds like herself. I sit across from her at the tiny balcony table. "Honestly? I really was. I've never seen a seizure and didn't know what to do. I'm so glad you're okay. Did you even know what was going on?"

Paige wolfs down a cupcake and bites into another.

"Not really. It's hard to explain. After, I felt groggy like I was sedated. I'm still kind of out of it. It's a crappy feeling. The doctors are tweaking my medication, and I'm amping up the cannabis oil. I'm not missing Rio for anything." She blinks a few times like she's trying to focus.

"Can I get you something?"

"No, thanks. The cupcake was perfect, and I'll nap soon. I'm just grateful for amazing Uncle Babysitter. My parents can finally rest a bit, and Gracie doesn't have to see me like this. Anyway, tell me something good. I'm tired of talking about sickness and all that boring crap."

"Let me think. How about gossip?"

"You know I love gossip."

"Your seizure outed my brother's sordid affair with Camilla."

"No way."

"Yup. I yelled for help, and Jeb and Camilla came running out in their underwear. You need to stay a little more alert during these seizures, Paige. You're missing all the scandal."

Paige laughs.

"We won't tell Camilla that Jeb's a chronic masturbator. He'll never live down the time in Bermuda when Janie and Brit walked in on him with Gram's *Redbook* magazine."

"Oh my God, stop. My whole body is sore. It hurts to laugh."

I get up to go. "Are you coming tonight?"

"I'll be there. I'm not letting a little seizure hold me back."

If that was a little seizure, I'm thinking a big seizure could take the whole ship down, but just being around Paige makes me feel better.

Now I'm ready to dance.

—&° THIRTEEN °&—

THE CANDLELIT BALLROOM is decked out with tropical flowers and oversized feathers for the Latin dance party. Janie sipped champagne and did my hair in a slicked-back bun to go with my flouncy electric-blue flamenco dress.

None of the patients are here yet. They've disappeared to their mysterious group, now joined by the alleged Nazi. Nobody knows what they're doing down there. They could be painting one another's genitals with maple syrup, for all I know, or building a time machine. We're blindly following them around the globe, and they're keeping secrets.

"Where is everybody?" Mom and Dad arrive with Aunt Rose.

"Billy and Wes just finished taking samba and tango lessons in the dining room," Bob says. "Although they could be giving the lessons. Those guys can dance."

The band starts with a samba song, and I'm stuck dancing with the minister. He's half my size and so rhythmically challenged it's painful. I scan the room for Enzo, but all I see are a gaggle of Ornaments dancing in a group, my parents attempting the samba, and Bob Johns and Marshall drinking at the bar. Janie's outside with Ty. I'm beginning to think the patients are the fun ones in the group.

Enzo finally arrives with Jeb and Burt, who look baked out of their minds, and cuts in on the minister. He flings me out and pulls me in and flings me around the dance floor like a professional.

"How did you learn how to dance like this?" I'm breathless.

"My mother forced me to take lessons on our Wishwell trips."

The music slows, and he holds me close. He's wearing fitted black pants and a crisp patterned blue shirt. I tell Dad to go get his bee. I want a picture of us.

The wheelchair brigade pushes its way in. Paige is in the wheelchair tonight. Janie points to Holly and gives me a thumbs-up. She looks regal, with a sparkly headband on her short hair and a shimmery princess gown. Marshall pushes Holly out to the dance floor as Uncle Billy gets up on stage.

"Wishwell friends, it has come to our attention that we have a dancer in the house. Mr. Bob Johns has asked to do the honors." Bob climbs up with his trumpet. Billy holds the mic to Bob's mouth.

"Holly, this one's for you," he says in his deep voice.

Bob plays "At Last." We gather in a circle around the dance floor, listening to the trumpet tell a love story that's sad and soulful all at once. Marshall stares down into Holly's eyes and bends to kiss her lips. He takes his place behind the wheelchair and spins her around and around—this time, Holly moves, and we stay still. Enzo drapes his arm around me and grips my shoulder as if his hand is saying, *Please don't get sick,* or maybe that's what I'm saying to myself.

The band takes over when Bob finishes, and the dancing goes on for hours. But even as Uncle Billy and Wes and the Ornaments and the "kids" are energized, the patients drop off early, one by one, as if to say, *This is how it'll be.*

And still we dance.

$$-\text{\textsection}o\text{\textthreesuperior}-$$

It's our last night on the Wishwell before Rio, and I have cramps. Enzo and I go back to his cabin, and we start kissing. His hands move under my dress, and I feel myself tense up. The same thought keeps running through my mind: *I haven't told him I'm a virgin.* I can't enjoy anything we're doing right now, with the period thing and the virgin thing and all the Wishwell drama. It's not happening tonight, that's for sure. But I have to tell him. I feel like I'm driving a car without telling my passenger I don't have a license.

I pull away and clamp my legs together. "Enzo?"

"Yes?"

"I'm a virgin."

His hands stop. His breath stops. "Uh. Wow."

"Yeah."

"I'm actually speechless."

"Why? Do I look like a slut?" It's too dark to read his face.

"No. Not at all." He pauses. "I just assumed you'd have…been with somebody by now."

"I've been close. It's a long story." I almost tell him about Ethan, but what if he has the same problem? I need to change the subject. "But if we do, eventually, I'm not going to be weird about it or anything."

He rolls onto his back and reaches for my hand. We lie still, side by side.

"Do you think it might be tonight?" he finally says.

"No. I mean, it might have been. But female issues. You know."

"Oh. Got it."

I want to ask, *Is this our last night together, because we haven't really discussed that?* Instead, I fill the awkward silence with "We're docking in Rio, and I have no idea where Gram's taking us. She loves to be mysterious. I'm not even sure who else is coming with us."

"Mum has to go back to England for a bit, and I have odds and ends to do for school." I'm sure he feels my entire body go rigid. "But I might be able to rearrange my schedule and meet you in Rome, if you're up for it."

"I'm not exactly able to jet-set around on my own at this point."

"No, but I might have connections on this ship who might have given me access to your gram's itinerary."

I realize what he's saying. "We're going to Rome?"

"You're going to Rome."

I shriek and roll on top of him. I sit up and hold his hands down and look into his eyes. "Swear? You're not messing with me?"

He pulls himself up and flips me over. "I'm not messing with you. But don't tell anyone I told you. I don't need Eddie giving me grief."

The thought of never seeing Enzo Ivanhoe again had been weighing on me. Suddenly I feel a thousand pounds lighter.

We eventually get up and eat peanut butter with our fingers on the balcony.

"Question," I say.

"You're full of questions, aren't you?"

"What's group?"

"What do you mean?"

"What do they do on the patients-only floor?"

"It's not that exciting."

"Don't tell me they sit in a support group and talk about their feelings."

"Not exactly. Do you want to go and have a look?"

"Now?"

"Yeah, now. We just can't get caught. My mother will punish us by making us talk about our feelings for hours," he says, pulling his hoodie over his head.

"In that case, we'd better be careful."

$$-\mathcal{E}\circ\mathcal{Z}-$$

I'm chilly in my rumpled flamenco dress and bare feet, walking down the fluorescent-lit halls. We descend the stairwell to the underbelly of the ship. I've gotten used to the wave sounds constantly swooshing under my window. Here, it's only eerie creaking.

Enzo opens the door and sticks his head out. He grabs my hand, pulls me into a dark room, and flips on the light. It's bright and cozy with plush carpeting and couches and a long table with neat stacks of paper and bins of sharpened pencils. There's a whiteboard, a black-board, and a Smart Board.

It's boring.

"This is it?"

"This is where the ideas are born." I can't tell whether or not he's joking.

"What do you mean? Stop being a little clue-giver."

"So, they're making a movie. Lots of movies, actually, but one big movie. Mum fancies herself a Hollywood director."

"What kind of movie?"

"It's for the movement. There's a video room down the hall where all the patients make personal films, for family and friends, memoirs, words of advice—whatever they want to get off their chests." Enzo laughs. "My sister and I used to sneak in and watch the films. One guy confessed a twenty-year affair with his daughter's best friend. Why would he do that to his wife and daughter?"

He digs through a random bowl of hard candies and settles on butterscotch.

"Focus, Enzo."

"Right, they come down and talk about why they want to do this, their lives before the illnesses struck, and how it's not a depressing thing. One woman explained it as wanting to find as much meaning in the act of dying as she did in the act of living."

"Will this movie be released, like, in theaters?" I can only imagine what Gram is contributing. She loves being on camera.

"Someday. They're waiting for the right moment."

"I guess that's more interesting than 'group.'"

"It's fascinating, actually, what people will say when they have nothing left to lose. The way they laugh and carry on down here, you'd never know they were terminally ill. Oh, and they also do graffiti. You have to see this."

I follow him through a room with video equipment and what looks like a recording studio into a dimly lit corridor so long it must span the entire length of the ship. I can't even see the end. There are layers and layers of colorful garlands hanging from the ceiling and graffiti covering the white walls. I've never seen anything like it.

"They call it the Gathering Wall. Somebody got angry at the world one day and went on a rampage with a Sharpie. I guess it went viral."

As we get closer, the colors and shapes turn into words:

I'm not afraid of dying. I'm afraid of being a burden even one more day.—*WW*

"In the book of life, the answers aren't in the back."—*Charlie Brown*

And soon I'll return to the white rose of Yorkshire, where the
sky bathes my soul with a watering can.—PJS

When I was a little girl, I stomped on a baby bird. I've
regretted it for sixty-seven years.—MJR

I thought my last meal would be filet mignon. But all I really
want is an animal cracker.—EM

My child is a murderer. I wish I had aborted him.—Anon

I look at Enzo, flipping through his bee as if he's waiting for the bus. The shock of this wall, mixed with everything else, is wreaking havoc on my stomach. I am too young for this shit. I want to run up to my bed, but I can't take my eyes off the Gathering Wall. Some of the clusters of words look like flowers from a distance. But they are sentences surrounded by *me too*s.

I can't wait to die so I can finally be free.—JD
Me too. Me too. Me too.

I feel my soul stirring, itching to be released.—WFG
Me too. Me too. Me too. Me too.

It is humiliating that I need a nurse to write down my deepest thoughts because my fucking hands died before the rest of me. —Jo
Me too.

You would think the pain would be the worst part. But for me, it's the diaper changes.—M

Somebody wrote:

LOL.

It goes on and on.

Quotes from Shakespeare. Quotes from Maya Angelou. Quotes from Lao-tzu. Quotes from Bob Dylan.

Hanoi was a lovely place. Why did they make me bomb it?—CR

I'm going home now, friends. Wish me well.—Mel

"Oh, what a beautiful morning! Oh, what a beautiful day!"—ST

The funny, the heartbreaking, the profound phrases continue on and on and on. I scan the walls for Gram's flowery handwriting. What would she write? I want so badly to know her secrets.

"You all right? You're quiet," Enzo says.

"I'm okay. Just overwhelmed."

"Let's go. It's late." Enzo leads me back to the stairwell. I've seen only a tiny fraction of this Gathering Wall. I pause for a second to look at a drawing of a hot-air balloon carrying a load of smiling people through the clouds.

I can almost hear the voices of the dead, echoing through the creaking sounds. "Get the hell out, you healthy asshole kids," the whispers say. "This is sacred ground, and you don't belong here."

Enzo points up at the garlands suspended from the ceiling.

"Can you see what those are?"

I try to make out the perfect circles hanging from fishing line. I realize they're the rubber bracelets people wear for causes. Pink for breast cancer. Gray for brain cancer. Purple for pancreatic cancer. Yellow for every cancer. Hundreds and hundreds of bracelets.

They've left their diseases behind.

-ૄ૦ૠ-

Gram's sitting on the edge of my bed with her Bermuda shorts and spider veins and mug of lemon tea. She's barking orders at Janie and me to pack faster because we both overslept in our boyfriends' beds.

"Bring the wool sweaters and parkas."

"What? Are you serious? Oh my God. We're going to Antarctica, aren't we?" Janie says.

"Just do it," says the loudmouthed secret keeper.

We get a text from Eddie.

Wishwell guests: Just a reminder to turn in your clearly

labeled medicinal "herbs" by three pm. We will store them in the vault until departure from South America. Wishwell policy requires us to hold on to your electronic devices until we complete our journey. Safe travels to our adventurers.

We meet in the dining room for brunch before we get off the ship. Dad's eager to tell us about his new buddy.

"His name isn't Gollum, Maddie. It's Heinz."

"So is he a Nazi or not?" Wes asks.

"I didn't think it was necessarily appropriate to ask him over coffee at seven AM," Dad says. "He mostly talked about his nephews and nieces. And his failing heart. He seems like a nice man."

"I wonder if that's what the Bergen-Belsen side of the family thought," I say.

"Not fair, Maddie," Dad says.

"Enough, honey. Give Daddy a break," Mom says.

Janie's pouting. After all her debating, Janie's hooked on Pickle. She's in a terrible mood because she's leaving him on the ship. Gram can't take it anymore.

"For Chrissakes, Jane Margaret, stop it. We are going to Rio. Dr. Do Me will be waiting for you in Asia."

"It's too long," Janie whines.

"Oh, for the love of God," Dad says. "You kids are running around like it's spring break in Cancún. Have some goddamn respect for your grandmother."

"It's okay, Aaron," Gram says. "I wanted it to be a little like spring break. I was afraid the kids would follow me around like I was a two-legged stray. Why should I be the only one having fun?" She holds her hand up to silence the table. "I do have one request. As we go off on our adventures, no pining away. When you live inside each moment, it's hard to have regrets. Okay, kids?"

"Yes, Gram," Jeb and I say.

"Jane Margaret? No pining."

"No pining,".Janie mumbles.

"Good. Now, sit up straight," Gram says. "You look like a pack of hunchbacks at a pity party."

—⚯◦ FOURTEEN ◦⚮—

THE RIO BUSES are almost as unnerving as Tits's Jamaican bus. We're on our way to see the giant statue of Christ. Gollum stayed behind. I guess we'll have to wait to see if the Nazi thing pans out. We left Holly and Marshall behind, too. Janie planted kisses on Holly's head and told her they'd be friends forever and they would see each other soon. Holly blinked twice. Then Janie mauled Ty on the gangway until Eddie had to pry them apart so we could get Janie onto the bus.

Rio is vibrant and electric. We pass stacks of buildings piled on other stacks of buildings like mismatched LEGOs stuck haphazardly together. The colors are mismatched, too, with burnt orange, bright orange, turquoise, yellow. There are kids everywhere, kicking soccer balls, riding two or three to a bike, racing barefoot on the crowded street.

Enzo holds my hand a little tighter now that we're about to say good-bye.

Gloria's talking nonstop about her recipes. "Oh, it's going to be epic, Gloria," Mom replies, referring to the recipe book they're making. I don't know if *epic* is the word I would use.

I texted Skinny Dave's mom before we got on the bus just to tell her I think about him often and to wish her a safe trip back home. I bet Skinny Dave didn't even write on the Gathering Wall. What would he have written?

What would I write?

"I'm going to miss you, Maddie Levine," Enzo whispers.

"So how shall we proceed?" I sound like an idiot, but I don't know how else to say *I know you said we are meeting in Rome, but I don't know when that will be, and I'm getting anxious because I like you.*

"Text me when you get to Rome, and we'll meet up. I have to say, I'm not the most brilliant long-distance communicator. I've gotten in trouble for that in the past."

"I mean, we don't have to text back and forth a million times a day, but it would be nice to know you're still alive."

"I think you would know if I were no longer alive."

"Ha-ha." I turn my head toward the window and watch a woman plastering a guy's face with kisses.

"I've got an idea. What if we text each other three interesting things each day? It could be something we want to share or something we did that day." He must sense my anxiety. "That way we have something to look forward to."

"That works," I say.

I know he's right, but three texts a day will feel like three sips of water. Not nearly enough.

-&o&-

I don't know whose idea it was to take a tram up Corcovado Mountain, but the wait is hot, long, and annoying. It takes forever to chug up to the top, and I don't even get to sit with Enzo because he's helping brace Mark's wheelchair.

We finally make it, and the view from the mountain and the statue of Christ the Redeemer is breathtaking. Rio's domed mountains remind me of alien pods in one of Rachel's sci-fi movies. Below us, the sea meets the city, and the energy churns upward toward this very spot. I'm feeling especially Zen as Christ and I keep watch over Rio de Janeiro.

Paige and Lane hug baby Grace between them and gaze out at the view.

"I'm so glad we're here," Paige says when we're all assembling for a picture. "It's more spectacular than I imagined."

We pose for a group shot in front of a backdrop so spectacular it looks fake. Enzo leaves Mark and Burt and runs over. He squeezes in between Gram and me.

"Say snow globe moment," Dad yells.

"Snow globe moment!" everybody yells.

I wonder what the guy taking the picture thinks of our unruly crowd.

"I like that," Paige says. "Snow globe moment, like we're suspended in a snow globe."

"It's our family saying," I explain. "One of them. Our family also likes the phrase 'you're an asshole.'"

Paige laughs so hard she snorts, and for a second I feel panicked. I don't want my joke triggering another seizure. I turn to go and notice Gram and Aunt Rose sitting side by side on a bench, heads together and chatting away. They look like they could be forty. Or fifteen. Or five.

On the tram ride down, we all stand in a human blob in front of Mark so he doesn't slide away into oblivion. Vito plops down on Mark's lap with his oxygen tank, and Mark starts laughing uncontrollably, which ignites a chain reaction. Even the strangers laugh.

We get to the bottom, and it's time for good-byes. Good-bye to the Corcovado. Good-bye to Gloria and the minister. Good-bye to my sorority sister and her adorable family. "Wave bye-bye to Uncle Babysitter," Paige says. Wes kisses Grace's plump little cheeks and rushes onto the bus, a hot mess. Good-bye, Vito and the Ornaments. Good-bye, Surfer Mark and Buffoon Burt. Good-bye, Wishwell, for now.

"Hey, Vito," Dad yells as Roberta lugs the oxygen tank onto the bus. "Bob and I are going to practice our poker and get you good when we're back on the ship."

"Not a chance," Vito yells back. "You'd better save your money, chumps."

It's time for the worst good-bye of all. Enzo puts his arm around me, and I look into his eyes. My lip trembles. *Don't cry. Don't cry. Don't cry.* It's harder to hold back than a sneeze, but I do it.

"Until Rome, beautiful Maddie," he whispers. I nod.

There are no words.

He helps hoist Mark onto the Wishwell bus. I wave at the tinted windows and hope he's waving back.

—ξοζ—

A guy with gold teeth stands to the side of the trolley entrance with a misspelled sign for the NORTH-ONELL PARTY. We all pile into a white van and set out past the brightly colored slums where people live in layers; *favelas,* they're called. Gold Teeth tells us boring stories about the history of the city in a Portuguese accent so thick it sounds Yiddish.

"How do they let this go on?" Wes says. "Look at those kids begging. This is horrible. I wish we could do something. I feel so bad for them."

"So stop the van and give them some money. That would help," I say.

"Yes, but it wouldn't solve the deeper problem of poverty, Maddie."

"I doubt those four-year-olds care about the deeper problem of poverty."

Wes furrows his eyebrows at me. "Oh, wow," he says in a blatant attempt to change the subject, "look at how the poor people have found a way to bring beauty to the Favela with art."

"And this is the upscale Copacabana Beach, home to the rich

and famous," Gold Teeth proudly announces. Crowds of people dot the white beaches between the busy streets and the sea. Sweaty girls around my age are drinking from a fountain on a volleyball break.

"Her name was Lola. She was a showgirl." Uncle Billy belts out our family's favorite karaoke song from Barry Manilow's *Greatest Hits,* and we all join in. Even Jeb's singing. Gold Teeth chair-dances, and we sing the chorus again.

We speed past the crowds of people and fancy buildings, then more slums, and arrive at the foot of a steep rain-forest hill. We drive into the canopy, surrounded on all sides by massive palm trees, ferns, tangles of vines, and multihued flowers. Gold Teeth finally stops talking long enough to let us out. We buy Coca-Colas from a roadside shack and pile into two pimped-out mega Jeeps. I squeeze in between Mom and Bob, who smells of incense and lime. Bob tells us about his trip to Mozambique, where he almost died from a staph infection after he got a hangnail. I did not know death by hangnail was a thing.

We stop at an overlook and take pictures of the view of Corcovado below us, where Christ looks like a tiny figurine made of soap.

"Let's do big trips like this every year, honey," Mom says. "I think I have the travel bug."

"Just don't let it get into a hangnail."

"Good one." She puts an arm around me. "You know what? I think I've figured out why we all like Bob so much. He's just like Grandpa Martin."

"Mom, Grandpa Martin was a short, pasty white guy who liked golf and Civil War artifacts. I'm not seeing it."

"Not looks or hobbies, Maddie. My father was quiet and kind and wise. He let Mother do her thing without complaining. He was always there, but he didn't need to be seen." She raises her eyebrows and nods toward Bob, who is taking a selfie with Gram and Aunt Rose.

"Whoa, Mom. You are so right. Bob is exactly like Grandpa Martin. I guess Gram does have a type."

—§o§—

We stop again at a fierce torrent pouring down the side of a steep ridge. A crowd of American tourists blocks the view of the waterfall with their big heads, and we wait for them to pile into their tour bus. The forest buzzes with insect sounds.

"I need a little boost," Gram says, taking my hand. She's breathing heavily.

"It's a magic waterfall," Gold Teeth says. "Make a wish."

This guy has no idea that our gram is dying. Mom stands at the edge with her eyes closed. She's falling for this—she must really believe this magic waterfall will make everything better. I can't stop wondering how many people like us have stood here wishing for miracles, only to have their wishes fall like bricks to the bottom of the swirling whirlpool.

Gram taps my shoulder and points to a nearby tree. A little monkey is sitting on a branch. We watch it peel a piece of fruit, then devour it intently. We all fixate on the monkey. It doesn't seem to give a damn about us as it looks around and licks its tiny hands.

"We should give it a name," Uncle Billy whispers.

"How about Lola?" Gram says.

"Her name is Lola. She is a showgirl," Wes sings. We shush him, but it's too late. Lola disappears into the forest canopy.

We are too much for the little monkey to handle.

$$-\xi\circ\xi-$$

After spending all that time in a moving vessel, it feels like I'm still moving, even as I linger in the shower at the Copacabana Palace Hotel slathering fancy soaps all over myself. Janie flings open the shower door to tell me she just had a nightmare about bats gnawing through her suitcase. We spend the next hour writing postcards to our friends. I end Rachel's postcard with: *Gram is hanging in there. She's a trouper.*

We're dressing for dinner when I get a text from Skinny Dave's mom.

Thank you for thinking of me. I'm missing my boy, but ready for the next chapter. Best wishes to you all.

$$-\xi\circ\xi-$$

Apparently the secret chemotherapy hasn't altered Gram's obsession with Brazilian meat.

I put on a short, very tight green dress and silver heels. Janie walks out in an even shorter, even tighter pink dress that highlights her voluptuous boobage. The gentlemen of the Copacabana Palace lobby swoon a little when we make our entrance. I'm disappointed in Janie and me—we should be taking advantage of the opportunity to hook up with Brazilian boys, but she's obsessed with Ty and I only have eyes for Enzo Ivanhoe.

I wonder what he's doing right now.

"Hubba, hubba. Our girls are all grown up," Wes says. Even Jeb shows up in nice clothes.

"My, my. Look at us. Aren't we sexy beasts?" Gram's wearing all her good jewels for this.

The *churrascaria de rodízio* restaurant, Brazilian for "so much meat you will puke," rests between Sugarloaf Mountain and the sea. We sit outside on a patio with hanging lanterns that glow dimly as the sky darkens behind the mountain. Waiters deliver platters of sausage, pork, chicken, beef, fish, fried potatoes, and salads. The wine and fresh passion-fruit juice flow, and Aunt Rose drinks cold beer.

Gram was right. The meal was so good, we barely said a word in two hours other than "yum" and "oh my God, this is so delicious."

We wander down a boardwalk made of snake-shaped mosaic tiles. We're all drunk on meat as we amble along. Janie and I struggle to keep up with Gram and Bob. Clearly the mosaic path wasn't meant for ridiculous heels.

"Will my babies be joining us at the jazz club tonight? It should be a great show." Gram looks back at Mom, Dad, and Aunt Rose, who are now a block behind us. "I can't wait to drop those duds and order my Rio drink. It's *caipirinha* time."

"What's *caipirinha* time?" Janie asks.

"Brazil's national drink. It's an elixir made with liquor, sugar, and lime. Only have one, Jane Margaret. We want you in one piece on the beach tomorrow," Gram says.

"Sorry, Ma. We're not spending our one night in Rio at a jazz club," Uncle Billy says.

"We are about to go dance off the five thousand calories I just consumed," Wes says.

I turn to Janie. "We could go three ways tonight. Coffee and cards with the duds, jazz with the eightysomethings, or dancing with the uncles. I'm going with the uncles."

"And I want to try a *caipirinha*," Janie says. "After I digest."

—&o&—

Usually Jeb blends into the woodwork and we forget he's with us. But after half a bottle of wine, he's in rare form.

"The chicks here are incredible," he says, trying to drum up enthusiasm from two gay guys and his sister as we wait outside the club.

"What about your girlfriend, Camilla?" I say.

"I don't have a girlfriend. We're hooking up. Speaking of which, how's your virginity?"

I ignore him.

Janie runs out of a souvenir shop with a Statue of Christ the Redeemer Christmas ornament. "Look what I got Vito. Don't you think he'll love it?"

"Vito will be dead at Christmas," Jeb says.

Janie stops abruptly. She has the expression of a little kid whose balloon flew out the car window.

"It's . . . I got it for his cabin," she says. The tiny ornament hangs on her finger.

"Why do you have to be a douchebag, Jeb?" I say.

We keep walking, following pulsing music into a club. The bouncer is hesitant to let us in. I don't know if it's because we're too old, too young, not cool enough, or annoying Americans. But he starts talking to Jeb about his tattoos and ends up waving us all in. My brother actually saves the day.

The club is dark, and the dance floor is lit with flashing colored lights. The women are dressed so scantily I can practically see their Brazilian waxes. My family insists on ordering multiple rounds of the elixir of Brazil, so I make my way onto the dance floor alone.

A tall Brazilian guy comes up behind me. I turn around and grind into his firm, muscled torso. What do I care? I'll never see any of these people again. The E's would be so proud. Janie finds me on the dance floor. Wes runs out of the DJ booth with a big grin, and Lynyrd Skynyrd's "Gimme Three Steps" comes on. I'm transported to the honky-tonk bar near Aunt Rose's Charleston house where we spent an entire afternoon last winter break choreographing a routine to this very song.

Janie and I fling off our heels as Uncle Billy and Wes grab us, much to the dismay of my partner, who soon realizes this is a group routine. The floor clears, and people jump in behind us, and within minutes, we manage to teach the entire club our routine.

Jeb two-steps behind me with a cute Brazilian girl while my guy is pulling me to the middle of the dance floor. We dance. We grind. He touches me. I touch him. It feels good. It also feels like I'm cheating on Enzo.

Janie's chugging yet another *caipirinha* at the bar while Jeb sucks face with the girl in the corner.

"Janie's puking." Wes grabs me.

I look up at my guy. "My friend, blah, blah!" I make the universal puking sound. I think my new friend thinks I'm about to puke because he lets go pretty quickly. I run over to Janie who is vomiting an impressive volume of meat mixed with liquor, sugar, and lime. People clear a wide path as Wes and I push her out the front exit. Janie trips and lands sprawled on the sidewalk, flashing her thong to the people passing by. Wes wipes her mouth with a handful of cocktail napkins. Uncle Billy and Jeb come out all sweaty and help lift her drunken body. We drag her to the Copacabana Palace and straight up to bed.

$$-8o3-$$

I wake up way too early and go out for a walk around Copacabana. The streets are much quieter than they were a few hours ago. I find a cute café and order coffee and a sweet bun. I open the *New York Times* and scan the headlines until a frantic text from Uncle Billy disrupts my grown-up moment.

Wes got beaten up last night. Police involvement. Please bring us an ice pack or frozen peas or something.

I run to the concierge, who is probably ready to kick us out of the Copacabana Palace. He finds me an ice pack, and I race up to discover Wes with a blue-green face, puffed up like a dead jellyfish.

Uncle Billy is furious. Once Wes has the ice, Uncle Billy launches

175

into the story of what happened after they dropped us off and went out for more drinks. "Wes got bombed and decided he wanted to go out and find poor people to help. We ended up in a deserted neighborhood in the bad part of Rio, where Wes saw a little kid pushing a shopping cart up the street. He tried to ask her if she needed help—as if she spoke English!—and out of nowhere, her grandmother started whaling on Wes."

"Wait, Wes got beaten up by a grandmother?"

"Yes," Uncle Billy says. "So then the grandma pulled out a knife, and I screamed for help. Building lights started going on, and somebody called the police. By the grace of God, the cop was relatively friendly and spoke a little English. Wes got out of it by giving the cop and the grandma five hundred US dollars each."

"Why did you have a thousand dollars cash on you?" I ask. Poor Wes is holding the ice pack to his ravaged face.

"I thought we might go shopping."

"Yes, he thought we might go *shopping,* and he thought we might help *poor people,* and he almost gets us killed!" Uncle Billy is livid and refuses to talk to Wes. He takes off to go hang gliding with the other daredevils—Jeb, Bob, and, wonder of all wonders, Dad. Dad is not a hang glider. I just hope he makes it back in one piece.

I'm stuck babysitting Uncle Babysitter.

Eventually, Rotten Plum Face gets into the shower. I text Janie: Beach? She texts back, No f'ing way. So sick. I can't believe she's pissing away her only beach day in Rio. Luckily, Wes rallies, plum face and all.

"What the hell happened to you?" are the first words out of Gram's mouth when she meets us in the lobby. She takes off her sunglasses and studies Wes, who expects me to tell the outrageous story.

"Wes, you could be dead right now. There are safer ways to help poor children," Gram scolds him.

"Assy, I was drunk. Do you think an old lady could beat me up if I weren't inebriated?"

"Yes," Gram and I both say.

"Can I not be the butt of jokes today? It's bad enough that Billy's not talking to me."

We agree to try really hard not to make Wes the butt of jokes and stroll along the snake-shaped mosaic path. I squint to make out the outline of three surfers paddling out. They remind me of Mark. And Enzo.

Gram wants to set up our stuff on the beach. Mom wants to sit by the pool. Gram wins. Gram and Wes comment on each person passing by, while Mom takes out her knitting magazine. Who can think about wool in eighty-five degrees? Although technically it is winter here.

Wes peeks out from under the oversized hat he stole from Aunt Rose to hide his deformed face. "How about that one, Aunt Rose? Inappropriate enough for you?" A woman prances by with a black G-string threading her bulbous ass.

"I want to wear a bathing suit like that," Aunt Rose announces.

"Okay, let's do it," Wes says.

"No, really." Gram pops up in her chair. Her skirted swimsuit hangs on her shrinking frame. "Let's do it. Let's all buy thong bathing suits and wear them. We'll just walk around a little. Come on, it'll be so liberating."

"I'll do it," I say.

"Me too," Aunt Rose says. I think of the *me too*s on the Gathering Wall.

I assume Mom will be the one to kill the moment, but she shakes her head and says, "Well, when in Brazil..."

We gather our stuff and walk a few blocks to a tourist shop, where I find my perfect suit for the day. It's a purple thong bikini with tiny seashells hanging off fringe on the top and bottom. I try it on in the changing room, which smells of mildew and feet. I look pretty good, all things considered.

I walk out to find Wes and Mom standing in front of the mirror. Mom's in a black one-piece thong suit and Wes is wearing a purple sparkly banana hammock thong. I am simultaneously impressed and disturbed by the size of Wes's banana. Mom doesn't even seem to notice. She's riffling through her bag looking for lipstick.

Gram walks out. She's a hairless, deflated mushroom. Her body is tiny and shriveled, and her ass tattoo hangs so low, I can't even make out the seahorse shape. It's just a blob of color. Her stomach distends like she's pregnant, and her boobs hang down and touch the swollen belly mass. Yet the shriveled, drooping woman standing before me in a shiny turquoise thong bikini looks beautiful. Her silver hair, pinned up in Chinese hairpins, frames her delicate features. Her devilish expression gives her a schoolgirl glow.

I love my gram.

Aunt Rose stands next to her sister in a ruby-red one-piece thong. She's a little taller and flatter bellied, but equally shriveled and even saggier. Gravity really does pull everything down.

"Wow, Wes. Billy never told me how large you are. Good for you," Gram says. Wes turns a perfect shade of purple to match his eye. "And, Trish, maybe a little laser hair removal would be good for you, dear."

"Thank you, Mother *dear,* but I prefer to look like a woman, not a baby," Mom says, adjusting her suit.

Gram pays the saleswoman, who doesn't bat an eye. She surely sees deranged people all day long. We don't hide behind our beach bags, afraid to show off our goods. No, the Astrid North O'Neill party struts. We work it. Wes is in the middle, flanked by Mom and me and Rose and Gram, walking the streets of Rio in thongs.

"We're sexy, and we know it," Gram belts. A man in a floral shirt gives us the thumbs-up.

We get to the beach, throw our stuff down, and march toward the ocean. We push against the waves, holding hands so we don't lose Gram and Aunt Rose, who probably weigh a hundred pounds between them.

"Woo-hoo-hoo," we shout at the top of our lungs, as the cold surf hits our bare skin. Aunt Rose's sun hat flies off Wes's head, and we lunge forward to grab it, causing all of us to fall in and yelp.

Wes runs up to get his bee as we stumble out, laughing so hard it hurts my side. We face the sea and pose for a nice lady who volunteers to take photos.

I'm exhausted by the adrenaline rush and from wrestling with the waves while laughing hysterically. Wes sends the photo of our bare asses with a text to Uncle Billy: I'm sorry for being an ass. Please forgive me. I love you.

Uncle Billy texts back, OMFG. I forgive you, you fool.

A few minutes later, he sends a close-up picture of Dad's terrified hang-gliding face with the caption SCAREDY CAT MADE IT!

Gram laboriously works on a text of her own, beneath the shade of our beach umbrella. It takes her five minutes to write two sentences. Be ready in the lobby at five sharp. We're going to Iceland, babies!

—ξoჳ—

I get Enzo's first three things just before we board the plane. I've been waiting; I wasn't going to go first. 1. My mum likes you. That's a first. (She called my other girlfriends flighty.) It's probably because you made me leave my cabin. 2. The best thing about being back in England is the prospect of eating large quantities of curry for lunch and dinner. 3. You have a perfect nose.

Enzo Ivanhoe said *girlfriend*.

FIFTEEN

IT TAKES EIGHTEEN hours, including a layover in Amsterdam, to make it to Iceland. The flight is so long we get warnings to walk around the plane so we don't develop deep vein thrombosis, another cause of death I was not aware of.

I switch seats with Bob and sit with Gram in first class for the second leg of the trip. Bob honks so loudly nobody can sleep. Gram doesn't know what's worse, Bob's snoring or Grandpa Martin's overactive bladder. "More reasons to embrace your youth," she finishes.

There are so many things I never knew about Gram. She can be as cryptic as she can be open and exposed. I ask why we're going to Iceland, of all places, and she whispers, "It's all because of a very old book." Then she pulls out a tattered copy of *Journey to the Center of the Earth* by Jules Verne. Gram had read us the story about the guy and his nephew who burrowed into an adventure through an Icelandic volcano one summer in Bermuda when we were freshly showered and lined up on the guesthouse daybed. I never knew how much it meant to her.

Gram hands me a folded, yellowed paper from inside the book cover. It says *Dear Mummy, I would like very much if you and Father could take me to the Sneffels volcano in Iceland so that I may take a journey into the earth. Very Truly Yours, Astrid North.*

According to Gram, who was ten at the time she wrote the letter, her coldhearted mother returned the letter and told her there was no such thing as a Sneffels volcano, the book was pure fantasy, and they would not be going to the wretched island of Iceland.

Despite Gram's parents, who were supposedly big assholes, the book became a source of inspiration for all her world travels. She's been to over sixty countries, but never got around to visiting the place where it all began. We're going to Iceland to prove Gram's mother wrong.

$$-\xi\circ\xi-$$

"This is psychedelic," Mom says as we drive down a solitary road surrounded by giant black boulders. There are no plants or trees, just an eerie lava rock graveyard.

I'm squished in the back of a tiny rental car with Jeb and the luggage. Our caravan pulls up to an oasis, a massive turquoise cauldron simmering in the middle of a vast boulder colony.

The Blue Lagoon.

"Pretty neat, isn't it?" Gram says as we climb out of our respective cars, groggy and grubby. "It's a man-made geothermic hot spring in the middle of a lava bed. These hot springs are the national pastime here in Iceland."

"It's freezing," Janie whines.

"It's Iceland, for Pete's sake," Dad says. "Grab your suits. Let's check it out."

God forbid we actually get a chance to take a nap or eat a meal before we plunge into a geothermal lagoon. We riffle around already messy suitcases for swimsuits. The only one I can find is my still-damp seashell thong. Gram walks straight into the communal shower, a tiny shriveled raisin wedged among Nordic goddesses.

"I'm not getting naked with Aunt Rose," Janie whispers. "This is just wrong. And what in hell's name are you wearing?" Janie stares at my seashell thong.

"A Brazilian souvenir." I've barely talked to Janie since we left Brazil, where she puked three more times at the airport and slept the whole trip.

A tunnel connects the locker room to the Blue Lagoon, so we only need to freeze for a few seconds before wading into the steaming cauldron.

"Kids, kids, over here," Dad yells. There they are, the misfits, sticking out like sore thumbs. Janie and I slowly wade over to them through the chest-deep pool that stretches as far as I can see.

"What is that awful smell?" Janie says.

"Sulfur. Because of all the volcanic activity," Dad says, floating on his back with his hairy belly sticking out of the water.

The mystical properties of the Blue Lagoon lull us into a collective trance, and we float aimlessly for an hour. Nobody wants to get out. It's probably fifty degrees, but the arctic chill feels subzero against the steamy water.

Back at the rental cars, we look like a pack of mole rats, shivering with sulfured hair shellacked to our heads. It's hard to believe yesterday morning we were strutting on Copacabana Beach.

-ε°ξ-

By the time everybody gets to the hotel lobby for dinner, Wes has made friends with an overly pierced couple, Helga and Magnus, and they've made a date to go out next Saturday night. I'm envisioning another pukey ride for Janie to the next destination.

We find a quaint restaurant with paper napkins and miniature lobsters. My family eats enough lobster to deplete the North Atlantic. We lick our fingers clean while Gram pulls out her tattered copy of *Journey to the Center of the Earth* and tells the story of the book, the note, and her asshole parents.

"I'd like to leave the book at the volcano if I can, as a tribute to Mr. Jules Verne."

"We can make that happen, Mom," Uncle Billy says.

I picture lava streaming down a monster volcano and trapping us for eternity in twisted poses like the Pompeii victims. People will discover us in a thousand years and make stupid guesses about who we were and what we were doing there.

We check out the wool sweater shops and modern street sculptures, then stop to feed the swans at a lake in the city center. Compared with vibrant Rio, Reykjavik is a watercolor of muted blues and grays.

Jeb and Janie and I go into a café for hot chocolates.

"I'm so excited. If Ty and I last another month, it'll be my longest relationship ever," Janie says.

"I'll believe it when I see it," Jeb says.

"Why do you have to be so negative, Jeb? That's rude." Janie gives Jeb the death stare.

"I'm not rude. I'm a realist. Number one: There's too much temptation." He slurps his hot chocolate. "Number two: You're weak," he says with his jackass smile. "I bet you'll hook up right here in Iceland."

"Shut up, Jeb. You're just feeling guilty for cheating on Camilla with that Brazilian girl," Janie says.

"I didn't cheat. Camilla is not my girlfriend. She's not even my type."

"Yeah. She's normal," I say as I get up to venture out by myself. I need a little break from the family. People are laughing and strolling next to the bay. Nobody strolls in Connecticut. The island is so volatile, the ground below me could erupt any minute, sending me into a Jules Verne dimension.

Gram always says there's a difference between being alone and being lonely. Tonight I'm by myself on an island of light and cold and heat and stark beauty, but I'm only lonely when I allow myself to think of life without my gram.

Wes texts: The Jeeps have arrived to journey us to the center of the earth. Move your behinds.

Janie and I pull our still-shellacked hair into buns and bundle up. Our guide Kristian is dirty blond with a gleaming smile and Bermuda-blue eyes. He's cute.

Another guy pulls up next to us in a matching mega Jeep. He's cute, too, in an elfish kind of way. He's slighter and more delicate than Kristian, who must be a direct Viking descendant. I climb into Kristian's Jeep and wave to Mom, who has decided to stay at the hotel with exhausted Aunt Rose.

Kristian takes us on a sightseeing detour, narrating the whole trip. We pass mist-shrouded waterfalls and grass-thatched cottages, simmering calderas and geysers. Kristian tells us the Icelandic people believe Iceland is full of elves.

We stop on the side of the road next to a mammoth waterfall pouring over a jagged cliff. Dozens of seals bob in the sea across the road. We walk down to the black sand beach and watch the seals ride the choppy waves.

A seal waddles right onto the beach, unafraid of our raucous family.

"What shall we name him, Assy?" Wes calls.

"How about Jules Verne?" she calls back, just as the waves pull Jules Verne back out to sea.

—ℰ∘Ⅎ—

After hours of Gram badgering Kristian to slow down, it appears in the distance—Snaefellsjökull, Jules Verne's Sneffels. It's a snowcapped mountain with no signs of spewing smoke or flowing lava, which is a letdown and a relief at the same time.

Gram asks Kristian to stop. She crawls up on top of a boulder, supported by Uncle Billy, and shouts, "See, Mummy? It really does exist. And Iceland is not a wretched place at all." Her voice is full of residual resentment.

We drive awhile longer, stopping to let a painfully slow and distracted herd of sheep cross the road. Wes stands on the seat of the Jeep behind us and frantically points toward the mountain. "Rainbow! Look, guys, it's a double rainbow!" Two iridescent domes of color and light hover above Gram's volcano, an unexpected gift from Jules Verne or Gram's mother, or both.

The off-road ride to the base of the volcano fuels everybody with adrenaline. The other Jeep flies with the top down. Dad's bald head pops up, and he lifts his arms like he's on a roller coaster. Jeb and Wes pop up next to him, three fools on a joyride, screaming at the top of their lungs. When we get to Snaefellsjökull, Kristian offers up a little surprise.

"Anyone interested in visiting the underworld?" Kristian leads us to a tin spaceship thing sticking out of the ground attached to a sign that apparently says THE UNDERWORLDS in Icelandic. He fumbles with a lock and opens the door. "This is an ancient lava tube that descends several hundred meters. Maybe Grandma and Grandpa over here want to stay and wait?"

"Not on your life, Blondie. We're going down," Gram says, marching to the front of the line in her hiking boots.

The staircase to the depths of the earth is uncomfortably narrow. The good news is that there aren't any bats. The bad news is that there is a good chance the volcano will regurgitate lava through this lava tube and singe us all beyond recognition. It's cramped down here, and I am not getting enough oxygen.

We stop to rest at the bottom of the first landing. Stupid, embarrassing Jeb has to pee on the wall right in front of us. Dad puts on Elf Guy's headlamp and looks around for a good spot to plant Gram's book.

"I think we should have a ceremony or something so Mom can say her farewells to the letter," Uncle Billy says.

"This volcano is believed to be a very powerful healing energy spot," Elf Guy says.

We form a circle, lit by headlamps and surrounded by ancient lava rock, and stand shoulder to shoulder, bathed in the energy of this underworld lava tube. Gram chooses Wes to lead the ceremony.

Wes clears his throat for dramatic effect. He is clearly flattered that Gram picked him.

"As we stand here beneath this powerful volcano that has stood longer and stronger than any human being, we are humbled and emboldened by its strength, beauty, and endurance." Wes pauses. "Astrid North O'Neill, you are a gift to every person you meet. Like the volcano, you bring strength, beauty, and endurance to the world. By leaving your cherished book behind, you join us all with the volcano and Jules Verne for eternity."

Everybody hugs in a lava tube moment of solidarity.

"You should be a preacher, Wes," Bob says. "That was eloquent."

"I need a little air," Uncle Billy says. He disappears up the stairs.

Gram burns the letter with Jeb's weed lighter. We surround it, mesmerized, as the yellowed page curls and disappears into ash. Gram kisses her book and leaves it in a dark space near the staircase. It's a heartfelt farewell to little girl Astrid at the end of her long, fabulous life.

We find Uncle Billy sitting on a boulder with his face in his hands. He's sobbing. Wes and Gram put their arms around him, and we watch from the Jeeps as the three of them hold one another under the changing Icelandic sky.

−ξ∘ƺ−

After the long ride back, I decide not to go clubbing with Helga and Magnus. I leave Jeb and Janie with their vodka shots and make my way down to Gram's suite.

Gram is tucking Aunt Rose in, so Bob and I order pastries from room service. While we were gone, Mom took Aunt Rose to a clinic and got her antibiotics for a urinary tract infection. They said it was good she went in, because people her age die from urinary tract infections.

Bob tells me about his four kids and seven grandkids and seventeen great-grandkids. All but two have the music gift.

"What do the ungifted do?"

"One's a banker. One's a lawyer," Bob says. "We've got the United Nations in our family. Two kids converted to Islam, we have one

Buddhist, and one atheist by marriage. And I love the whole bunch of them."

The pastries arrive, and we spread them out on the coffee table.

"Hey, Gram. Remember when we used to play that game where we would say a word and you would connect it with one of your adventures?"

"Of course, Maddie girl. Let's play. Bob, you'll love this. Go ahead. The first word that comes to your mind."

"How about *parade*?"

"Let me think." Gram's lips pucker as she sifts through volumes of memories. "Got it. One time Martin and I went skiing in Switzerland and ended up walking around a darling little town. A parade popped up out of nowhere with the horns and floats and people marching. After a few mulled wines, Martin had the idea to jump in and join the parade. And there we were, marching along. It was so unlike your grandfather to hoot and holler like that. What fun we had."

"That's a good one, Gram."

"You're a traveler, too, Bobby. Let's give you one." Gram slaps Bob on the arm. "How about noodles?"

Bob smiles. "Oh, I've got a good one. And what's nuts is I haven't thought about that night until this very minute."

Aunt Rose shouts something from the bedroom: "Okay, babe! Okay. Okay, babe." I jump up to see what she wants.

Gram follows me into the bedroom.

"What's she saying, Gram?"

"She's talking to Karl. She does this all the time."

"She called Uncle Karl *babe*?" I whisper.

"Yes, she did." Gram covers Aunt Rose with the puffy white comforter, and I softly close the bedroom door. "Go on, Bob. I want to hear about noodles," Gram says.

"So I was in Hong Kong with the band doing gigs at big clubs. One night I had a craving for lo mein and I ended up at this dinky restaurant. The owner saw my trumpet and invited me to this dark, seedy back room where guys were smoking pipes, probably opium. They didn't speak any English, but somehow they managed to belt out those Sinatra tunes in Chinese until sunrise."

"God, you guys are soul mates," I say. "Seriously."

"One more, Mads. Your gram's getting loopy."

"How about the hind legs of a boo shoo bird?"

"You're not going to stump me on that one! That's the one Jebby made up when we were playing this very game many years ago. We were in stitches that night."

—&o&—

I tuck Gram in next to a restless Aunt Rose and stretch out on the couch. I'm not ready to go to bed. I eat the rest of the pastries with warm Coke and write a bunch of Iceland postcards to my friends. I scroll through the volcano pictures and text the best to Paige and everybody.

Burt texts back right away, Those sheep better watch out with your crew. LOL.

Paige texts: Never have I ever seen the hairy ass of a guy named Burt five times in one week. (Insert jelly bean.)

I expected Enzo's three things when I got back from the volcano, but all I had was a photo of Paige and Grace surrounded by Patagonian penguins. I sent my three things this morning, but I decide to send three more. Maybe he needs a reminder. 1. I just emerged from the Snaefellsjökull Volcano lava tube. 2. I love 80s movies and music. 3. I put a popcorn kernel up my nose when I was six, and it came out two weeks later.

It's the middle of the night, and the relentless sunlight still streams through the heavy curtains. I'm tired and cranky and annoyed that Enzo's blowing me off. I tiptoe out of Gram's suite to crawl under my own fluffy comforter and get a few hours of sleep. With the swipe of a hotel room key, I walk into a live porn movie that might be called *American Barbie Does Icelandic Elf.* I close the door and slap my hand over my mouth.

I did not need to see that.

With no way to get back into Gram's room, I'm forced to lie down on the leather lobby sofa, cold, exhausted, and cursing out my cousin. A text arrives as I'm drifting off with my face against a burlap pillow. 1. I'm very forgetful. For instance, I visited my cousins in Scotland and left my bee at home. 2. While in Scotland, I laughed out loud at the thought of our Wishwell conga line and my cousins thought me daft. 3. Caveman misses hot girl.

—ℰ∘ SIXTEEN ∘ℨ—

IT'S RAINING HARD as the plane touches down outside Venice. By the time we get to the gondolas, it's hot and steamy. Venice would be romantic, if not for the stench.

Gram had texted us at seven in the morning with her not-very-mysterious clue. Gelato. Gucci. Gondolas. Guess where? I got to sit between Janie and Aunt Rose on two flights. I preferred Aunt Rose telling me about meeting Karl in Central Park and her dog, Tippy, to Janie's sullenness and dry heaves. I don't know if she saw me walk in on her and the elf. I hate to admit it, but Jeb was right. She couldn't be faithful to Ty.

The canals stink of garbage bags filled with fish corpses. But it's a pretty city, in an Old World, rusty antique kind of way. We snake around the buildings teeming with life. Clothes hang from windows where garlic wafts abundantly. I'm just hoping our gondola doesn't tip me into this putrid water.

Janie and I waste our only day in Venice asleep. By the time we get our act together, it's dinnertime and I'm starving.

We leave our ornate Renaissance-era hotel room overlooking the Grand Canal and make our way through St. Mark's Square before dinner. There might be more pigeons in this Italian square than in all of New York City. The nasty birds have formed aggressive gangs to attack yelping tourists. Janie thinks they're cute. Maybe she'll hook up with them, too.

"Shrimp, please." That's what we say. We're a family of hogs sniffing out the best food wherever we go. According to Gram, the food to eat in Venice is shrimp.

Wes makes us go around the table and say what we're grateful for.

"I'm sorry. Is this Thanksgiving?" Uncle Billy says.

"No. I just want to say I'm grateful to be in this family, as high maintenance as it is, and I'm grateful for every minute I have with you, Assy."

"And I'm ever grateful for my Wessy."

"Who's next?" Wes says.

"I'm grateful for the wisdom you have imparted as a mother and grandmother," Mom says with a quiver in her voice. Gram blows her a kiss.

"I'm grateful for the ability to tune out this cheesy conversation," Jeb says.

"Stop being a wiseass, Jeb," Dad says. "I'll go. I'm grateful for Mr. Bob Johns. Bro, you are my poker buddy, and I'm damn glad you're here."

"Thank you, Aaron. Same here. I'm grateful this family has welcomed me with open arms."

Did he just call Bob bro? Jeb texts me. I laugh out loud and text back Aww. Dad finally has a friend.

The chorus of gratitude and snide comments continues through the piles of buttery shrimp and loaves of crusty bread dunked in olive oil.

"Maddie's turn," Wes says. His face is red from the wine. They all turn to look at me. I'm not feeling philosophical or particularly grateful. But I don't want to be a douchebag like Jeb.

So I decide to sing. It only takes one line of Louis Armstrong's "What a Wonderful World" to get them going. We sing the song, beginning to end, in our terrible voices. The group of Bulgarian tourists at the table next to us don't crack a smile, but that is their problem.

Gram motions to the waiter and hands him her Amex platinum card. Where will we be in a year, when Gram is no longer telling us to get our asses to dinner or brunch? Who will grab the arm of the maître d' and whisper, *We'd like a corner table and your best server, please*? Who will make the reservation in the first place?

On the way to the hotel, we stop at a Venetian glass shop with a delicate menagerie of blown-glass creatures, each more exquisite than the next. I spot a marble-sized glass soccer ball hidden behind a school of orange fish. I buy it for Enzo.

It pours again on our walk through Pigeon Shit Square. The

downpour has caused the bay to swell and flood the sidewalk in front of our hotel. I start to panic.

"Maddie, relax. Venice has been flooding for hundreds of years," Gram says.

"Gram, do you seriously love this city?" My feet squeak on the marble lobby floor.

"I love the grand idea of Venice sinking before our very eyes." She holds my arm and we shuffle toward the elevator. "It's fascinating to think we might be part of the small fraction of humans who will get to enjoy this place before it returns to the sea."

"Is that why you chose it?"

"That and because it's on the way to our next destination. Also, I had my heart set on a fabulous Venetian dinner. But between you and me, I could barely taste the shrimp. My palate is gone."

"I'm sorry, Gram."

"It's okay, honey. The company was good."

We go to our rooms, and I sink into my gilded Renaissance bed, desperate for sleep. I try to think of clever things to write Enzo, but I'm too tired. So I wing it. 1. I had a plane dream that I forgot to take gym class and they wouldn't let me graduate. High school forever! 2. My family is obsessed with food. 3. I liked you a tiny bit more when I saw your legs in soccer, excuse me football, shorts. Bonus Question (you know I like questions): Is there anything about you that isn't perfect?

I hold the glass ball to my cheek and hope the flood doesn't rise above the second floor.

I'm too tired to swim.

-ξoξ-

"Why the hell are we going to a place called Bled? Why don't we stop at Clot and then Barf and maybe have lunch at Tumor?" Janie is in rare form. She sounds like Brit, the evil twin.

Dad keeps bugging us to move up a few rows in case we get rear-ended. We're on a private coach bus, and the roads in Slovenia seem safe, but we humor him anyway.

"Who goes to *Slovenia*?"

"It's still the Alps. It can't be that bad. What is wrong with you, anyway? I'm just going to ask you one thing, and I don't want you to get mad."

"What, Maddie?"

"Are you mad at me because I'm still a virgin?" I whisper, in case Dad is listening.

"What? That's idiotic. I'm mad at you because you're annoying."

"Because I was totally about to have sex, and then I got my period."

"I don't care," Janie says, picking at a split end.

I decide to blurt it out. "You saw me walk in, didn't you? In Iceland."

"I don't want to talk about Iceland." She turns away and presses her face against the window.

"Why not?"

She turns back and gives me a snide look. "Because I'm a slut, Maddie. I promised Ty I would be faithful, and I did way too many shots and slept with that guy, okay?"

"Stop doing this to yourself," I say. "It's not like you have a ring on your finger."

"Did I tell you Ty's mom died on the Wishwell? That's why he became a doctor. And he cares about the environment and fosters pit bulls when he's not on the ship." She shakes her head. "He's a saint. And I'm a horrible person."

"Seriously, stop, Janie."

She whips her head around and stares at me. "I made fun of his penis, and I slept with somebody else."

"But you are not a slut. You're just a sloppy drunk. It's the O'Neill gene."

"It doesn't matter that I was drunk. I feel awful. Like, sick-to-my-stomach awful." She pulls her hair out of the ponytail and picks furiously at the split ends.

I feel bad for judging her. "You know, maybe this trip would be a good time to turn over a new leaf," I say. "Everyone has a slutty phase. There's plenty of time to become a big sober prude."

"That's easy for you to say, virgin."

Janie rests her head on my lap. I play with her hair and remember the days when our biggest problem was where to set up our Barbies. When did life get so complicated?

I lean down and whisper, "I'll stop being a virgin if you stop being a slut."

"That's why I love you so much." Her voice softens a little. "You come up with crazy deals that I can't refuse."

—ε₀ϑ—

Enzo texts me: I am far from perfect. 1. I am an insufferable slob. 2. I didn't learn to read until I was 8 and as it turned out I had a learning disability. 3. Every now and again I go through a dark period where I sit on the chair in my briefs and count starlings at the bird feeder. I'm sure there's more. So there. You're the perfect one.

We stop at a red light in a sleepy village where three girls around my age are dancing up a steep hill. I wonder what the E's are doing right now. It's late in Connecticut, so they're probably sitting on the lifeguard chairs, making fun of Abby's obnoxious burps. Maybe there's a party and they're all hooking up. They've probably recycled some boys already.

The bus rolls into a fairy tale.

"I think this is where the snow globe makers get their ideas," Mom says as we drag our luggage off the bus. "It's breathtaking."

The town overlooks an island in the middle of a pristine Alpine lake, below a cliff where an actual castle sits suspended in time. Gram sends Wes and Uncle Billy into a store for food and leads us all down to the lake. Flat-bottomed boats glide back and forth to the island. When we get to the end of the dock, Gram takes Aunt Rose's hand.

"Rose, do you remember this place? It's Bled. We came here years ago with Karl and Martin. Look at the castle, Rose, and the island. Does this ring a bell?"

"Yes. It's lovely," Aunt Rose says. But there's no recognition on her face.

"It's Bled, our most special sister place on earth, remember?" Gram's getting frustrated. "You must recognize it. It hasn't changed a bit."

"Astrid, come. The boys are here with the food," Bob says. He leads Gram and Aunt Rose to a table under a tree. Wes spreads out napkins and sandwiches while Uncle Billy sets down a box of cream-filled pastries covered with powdered sugar.

Gram tells us all about her secret trip to Bled with Aunt Rose and Uncle Karl and Grandpa Martin, about how their parents didn't want them to marry an Irishman or a Slav, so they sent them off to tour Europe and hopefully forget about their boyfriends. Their parents never knew Uncle Karl and Grandpa Martin went with them on their European adventure.

"How scandalous, Assy," Wes says.

"Oh, it sure was," Gram says. "We traveled all the way to Slovenia to meet Karl's rather large-boned, brutish family. Then the four of us came here to Bled." She pauses, as if she's deciding whether to say what she's thinking. "We did the old hotel key switcheroo, if you know what I mean," she blurts out.

"No, we have no idea what you mean, Mom," Uncle Billy says, shaking his head.

"Oh, it was heavenly," Gram says. "We were young and brave and glamorous, and the clothes were well made back then. And"—she points toward the island in the center of the lake—"Rose, it was right over there that Karl asked for your hand in marriage."

Aunt Rose looks confused. "I, I don't know. I remember Karl asking me in Central Park." She taps her foot nervously and furrows her brow.

"That's what we told Mother and Father, but it happened right here."

We're all feeling the tension. We know Gram wants to share this with Aunt Rose so badly. We just don't know if Aunt Rose can do it.

"Come on, guys. Let's take a boat ride," Dad says, nodding toward the island and taking Gram gently by the arm. "Let's take Rose back to your island, Astrid."

The man rowing the covered boat speaks enough English to tell us the island has magical properties. Does every place have magical properties? We climb the steps of the old church and sit awhile, taking photos of the lake and the castle.

"Come, Rose. I want to show you something." Gram takes Aunt Rose's hand and leads her slowly back down the steps and into the forest. She opens her oversized pocketbook and pulls out a photo from a Ziploc bag.

"This is the spot where we took this." She shows Aunt Rose a worn black-and-white photo. I've seen the photo many times on Gram's bedroom wall. It's Gram and Aunt Rose, joyful sisters in A-line dresses and starlet hairdos, with arms joined and legs kicking out.

Aunt Rose studies the photo intently. She looks at Gram. "We looked like Rockettes," she says.

"We sure did."

"Where's the tree?" Aunt Rose cranes her neck toward the water.

"What tree, Aunt Rose?" Mom says.

Aunt Rose wanders toward the lakeshore, thick with trees and brambles. We all follow as she walks down to a tree hanging over the water. Jeb holds her around the waist and she steps into the water in her orthopedic shoes. "Here it is." She tries to move some brush aside.

"What the hell is she doing?" Wes says. We hang back a little and watch the rest of them digging around this tree.

"I knew it!" Aunt Rose says, with a smug expression.

We can barely make out *R+K and A+M Forever* in the middle of a faint heart shape at the base of the tree.

"Oh my God, Rose. I completely forgot about our forever tree."

We let Gram and Aunt Rose have a lucid sister moment standing in front of the tree, whispering and giggling, with water up to their ankles.

"Come on, girls, let's get a photo," Dad says, pulling his bee out of his pocket. Gram puts her arm around her big sister.

"Rockettes," she shouts. They manage to kick up their legs as Dad takes the picture. It's as if Bled's magical properties have just swallowed up six decades.

On the way back to the boats, we pass a public restroom. "Hey, Janie, you see that bathroom over there?" Gram says.

"Yeah, Gram. I don't have to go."

"I just wanted to let you know that's where we conceived your mother."

A chorus of *yuck* and *too much information* and *classy Assy* rings out.

"That explains a lot," Uncle Billy says.

$$-\xi \circ \xi-$$

We spread out and crank jazz music on the coach ride from Slovenia to Rome. As we pass through the burnt oranges and deep greens of the Tuscan countryside, we get a text from Eddie.

Astrid and Family, I thought you should know that our lovely dancer passed away this morning in her sleep. Holly had hoped to hold on a little longer. Services are tomorrow on the ship. So sorry to deliver the news during your travels. Eddie

Everybody looks at Janie.

"It wasn't supposed to happen this way," she says, with tears streaming down her face.

Marshall texts us a couple of hours later.

All, I am heartbroken. Holly was my best friend and my light. Even at her sickest, she showed me how to be a better man. Thank you for giving Holly a wonderful last hurrah and for allowing her the dignity of one last dance. And most of all, thank you, Janie, for being the friend Holly needed and deserved. You are an incredible young woman. Don't you dare change. We need more pure spirits like you and Holly on this earth. I plan to fly home from Asia to be with Holly's family. Please stay in touch. Love, Marshall (and Holly)

As sad as I am that Holly is gone, I'm glad she's free of the body that betrayed her, just like Skinny Dave. I try to comfort Janie by telling her how unique she is in a world where most people, myself included, don't know how to treat the dying. She soaks my shirt with her tears and tells me it wasn't like that. She just liked Holly.

The bus is silent the rest of the trip.

-&° SEVENTEEN °3-

DAD AND I share the same first impression of Rome: The drivers are lunatics. My second impression is that Rome is our kind of city. Start with art, shoes, and food, and throw in Gram and Bob's favorite jazz singer, a lady named Celia Hobbes, and we're all happy to be here.

Our hotel sits at the top of the Spanish Steps. Gram wants to spend a few hours of alone time with each one of us while we're in Rome. She picks Janie first, probably because she feels bad Aunt Mary ditched her own child and because Janie's still pretty shaken up about Holly.

Mom, Dad, Jeb, and I embark on a whirlwind sightseeing tour. We walk at a fast clip, the way we did in the old days when we took family trips to boring places with too much rich history.

"This is a strange crumbly formation," I say as we wander into some ancient ruins.

"This, Maddie, is the Roman Forum. My God, look at this." Dad gets down on his knees and touches the ground. "It's utterly amazing. The Romans constructed roads and hydraulic systems two thousand years ago." Dad can barely contain his excitement.

"Okay, even I'm blown away by this," Jeb says when we get to the Colosseum.

Two guys dressed as gladiators stalk us until we take a family picture with them.

If the lava tube felt mystical and energizing in a cool, spiritual way, the Roman Colosseum feels mystical in a terrifying, bad-demon, sinister way. It's like I can sense the screaming souls of the people ripped apart by lions. I shriek.

"What the hell, Maddie?" Jeb jumps and falls onto a slab of stone.

"I felt something graze my leg. I think it was a giant rat."

"Moron, it's a cat." Jeb points to a scraggly orange cat with dead eyes.

"Look, guys. I guess they don't do a lot of spaying and neutering in Italy." Mom nods toward a swarm of cats pacing and lounging behind a rickety gate.

"Hey, kids, maybe they're reincarnated from the lions they kept chained here, ready for battle."

"Stop, Dad, that's annoying," I say, but part of me wonders if he's onto something. Cats creep me out with their claws and sneaky prowling.

"Can we go?" I say.

We track down the fake gladiators and pay thirty bucks for a five-by-seven photo of the four of us half-smiling. With everything that happened in ancient Rome, it ends here with a cheesy souvenir photo.

It only takes pit stops in four piazzas for us to realize they're pretty much all the same. But we discover the true draw of these cobble-stoned squares: gelato. We sit four in a row on the edge of a fountain.

"I gotta say, kids, I'm proud of you two." Dad sets down his gelato cup and puts his arms around us. Mom jumps up and fumbles in her bag. "None of this has been easy, but you're both going with the flow." Dad pats us on our backs.

"Thanks, bro," Jeb says. I stifle a laugh.

"Let's do a selfie." Mom has wrestled her bee out of her bag, and plops herself down on Dad's lap.

"Mom, you have wicked BO," Jeb says.

"I'm sorry, it's hot." She clicks the bee and gets the top of our heads.

"Well, there's a memory," Jeb says.

Mom takes out a lipstick and applies it to her lips and mine. Jeb grabs the bee and takes a bunch of pictures.

"We'll title this one *Italians make fun of loser Americans taking endless selfies,*" I say.

"Onward and upward." Dad gets up and dabs at the giant gelato stain on his golf shirt.

Mom and I have had it with the ancient rubble piles and creepy cats. We send the nerd archaeologist and his sidekick on their way, and sniff out the unmistakable scent of soft Italian leather.

We try on gorgeous Italian shoes in a little shop. I am confident nobody at college will own these shoes, and I will stand out as Maddie Levine, shoe goddess. Mom walks over with a low-heeled black pump.

"Is this not Gram's dream shoe?"

"She'll love it. You have to get them for her."

Mom's face drops. She staggers slightly, then grabs the edge of a display case and pulls it to the ground as her knees buckle. It happens in slow motion. By the time I realize what's going on, she's sitting in a pile of stilettos in her khaki skirt and kitten heels. And she just sits there, staring at the shoe.

"Mom, are you okay?"

The portly little saleswoman rushes over. She talks a mile a minute in Italian, then runs back to her post when Mom still doesn't move.

"Mom, try to breathe. Do you want to get some air?" It's like she's in a trance. She doesn't take her eyes off the shoe.

The saleswoman comes back over with a bottle of water. I wish I knew how to tell her that my mom is okay, just grieving in the way people do when they're about to lose the most important member of their family.

And soon, Gram won't need shoes.

I clear a path in the shoe pile and kneel on the floor next to Mom. We sit together in silence for a long time. I rub her back the way Dad always does.

"I'm so sorry, Maddie. I just, I . . ." She shakes her head.

"It's okay." I lean over and kiss Mom's flushed cheek. I don't know what to say. My mind is playing tricks on me, saying, *Don't think about it. It's not happening yet. Don't think about it until you have to.*

We stand up and dust ourselves off. The saleswoman treats us as if nothing happened. She won't even let us help clean up the mess. We thank her by buying an excessive amount of footwear, including Gram's low-heeled pumps.

-&o&-

I sleep well our first night in Rome, despite the heat and lack of air-conditioning. Gram meets me in the lobby at ten AM sharp for our date.

"Shall we sit awhile?" She's wearing her giant beetle sunglasses. People are sipping cappuccinos on the Spanish Steps. I miss my Starbucks chai.

"So, Mads, Janie and I had a good long talk. Your cousin is a complex, sensitive, bright young lady."

"She is?"

"Yes, she is, wiseass. You, on the other hand? Pure bimbo."

"It takes one to know one." Gram acts like she didn't hear me and puckers her lips. It's her thinking pose.

"I'm trying to get a mental picture of the future Maddie. Formal wedding or elopement? I suspect formal for you."

"Of course. I want to design my own wedding dress."

"You can still elope if you design your own dress. My friend Ruth eloped in a custom French gown at a Vegas chapel in 1969. Second marriage, though." Gram lifts her sunglasses to check out a very hot guy fifty years her junior. "Anyway, we need to figure out your something old, something new, something borrowed, something blue. It's my very favorite wedding tradition."

"What did you do for your wedding?"

"My grandmother's blue handkerchief for old and blue. I don't know where that thing went. Rose's drop diamond earrings for borrowed. And new, of course, was my grand gown." She pinches my stomach. "Your waist would never be small enough to fit into that dress."

"Hey, that's mean. Are you calling me porky?"

"No. Our waists were freakishly tiny back then. Women—such odd creatures we are. Anyway, it would give me great joy to plan your wedding somethings."

I want to say, *Let's worry about that some other time.* But she wants to do this now, because now is all we have left.

"I would love that, Gram. What are you thinking?"

"Let's stroll awhile. It'll come to us."

We stop at the Trevi Fountain, where people are supposed to throw a coin to guarantee a return to Rome. Gram hands me a coin like she did for the gumball machines when I was little.

"If I recall," she says, "you throw with your right hand over your left shoulder."

"Am I supposed to make a wish?"

"It can't hurt, can it?"

I should wish for a miracle. I should wish for Gram and the other

Wishwell patients to get better. I should wish for peace or gay equality or an end to fossil fuels. But the coin slips out of my hand and flies over my left shoulder before I can change my impulse wish.

Enzo, come back to the ship with me. I am an evil person.

"Now, then. On with our wedding shopping." We weave through the crowded streets. "I won't be around to choose the husband, so please, dear, use your brain, not your body. The content of a man's semen is very important."

"Gross, Gram."

"Hear me out. First, the little buggers need to be able to swim. You can't know that ahead of time. Personally, I think it was Karl's plumbing that didn't work, not Rose's. We North women are very fertile." She hesitates. "I even got pregnant the first time with Bobby," she blurts out.

"What? Are you serious? You had an abortion?"

"No. Abortion was illegal. I could have paid big bucks for an under-the-table one, but I wasn't sure if I wanted to do that. I lost the pregnancy early on. That's when I started believing in God." She reaches over and pinches my arm really hard.

"Ow."

"You need to use protection. I don't ever want you to be in that position. It's hell."

"Got it."

"Anyway, we're missing the point," Gram says. "*Sexy* is good for dating. But it's best if you marry somebody kind and honest, somebody who can give you smart, well-adjusted children. Someone like Martin or Bob."

"Okay, Gram. I'll be sure to do careful semen sifting."

We walk slowly because the heat and exertion are already getting to Gram.

"Oooh. That gelateria is open. Sit, Gram. I'll go get us gelato."

"If you're not porky now, you will be after this trip," Gram calls after me.

-&o&-

We lick the tiny flat spoons.

"Do you have any regrets, Gram?"

"I've made mistakes. Who hasn't? But I do not have one regret."

"Not even the ass tattoo?"

"I love my ass tattoo. My ass, however, has a mind of its own. Trust me. I don't know what it's trying to do back there, all flat and flabby. Maddie, I've got it!"

"What?"

"Your something borrowed and blue will be an ass tattoo."

"Hilarious, Gram."

"No, this is it. You'll *borrow* the idea from me, and do a *blue* sea star tattoo on your ass. Let's go find a clean tattoo parlor."

"Wait, you're serious. Gram. I would totally do it, but I don't like pain—tattoo pain or Dad pain. Because you know my dad will literally kill me. He'll string me up by my ass tattoo in that piazza."

"Maddie, how often does your father see your behind?" She squeezes my butt cheek. "If I listened to my parents, I'd be sitting in a country club in Greenwich about to play bridge with some red-nosed old fart." She laughs. "My life has been fabulous because I never listened to my parents."

My grandmother is peer-pressuring me.

"Yeah, but what about the pain? I can't even wax my eyebrows without nearly passing out."

"Stop being a drama queen. Yes, it hurts a little. But no pain, no gain. If I hadn't pushed your giant mother out of my vagina, you wouldn't be here. You can get a tiny tattoo. Come on, live a little."

"Fine. I'll do it. I will suffer for you, you sadistic old nut."

"There it is." Gram points at me.

"What?"

"The scrunch face."

—ξ◦ვ—

Gram sends me up the Spanish Steps to whisper our request to the concierge. "This is the one the rock stars use," he says with a wink.

Between the death-defying cab ride and the anticipation of the searing pain I'm about to feel on my tender ass skin, I'm violently nauseated. Gram is busy sketching out my tattoo on a napkin.

"Here. How's this?" She holds up a perfect sea star. I've forgotten how gifted Gram is.

A woman, tattooed in watercolor from neck to ankle, greets us in front of a charming storefront brimming with potted flowers. Ink Woman loves Gram's sketch. She makes Gram sign a minor release. Gram makes her show us her hygiene routine, so I don't get AIDS or hepatitis. Great, more diseases to worry about.

"Holy fucking shit," I scream. Gram holds my hand.

"I know, honey. It hurts. But it's looking fabulous. Just keep thinking about your wedding day."

"I'm a teenager. I don't care about my wedding day. This is abuse."

"Almost done. Shh. She's just doing the shading now."

"Ow. It's worse. How did you do this to your whole body? This is insane."

Ink Lady finally stops.

"Just wait until childbirth." I hate it when Gram says that.

I hold a hand mirror to my butt. The area around the tattoo is red, but there it is, my delicate starfish in shades of blue. It's barely the size of a quarter, but it looks like it's floating on my skin, brought to life by Gram's creative genius and a stranger's steady hand.

"Oh, honey. It's fabulous. It's so you."

"It's a companion for your saggy seahorse. I love it."

Ink Lady takes a picture and emails it to my friends for me. I'm sure the lake club could use some good gossip by this point in the summer.

"Now we have your something borrowed and something blue. The new will be the dress. Even if you don't design it yourself, buy it new. You don't need some vintage thing with another woman's secrets stuck to the seams."

We stop for real Italian pizza, and Gram makes a toast with sparkling water or, as the Europeans call it, "water with gas."

"Cheers to all the fun we've had. There are no words for the joy you have brought me. I love you, honey." Her eyes fill with tears. I shake my head. I can't do this now. If I start crying, I'll never stop.

We barely make it up the steps. Gram is breathless and holds her lower back as she crawls into bed.

"I need to nap if we're going to the jazz club tonight. But come here. I have something." She reaches into the nightstand drawer and hands me a macaroon from her stash. "That's not the something. Here it is. Come to think of it, you could have used this as your blue and your borrowed." She passes me a small, square box. "Oh well, the tattoo is divine. This isn't borrowed, anyway. I'm giving it to you for keeps."

I open the box. It's Gram's sapphire.

"No way. You can't give me this. This is your favorite thing in the world."

"My babies are my favorite things in the world. This belongs to you. My fingers are too skinny now."

"But, Gram—"

"You've loved this thing since you were an infant, and I let you teethe on it, much to your father's dismay. He was afraid you'd get it lodged in your trachea."

She smiles. I slide the ring onto my finger. It fits perfectly.

"Wear it in good health, my dear."

"Oh, Gram. There are no words."

"It's good luck, by the way. Right after I bought it at a shop on Madison Avenue, I vomited all over a man's foot. That was my first sign that I was pregnant with your mom. Whatever you decide to do for your wedding, wear the sapphire. Then I'll be there."

I'm a little queasy. I can't tell if it's because of the ring or the butt soreness.

"You should know how proud I am of you, honey. Going sleepies now." Gram closes her eyes. I draw the curtains and kiss her on the forehead. She's already asleep.

—&o&—

I just got a text from Lane. It's a video of Paige and Burt on the beach, pushing Mark into the ocean on a wheelchair surfboard with Gloria and the minister photo bombing in the background. I reply with a picture of all of us on top of the Spanish Steps with the caption The Wishwellians are taking over the world!

"I thought you had to have a lot of sex to get a urinary tract infection," Janie says, after Mom texts us that she's skipping the jazz club to take care of Aunt Rose.

"You can get urinary tract infections from sex?" I can't believe how little I know about these things.

"Duh."

"Maybe she was banging Eddie," I say.

"Or Burt."

I'm getting anxious. We're out on the hot sidewalk, waiting for the rest of the family to come out of the Sistine Chapel so we can go back to the hotel. It was breathtaking for the first hour and a half, but I got a neck cramp from looking up.

Gram gave Janie her diamond studs. They're her something old, since the diamonds go back as far as the North family estate. Janie feels special because they're worth more than the sapphire, but I know who won this contest.

Jeb got Grandpa Martin's vintage Rolex. I doubt Jeb will ever find anyone to marry him, but he can wear the Rolex to my wedding. Who knows, maybe he'll surprise us.

Bob comes out, and the three of us ditch the others. Bob tells us he can't wait to go to the jazz club to see their old friend Celia Hobbes.

"So who is this Celia Hobbes person?" Janie asks. I grip the door handle of our microcab.

"We met her at the Birdland jazz club. Your gram and I pulled a lot of strings to get in, and the vibe in the club was electric. After that, we went to Celia's shows all over town. She was way up there with Ella Fitzgerald and Billie Holiday. Man, those were the days."

Bob is so animated when he talks about the old days.

"It was Celia who gave us a nickname, *Cookies*. She once joked that we looked like a half-moon cookie. People would say, 'Are the cookies coming out tonight?' That was us: black, white, and sweet on each other."

"Aww. You still are," Janie says, climbing out of the cab.

"Yes we are." Bob smiles like a schoolboy. "Yes we are."

—໌o໌—

1. I have a date tonight. 2. She's kind of cute. 3. I'm not excited at all.

I text back. 1. Strange coincidence, me too. 2. He's not bad, if you like the exotic Euro type. 3. But he sucks at Whac-A-Mole.

"I would do you," Janie says when I twirl for her in my forties dress.

"What if he was beer goggling the whole time on the ship and he's disappointed when he sees me?"

"Stop. Don't turn into one of those annoying insecure girls. Repeat after me: He's just a boy."

"He's just a boy," I say, so aware that he is not just a boy.

"I don't even know what I'm doing. I'm going to see him at the jazz club and hang out. Then what? Never see him again?"

"Just live in the moment, for once. God, you worry way too much. You're hooking up with a hot guy tonight. That should be good enough."

Gram texts, Our chariot awaits.

Francesca sent a limo to pick us up. Uncle Billy and Wes scroll through pictures from Paige and Burt and the Ornaments. It's nice to see my uncles being nice to each other.

My ass is sore. I can't believe I have a tattoo.

"Don't do anything to embarrass me tonight, kids. I worship this woman," Gram says, checking her lipstick in a hand mirror.

"Mom's telling us not to embarrass her. That's a good one," Uncle Billy says.

The basement club has black-and-white checkerboard floors and posters of famous jazz musicians on the walls. We sit to the side of the stage and, within seconds, the drinks start flowing.

"Cheers to good people and great music," Bob toasts. I take a sip of champagne. It tastes like my constipation medicine.

We tap feet and fingers, and my curls bounce to the beat of the horns. My head is on a permanent swivel, searching for Enzo. Celia Hobbes walks out during an instrumental set. The crowd cheers. She's a tall, thin African American woman with a platinum-blond wig, lots of bling, and a voice that defies her ninety years. Gram and Bob jump up to grab her after the first set.

"Still drinking straight bourbon, Miss Celia?" Bob shouts.

"You bet. It has preserved my insides like a jar of pickled beets. Oh, lord! The Cookies are here, ghosts from a Fifty-Second Street graveyard. It is good to see you two." They walk off to catch up as a young Italian woman belts out one of our favorites, "The Man I Love."

"Why don't you dance with your sister?" I can tell Dad's a little tipsy on half a glass of champagne as he pushes Jeb toward me.

"Care to dance?" Jeb's tipsy, too. I reluctantly dance with my old ballroom lesson partner and try to ignore his alcohol garlic breath. Bob gets up and serenades Gram and Celia Hobbes with a trumpet solo.

A group of people enters through the dim back entrance. I see Enzo right away. My stomach flips. He's wearing a gorgeous suit and a boyish grin. I push Jeb out of the way and smooth my dress. I want to run toward Enzo and leap into his arms, but I wait for him to come to me.

He stares at me for a few seconds and smiles. "Hi, Maddie."

His smell, the slight scruff on his face, the smoothness of his hand when he grabs mine and leads me over to meet his sister—everything makes me feel faint.

I meet his sister, Claudia. She's stunning and elegant and perfect. Francesca talks about Holly, but I can't think about that right now. I need a break from all the sadness. I need to be with Enzo.

Gram and Francesca and Claudia and Dad and my uncles and even Celia Hobbes swarm around us. Enzo and I are talking to them, but we're looking at each other. The intensity grows. It's hot and noisy, and I'm panicking that the swarm won't ever leave us alone.

"Maddie." I love hearing him say my name. "Let's go. I want to show you Rome. Come on."

I tell Dad I'm going exploring with Enzo. Dad is buzzed and embarrassingly silly, and he lets me go. Enzo takes my hand and leads me up toward the lively sounds of Rome on our perfect summer night. The fountains cast a filmy light over the city. We walk a minute or two before he pulls me into the shadows.

"Maddie," he says into my ear.

Then come the kisses. It's more like one long, delicious kiss infused with the smell of subtle European aftershave and him. He has a smell all his own. We can't stop kissing. I let out little sounds, and he kisses me harder. I feel his hands on my back, up my back, in my hair, on my ass.

"Ow." I grab his hand and step backward.

"I'm sorry."

I laugh. "It's fine. This is going to sound ridiculous, but...Gram kind of forced me to get a tattoo on my ass today."

"Today?"

"Yeah."

"Can I see it?"

"Later." We walk toward a busy square.

"Would you like to see my house?"

"Sure." Of course I want to see Enzo Ivanhoe's house. I want to see his bed, his sock drawer, his baby pictures, and the spoons he uses to eat cereal.

-ε○ҙ-

The streets buzz with people who don't seem to realize it's two in the morning. Enzo's house is a giant villa in the middle of Rome, with an open-air patio in the center of the building. A fountain gurgles between two terra-cotta benches, and crisscrossed vines of flowers fill the courtyard with color. This isn't a house. It's a palazzo with its own piazza.

"Let's have a bite to eat." He leads me into a cavernous marble and rustic wood kitchen, with cured meats and cheeses and fruits lined up on a cluttered counter. Enzo selects a hunk of cheese from under a glass dome.

"Here, try this. It's infused with truffle oil." He feeds me the cheese, and then a red grape and a bite of sausage. We share a lemon soda and a biscuit, which turns out to be a cookie. I haven't quite finished chewing when he pushes me up against the counter and kisses me again. Our kisses move to the rhythm of the courtyard fountain. He presses against me, and all the nerves in my body respond.

Francesca and Claudia burst into the kitchen. I jump awkwardly toward the sink.

"Look at our lovebirds!" Francesca is as over-the-top as Gram.

"We're eating, Mum. Do you want to join us?" he says in a polite tone.

"No, darling, you two enjoy each other, but not too much. Astrid will murder me if you get her granddaughter pregnant," says Astrid Junior.

"Mum, please. You never cease to humiliate me."

"Maddie, Enzo says you love fashion," Claudia says.

He talks about me.

"Yes. I've been interested in fashion since before I could dress myself." I want to impress her.

"I have, as well. I'm in merchandising for Gucci. It's a really nice job." Of course she has the best job ever. She's perfect. Maybe I should get pregnant, just to permanently attach myself to these people and their genes.

"I'm going to take Maddie back to the hotel." He moves closer and puts his arm around my waist.

Double cheek kisses and hugs good-bye, and I wonder if they can smell Enzo on me.

-ໃo໌-

I've never needed my friends so desperately. *Do it. Do it.* That's what they would say. Or maybe *Do him.* The stakes are so high. I can't think.

I tell Enzo to come back for me in the morning, and I'll be all his, at least for our last day in Rome. Part of me worries that I'll lose him, that some outrageous Shakespearean comedic tragedy will befall our situation and separate us before I can see him again. But if this trip has taught me anything, it's that the only thing guaranteed is this very moment. And in this very moment, I give Enzo a kiss he will most certainly want to repeat.

—ε∘ξ—

Enzo's text wakes me only a few hours after I fall asleep. I have a seven-thirty football match. I'll pick you up after. Or you could come watch. I reply: I want to watch . . .

"Get up." I tackle Janie. "We're going to watch hot Italians play soccer." That's all she needs to hear. I make her check my tattoo before we leave.

"You should pay me for these services. You're the grossest person I've ever met, other than Jeb. Who gets crust on their tattoo?" Janie got a tramp stamp of the New York skyline inside a snow globe before she left for college in Vermont.

Janie and I hate sports. We hate it when Dad and Jeb talk about scores and boring stats. I spent countless hockey, football, and lacrosse games making plans with the E's while pretending to give a crap about the games. Sometimes I even put on sunglasses and dozed off.

But this is different.

Janie and I take a cab to a spectacular Roman park where hot shirtless European men are doing sprints in shorts and cleats. They're all running back and forth wearing sweatbands and cute little ponytails. This is our kryptonite, and I have gotten my hands on a hunk of it.

Enzo gives us a wave as he runs down the field, but he's dead focused when the game starts. He's sweaty, fast, and so very skilled with the ball.

"This is almost too much to handle," I tell Janie. I can see it's too much for her, too, and she needs to sit. I'm afraid she's going to implode and dissolve into a pile of pheromone-laced ash.

We sit on the grass and, for the first time in our lives, pay attention to what's going on.

The game ends, and Enzo runs over and kisses me on the lips in front of the other guys. He says something to them in Italian as everyone gathers their stuff. A bunch of them say, "hi" and "*bella* something *bella*." Enzo is speaking Italian. There are no words.

One of the guys fixates on Janie. He whispers something to Enzo and gives Janie a "*ciao, bella*," before slowly strutting away.

"Janie, my friend Pietro wants a piece of you. I think that's the direct translation," Enzo jokes.

"*That* would be a deep and meaningful relationship," I say.

"Tell him I'm taken." Janie is resisting the kryptonite. She's blowing my mind right now.

"Well, that was fun. Now if you guys will excuse me, I have a date with my uncles." Janie puts her earbuds in and jogs away.

"Does she even know where she's going?" Enzo asks.

"She'll be fine," I say.

And here we are again. He puts his arms around me and kisses me.

"Sorry I'm sweaty," he says.

"I like it." He raises his eyebrows and smiles.

"Thank you for coming."

"Thank you for having me. I think you wanted to show off your stellar soccer skills."

"Actually, I wanted to show off my beautiful American girlfriend. Come on. Let's walk."

The park's vistas overlook all of Rome. It reminds me of the view above Corcovado Mountain.

When a girl is about to lose her virginity, she needs her friends around her for support. That is a universal truth, except maybe for people like Rachel. I can't picture Rachel having sex, but I'm sure it will happen during a Comic-Con. I am also pretty sure she'll be wearing pigtails and some sort of anime costume.

It seems terribly lonely to be enjoying this dream without sharing every detail with the E's. But I can't worry about that. Today is my day.

Enzo and I sit by a lake and share a water bottle. I love the intimacy of sipping from the place he just sipped.

He tells me about the internship he landed in Egypt, where he'll be working with world-famous anthropologists, and how he's learning Arabic online.

I tell him about the Blue Lagoon and the Jules Verne volcano and rainbows and elves. I tell him about Venice and Bled and the forever tree.

"And then, of course, Gram took me to get the tattoo."

"Was it a large lady covered in tats?" He pulls down the elastic of his shorts. Right in the crease near his hipbone, he shows me a tattoo of a red teacup with a soccer-ball-shaped tea bag coming out of it. I run my finger over it.

"I can't believe I haven't seen this yet. I didn't think you were the tattoo type."

"It's for my dad, you know, in his memory. It took him a long time to die. He fought hard. Every day at the end"—Enzo clears his throat—"I would bring him tea, and we'd watch football on TV. It was our thing." He lies down on the grass and stares up at the cloudless sky. "God, it's been years, but I miss him. I wish you could have met him. He had this charm. Everybody loved Dad."

"I'd love to see pictures sometime."

He shifts his gaze to me. "Sorry. I don't want to be a downer."

"Enzo, I'm on a death-with-dignity trip. It's kind of a downer theme."

"Good point." He laughs, then looks back to the sky. "Mum took it harder than all of us. She lost my granddad that same year. She's the type of person who needs to do something positive to deal with the grief. So Mum used most of Granddad's money to start up the ship."

"That's amazing. Gram says when bad things happen we should take the pain and grow something beautiful. Your mom has done that."

"She has. She works too much, but she's pretty fantastic." He moves closer and snaps the elastic on my shorts. "Hey, stop stalling. I want to see the tattoo."

"Okay, but it's a little red and crusty." I pull down my underwear just enough to reveal my little starfish.

"It's so cute. It's perfect." He looks at me with those gray-green eyes and leans in. We kiss and sink into the grass, and there is nothing left on this earth but Enzo and me and the salty sweat taste and the voyeuristic birds. He grabs my hand and pulls me up, and we walk up an embankment and behind a vine-covered temple building into a thick grove of flowering trees.

"I want to," I say.

"Here?"

"Yeah."

"Are you sure?"

"Yes. I'm sure."

So here, in the shade of this tangled grove in the middle of Rome, Enzo Ivanhoe fishes a condom out of his gym bag, and it happens. Just like that. It's kind of like getting the tattoo: It's a little painful and intense and, when it's done, my body is permanently altered in a very good way.

We lie on our backs looking up at the trees. I lean on my elbow and stare into Enzo's eyes. I run my fingertips up and down his tanned chest, and one word repeats itself in my head. *More.*

-ε∘ɜ-

I thought a whole day together would be a gift after all that waiting. But the soccer game and losing my virginity took almost two hours. Now my family wants me to go to some underground tomb outside of Rome so I can waste the last eight hours I may ever have with Enzo Ivanhoe.

I could ignore my bee, but they will surely send the *polizia* looking for me, and Gram does not like no-shows.

"Come on, it'll be fun. It's like a haunted house, only real," Enzo says.

"I want to stay here with you."

"Let's go. I have a little surprise. Trust me."

They call the place the Catacombs. It's hundreds of miles of tomb tunnels under the city. My family waves like a bunch of idiots when our cab pulls up.

Today, they're a swarm of mosquitoes buzzing around my head. Dad is wearing a ROMA ITALIA T-shirt. Wes is passing out granola bars and loose change to a pack of street urchins who probably pegged him as a sucker from a mile away.

"Yay, you made it," Mom says. She claps.

Francesca comes over with tickets. She's wearing a dress that belongs on a Greek yacht and sunglasses perched on top of thick layers of black hair. Nobody would suspect this woman is a mastermind of an illegal international death-with-dignity fleet.

"Where's everyone else?" I ask Mom, trying to act like I haven't just lost my virginity.

"Oh, Gram and Bob visited with Celia Hobbes until the wee hours of the morning," Mom says. "They are spent. The two of them, and Rose, are snoring away in Gram's bed."

I came to be with Gram. Now it's even more of a waste of time.

"Yeah." I "yeah" Mom when I'm not listening. I'm pretty sure she's going on about Aunt Rose's infection. I'm thinking that I left my virginity back in that park.

I look over at Janie. I'm desperate to tell her, but I can't. She's too excitable. She'll say something to tip off the mosquitoes.

The creepiest individual I have ever seen lurks around our group sporting a full priest dress and a buzz cut. He's gearing up to lead the Catacomb tour. I'm starting to panic. I can't walk through dark tunnels of tombs. I hate tombs.

"So what's after this?" Uncle Billy says. "Should we try to make it back to the Vatican?"

"Don't popes hate gay people?" Janie says.

Dad shoots her a look and nods toward the creepy priest.

"Sorry," she whispers. "I thought it was a costume."

"I can't do this," I blurt. "I can't deal with tombs. And I want to spend time with Enzo in Rome. Okay? Sue me."

Silence.

Why aren't they talking? Was I too bitchy? Is there a virginity stain on my shorts?

They look at Enzo.

"Am I missing something?" I say.

"I've decided to join you on the ship awhile longer," Enzo says. "I wanted to surprise you, but I had to make sure Astrid was okay with it."

"Are you joking?"

"Nope. Not joking. Want to come help me pack?"

We don't wait for the creepy tomb tour. We fly through the city, hand in hand, high on sex and anticipation. Not far from the banks of the Tiber River, we stop at a carousel, the old kind that has probably inspired thousands of love stories. The breeze. The boy. The smell of popcorn. The sound of a carousel song. We circle and circle.

—ଓ° EIGHTEEN °ଓ—

WE'RE TWO HOURS away from Taipei, Taiwan. Right before we boarded the chartered jet, I texted Paige: Never have I ever lost my virginity to Enzo Ivanhoe in a park in Rome (and liked it very much). She texted back immediately: OH MY JELLY BEANS!!!!!!!

Gram loves that Enzo is with us. She thinks he'll add a healthy dash of young man testosterone to the mix. I tell her to keep her knobby hands off him. I don't know exactly how Dad feels about the boyfriend travel companion. He can't mind all that much, since he spent the first three hours of the trip comparing Egyptian and Roman burial techniques with Enzo while I played UNO with Wes and Aunt Rose.

"Do you believe in life after death?" I ask.

Enzo and I are snuggled under a blanket on cushy reclining seats.

"Life after death? Yes."

"So sure?"

"Yes. I don't know about the heaven-hell religious stuff. That could be true." He shrugs. "I just know the stuff that's happened to me since Dad died."

"What stuff?"

"I'll only tell you if you can be open-minded. If you think it's rubbish, it'll piss me off."

"Okay, okay. I promise." I wrap my pinkie around his.

"So remember how I told you I used to watch TV with Dad and give him his tea? One day, it was springtime and kind of cold, but we opened all the windows to get Dad some fresh air. We both dozed off and woke to thousands of ladybirds in the house."

"That's terrifying. How did you know they were lady birds?" I'm picturing some freakish female bird mating ritual.

"The spots. How do you not know a ladybird?"

"Oh. You mean ladybugs. Okay. I get it."

"Yes. We say ladybirds. So I saw the swarm of bugs and screamed and jumped around. Dad laughed for a long time. I had to usher all the little beasts out of the house, but it was quite funny. Anyway, I was devastated after we lost Dad. I was ten years old, and I had lost my idol. Everything in the house reminded me of him, so I would sit on the front step every day. One day I was on the step and a ladybird landed on my knee. It kept me company for the best part of an hour. I knew it was a sign from Dad."

"How?"

"I can't explain it, but I just knew. They started showing up in the strangest places. One landed on the end of my toothbrush. One landed on the cheek of a girl I was kissing." He sees my face change. "I mean, it was a long time ago. One even flew onto my exam paper last year. I'm telling you, Maddie, the dead like to mess with you."

I don't want to know he kissed a girl. I snap myself back into the moment.

"In some weird way, this is comforting to me," I say. "Like Gram and I joked that she would come to me in the form of a chipmunk."

"Chipmunk, huh? I don't know that I've ever seen a chipmunk."

"They look a little like the moles in Whac-A-Mole, only spotted. Like ladybirds."

He laughs and takes a sip of tea. "There's other stuff," he says.

"Like what?"

"Like the dreams. The Wishwell used to trigger awful dreams, awful memories. I needed to get distance from that ship for a while." He exhales deeply. "But now when I have the dreams, they're visions of our holidays in Tuscany, and Granddad with his pet canary, and Dad grinning."

"Maybe heaven is another dimension, and our dreams are a portal." I sound like Rachel's friends.

"Sometimes it sort of feels that way," Enzo says, running his finger over the sapphire. I've decided to wear it for safekeeping. "Anyway, that was a long answer to your question. How about you? Do you believe in life after death?"

I shift in my seat and pause for a few seconds, distracted by the loud poker game behind us.

"I'll have to get back to you on that one."

"Fair enough."

Taipei, Taiwan, in the summer is hot, crowded, and as far from Connecticut as we could possibly get.

This leg of the trip has been the most mysterious of all. We know we're not here for long, because we're meeting the Wishwell tomorrow. But only Gram knows *why* we're here.

Gram asks the bus driver to show us some sites. The bus meanders through streets packed with cars and mopeds. Everywhere we go, we see the same building, about a thousand stories higher than all the other buildings, sticking up like a steel temple. I'm just grateful I don't have to find my way around, since I can't read one single street sign.

The hotel isn't terrible. It's the same decor as all the nail salons I've ever been to, with bamboo plants, peach-colored bedding, and cold floors. The problem is they overbooked the hotel, and Gram refuses to stay at a crappier place. I end up sharing a room with Janie and Mom, and poor Enzo gets Dad and Jeb. I pray he still likes me after rooming with those two.

"So? Can you believe this is happening? Is it sinking in that Enzo is with you right now?" Janie is holding me by the shoulders and shaking me, while Mom tries to figure out how the shower works.

"I have to tell you something, but if you tell anyone, ever, I swear to you I will punch you in the head."

"Okay, maniac. I swear."

"I'm not a virgin anymore."

"Can somebody help me figure out this shower?" Mom comes out in her underwear with her boobs flopping around. Janie runs in and says "shit" about a hundred times before she finally figures it out and comes back.

"Okay, when could you possibly have lost your virginity? Did you join the mile-high club while we were playing UNO?"

"No. Remember when you left us in the park in Rome? We did it there in a grove of trees. It was romantic and perfect, and in case you're wondering, he used a condom."

"Pain?"

"Probably like a four on a scale from one to ten." She nods like that sounds about right.

"Pleasure?"

"Probably a four on a scale from one to ten, but who cares? It was Enzo, and it's done. I don't have to think about it again. I mean I'll think about it, probably every day for the rest of my life. But I don't have to wonder anymore. I'm so happy, Janie."

"I'm so happy for you, Mads. I mean he's gorgeous and smart. He's like Ty."

Except for the pickle part.

Mom walks out in a towel. God, she takes the shortest showers ever. Did she even use soap?

We're so jet-lagged, we don't even know if it's night or day. Finally, everybody—even Aunt Rose, who is slightly more with it since she started antibiotics for her urinary tract infection—meets to go out for dinner. It's after nine at night, and we end up at a famous open market with stands filled with questionable-looking food. An Australian couple tells us it's called Snake Alley because they sell snakes, living and dead.

Wes strikes up a conversation with two local guys who are obviously desperate to practice English. They apparently have nothing better to do than guide us through this market. It smells so bad I gag at least twice. I'm trying to talk to Enzo and appreciate this experience, but it's awful. I won't try any of this stuff, even though I'm starving. Dad buys chicken feet, something called bean curd, and fried shark, which Bob describes as "chewy." I can't believe they're gnawing on actual shark meat and the bony little disembodied feet of chickens.

"Not bad," Wes says. "Kind of crunchy."

My bee buzzes. A little tip: You need to get some again soon or you'll forget how to do it and you'll be back to square one. My little Maddie is all grown up.☺ Janie gives me a wave from behind Aunt Rose, who is now also chewing on a chicken foot.

The random guys stop at a beverage stand and start laughing. They want us to try deer penis wine. What the hell is wrong with these people?

Finally we get to a bakery. I pull Enzo inside while the others are out in the street inhaling steaming noodles from plastic bags. He exhales like he's been holding his breath for an hour. I certainly have.

I look up at him. He leans down to kiss me, and they all rush in to kill the moment. They fawn all over the fruit-covered cakes and sugared pastries in the case. I'm so hungry I eat half a spongy, fruit-covered cake in the span of three minutes and chase it with a Coca-Cola. Even the Coke tastes bad. Uncle Billy makes a toast to great adventures, and we clink Coke cans and milk tea cartons, because half my family is drinking something called milk tea.

I've barely heard Gram talk the whole night. Maybe she's still recovering from her all-nighter with Bob and Celia. It's probably not easy to party all night when you're really old and dying of cancer. But Gram said it was one of the best nights of her life. Maybe it's all finally hitting her. Or maybe she's hurting more than we know.

–ع٥ڒ–

Gram was the last person to get to the lobby this morning. And she was holding a teddy bear. Mom and Uncle Billy worriedly whisper that she's regressing, wondering why else she'd suddenly be holding on to this teddy bear. It's making me nervous. She clings to Bob Johns like a security blanket—he's the binky to go with her bear.

This bus ride sucks. We're careening down roads with no guard-rails through the countryside of Taiwan toward an unknown destination. This morning Dad pressed Gram for information, until she got all cranky and called him an irritating little asshole. We pass through towns congested with smog from mopeds and cars. Then we go through a stretch of mountains, green and lush, with mist rising from the tippy tops and quaint temples dotting the landscape.

Dad gives us the speech about our bus getting rear-ended, but we decide to take our chances and sit in the back. Enzo talks to me so close, he's making it impossible to concentrate on anything but how he looked naked. How can his breath be sweet and fresh after the fried scallion pancakes we ate off a cart for breakfast?

"Is your gram always mysterious like this?"

"She likes to be dramatic, so she delivers these surprises all the time. But she's not acting normal. I have no idea what is going on. And that teddy bear is freaking me out."

He leans over and kisses me on the forehead. It's an innocent kiss, but it triggers a response from someplace deep inside me that fills my whole body. I thought lust was a fake thing somebody made up to be gross. I was wrong.

The bus stops near a pedestrian bridge in the middle of a street in a tiny village surrounded by mountains. A man wearing one of those wide-brimmed straw hats squats over a small patch of land next to the bridge. We all climb out and stretch as the bus driver pulls Gram over and points to a house halfway up a steep hill.

"Come on, we have to cross that bridge. Billy, help your aunt." Gram starts walking.

"Oh, come on. This thing doesn't look like it can hold a hundred pounds," Dad says. "Do you really think this is a good idea, Astrid?"

"Well, the Orientals have been doing it for centuries," politically incorrect Rose says.

"The 'Orientals' weigh a hundred pounds," Jeb says. Apparently we all have a bridge phobia.

The river below is not deep. That makes it even worse, because all the rocks stick out from the bottom. Two men stand ankle deep with fishing poles, not far from the bridge, but too far to help us if it collapses.

After several minutes of our complaining, the bus driver loses his temper. "Go, cross the bridge. Just go." He says it with such force that we listen.

We climb the steep dirt road and knock on the old wooden door of the mystery house. It looks like it's made out of concrete slabs, like somebody's garage.

A woman in her fifties or sixties with a short salt-and-pepper bob opens the door.

"Oh, hello, hello. Astrid." Gram holds up her hand, as she fights to catch her breath.

She leads us through a large room with white tile floors and bamboo furniture. There's a TV and a shrine on the wall with little statues and incense and oranges.

Before we even know what to say, we're in a back garden, if you can call it that. It's a patch of grass with two chickens running around. An ancient woman sits on a stool. She gets up with the help of the other woman, takes one look at Gram, and starts the lip quiver.

"Astrid." The two old ladies embrace. Now I feel silly for calling Gram a shriveled raisin. This woman is a shriveled raisin. She makes Gram look like an NBA player.

"Lin, I feel like I've embraced you a thousand times."

"Yes, me too. Oh, let me look at your family. Oh, who is Trish? And Billy? Jeb?" She looks at Enzo. Not even close.

"Sit, Lin," Gram says. "I have a very big mouth, but I wanted to wait until we were here to tell them the whole story." Gram sets the big teddy bear on her lap.

"Yes, Mother. I think we need to know everything." Uncle Billy's getting his bratty tone.

We all sit, on various chair-like things, if the rice bag I'm sitting on is a chair-like thing. The lady starts talking, but we keep saying "Excuse me?" and "Can you repeat that?" not because her English is bad, but because her voice box is ninety-something years old and barely works. So finally Gram says, "Lin, just let me tell them, and you can fill in the blanks."

"Your English is very good, ma'am," Dad says.

"I had a good teacher." Lin winks at Gram.

"Wait a minute. You were her English teacher?" Janie looks at Gram.

"No. Martin was."

"Martin taught English?" Dad asks.

"Oh, for the love of God, let me tell the damn story."

And the (damn) story goes like this: During World War II, Grandpa Martin and a group of other guys were supposed to sneak into Taiwan to get Japanese military information. But the Japs (as Gram calls them) sent everyone in the group to a copper mine prison camp, except Martin, who escaped into the mountains. In the meantime, Lin, who was a university student at the time, had been sent to live with distant relatives in a remote village to get away from the Japanese soldiers who were notorious for raping young girls. One day, a scrappy-looking American GI wandered into the village looking for shelter.

"We called Martin 'white ghost.' We had no food. Everyone was starving. Martin went through danger every week to steal food from Japanese soldiers. He almost died many times." Lin's face brightens. She holds up a shriveled hand. "But every time, he brought back food, and he kept us all alive. He was our white ghost. Martin O'Neill saved my sister, me, our village."

Gram rests her hand on Lin's back. "Martin and Lin exchanged letters for decades, and when he died, I started to write."

"Martin was a war hero. I can't believe he never told us," Dad says. "That's something to be incredibly proud of."

"You know Martin. He wasn't one to toot his own horn and, frankly, he was shell-shocked from the war," Gram says. "Sometimes, though, he would drink a little too much and tell me how those times he cheated death were the times he felt most alive."

After Lin's daughter, Bing, serves an entire fish, more chicken feet, and pastries stuffed with bean paste (the worst dessert ever), Lin wants to show us Grandpa Martin's favorite temple. We tread, single file, over the treacherous suspension bridge and board the bus.

"I can't believe you kept this from us," Mom says to Gram.

"You people are always telling me I talk too much, and if someone tells me a secret, I need to keep it. Now you're bitching that I kept Martin's secret? The one thing my WASP mother drilled into me was to ask myself the question 'Is that your story to tell?' It wasn't. It was Martin's. If he didn't want to share, he didn't want to share."

"Not everybody is an open book, guys," Wes says.

The bus crawls even deeper into the mountains on an unpaved road. As we approach the temple, I understand why this place was so special to Grandpa Martin. It's mind-blowing.

We walk up a stone pathway to a collection of bright red buildings with the orange curved roofs of all Taiwan's temples. It feels like the most serene spot on earth, like this is where the earth breathes when it's sleeping soundly. A lone Buddhist monk, completely bald and draped in a saffron robe, sits on a bench, his hands folded. A stray dog darts over to him and back to us, but the monk doesn't look up.

We walk to a gazebo, also covered with a curved orange roof and lined with benches, and sit to catch our breath. Lin's daughter pulls a stack of photos from her messenger bag. There's one old, tattered photo of Lin's sister and Grandpa Martin sitting together on a bench and laughing at something in the distance.

"We took this right over there." Lin points to a shady spot near the main building. "Martin had returned with food. He stole two bottles of rice wine from the Japanese soldiers, and we drank it, and we had a little party. It was so special, that day. War was dark and terrible all around us. Martin gave us little sips of laughter and light. Maybe that is what kept us alive. More than the food." Lin's voice drifts.

An ancient man and three women shuffle toward us. "Here they are," Lin says to Gram.

Gram's still holding the teddy bear.

"These are the last of the people White Ghost saved," Lin says.

None of them speaks English. Lin translates story after story of Grandpa Martin's selflessness and heroism as these people are reduced to tears. I wish so badly Grandpa could be here to feel their gratitude.

"So I brought you all the way here for a couple reasons," Gram says, pointing to all of us. "I racked my brain to think of a way to honor Martin and the people he helped." She makes her way over to Lin and Bing. "Bing, we'll need you to translate." Gram straightens her tailored navy blouse and touches her pearls.

She nods toward Bing. "I would like to announce the Martin O'Neill, White Ghost, Scholarship Program. Each year, a committee, chosen by you and your children, will select a deserving young person from your village to receive full college tuition, including room and board." She stops and waits for Bing to translate.

One of the women in the group claps. The others follow.

"I would like to appoint Martin's son, William O'Neill, as the North Foundation point person and ambassador to your lovely village."

Uncle Billy looks surprised.

"You good with that, Bill?" Gram says.

"Of course, Mom. I'm honored."

"Daddy would be proud," she says, reaching up to touch Uncle Billy's face.

Gram motions to the people to join her on the bench in the gazebo. We're all awkwardly standing around, ready to wrap things up, when Gram yanks the head off the teddy bear.

"What are you doing, Assy?" Wes says.

"I'm taking out Martin. Bobby, help me unscrew the top here. Surprise! Martin's been with us all this time. Bob said I'd have to fuss with Customs if I claimed his ashes, so I smuggled him in this bear."

My hands get sweaty. My grandpa's charred remains are inside a teddy bear.

"I gave Martin my word I'd find a way to scatter his ashes here."

"Here? You're going to scatter Dad now?" Mom says.

Gram nods. Lin and the others walk toward a steep drop at the edge of the temple grounds. I guess they were privy to this information.

I stay back with Enzo. "Are you okay?" he asks.

I try to take a yoga breath, but it gets stuck. "No."

"Maddie, you're shaking. What's wrong?"

"I don't want to do this. I'm freaked the fuck out right now. What if a finger falls out or a toe or his nose?" I sit on the bench and put my head between my knees. Enzo rubs my back.

"It's okay. I'm here. They're all down at the base of the lot saying a prayer or something. It'll be over soon."

That was not fair of Gram to smuggle Grandpa in a teddy bear.

It takes only a few minutes. They must have dumped the whole thing over the bank, like my grandfather was the remains of somebody's barbecue pit.

I give a weak bow to the old people as everybody says their good-byes. Now that I think of it, bowing might be more of a Japanese thing, but I can't really keep track of Asian customs at this moment.

Jeb comes over. "This is it, Maddie. You had better get your shit together and say good-bye. He's not waiting on the shelf in Gram's study for you to get over your issues." For once, my brother isn't being an asshole. He means it. I squeeze Enzo's hand and let go. I walk alone to the edge of the cliff.

"Bye, Grandpa Martin," I whisper under my breath as Gram hugs Lin a few yards away. They're two shriveled raisins in front of the orange-topped temple where my grandfather became a quiet war hero.

I write postcards to my friends on the bus ride back to meet the Wishwell. *The food in Taiwan is bad, but this place is pretty cool. We should take a road trip here someday.*

NINETEEN

WE ARRIVE ON the Wishwell late and go straight to Enzo's cabin. "I need a shower," I whisper. "So let's shower," he whispers back. Our bodies slide in the steam. He turns me around and holds my hands against the wall and kisses me, starting at the top of my head. I didn't know the human body could be heat-drenched and still shiver. We move to the bed, balcony doors flung open, moonlight streaming, breeze pushing in and drawing us closer, if closer were possible.

I use my finger to trace a newly discovered constellation: Maddie Major, the perfect semicircle of freckles on Enzo's shoulder. I can't even think about it without the sensation spreading outward from deep inside. I'm hooked on Enzo's smell.

We're starving. My knees buckle a little when I get up to answer the door. Enzo jumps up and puts on boxers. By the time Camilla comes in with breakfast, he's on the balcony, kicking a soccer ball between the chairs.

We lounge in our underwear and feed each other bites of buttered toast.

"Can I ask what happened back at the temple to upset you so much?"

He might as well get to know my crazy side.

"I used to get really freaked out about death. It started when I saw my dog get hit by my school bus. I went to therapy, which kind of helped, but then when they cremated my grandpa Martin, I couldn't handle it. I couldn't get the image of Grandpa burning in an oven out of my head."

"I get it." Enzo pulls the covers up. "I have to say, being on this ship, seeing the patients, always brings back memories of Dad." He stares at the ceiling. "Those images are tough to get rid of."

We sit awhile, lost in dark thoughts until Enzo finally turns toward me and changes the subject. "God, you're beautiful."

I burrow under the covers and lay my head on his chest. His heart beats against my ear.

Before I sleep, I think of Holly. When I was little, I was afraid that if I looked at a sick or disabled person, I would become one. I knew it was weird and wrong to feel that way, but I couldn't help it. Now I would give anything to look Holly in the eyes and tell her how brave she was and how her spirit inspired everyone. There will be a flood of emotions when we meet back up with the others. And there will be a life-size void where her chair belongs.

-&o&-

We're all gathered on the pool deck, swapping stories. It seems like baby Grace got bigger and more adorable while we were gone, and Paige says she has a big surprise for us.

"Go ahead, Gracie. Go see Uncle Babysitter." Grace toddles with a determined expression into the arms of a very emotional Wes.

"Yay, Gracie," we all cheer. "You walked!" She laughs and claps, very proud of herself.

It almost seems the same, with Burt making fart jokes and Gram gesturing dramatically as she describes our thong swimsuits. It almost feels normal, with Jeb trying to hide his obvious interest in Camilla, and Mom gushing over Gloria's snorkeling pictures. But something is off. The patients are weaker, grayer, yellower, quieter. And soon they will all be gone.

The elephant in the room hovers over our Wishwell reunion like a sinister pervert waiting for the right time to grab another innocent ass.

-&o&-

"Tomorrow's my birthday," I say to Enzo.

"I know tomorrow's your birthday. I wish I could take you to Paris for the night."

"I've had enough jet-setting for a while. I'll settle for cupcakes."

"Come on, we have to have a party. Eighteen is big. Let's make you a birthday playlist to get you in the mood."

"That would require getting out of bed. Although I do need a break. You've worn me out."

"Would you believe you've worn me out, too?" He gets up and smooths down his hair in the mirror. "Let's have a Wishwell day."

We go up to the deck and steal pizza from the Ornaments while they play pool volleyball with Burt and my uncles.

"That's it. A pool party," Enzo says. "I'm sending out an invite."

"Do you think that's appropriate at this point in the trip?" I step into the Grotto.

"Sure. Things will be pretty uneventful until after Wishwell Island."

"What's the point of Wishwell Island, anyway?"

"Life. That's the point. Mum created the ship so people don't have to suffer in the end, but the goal of the Wishwell movement on the whole is to prevent diseases altogether." Enzo looks down at his bee. "They actually have a party invitation app on these things."

"Enzo, focus. I want to hear about the island."

"They recruit the best doctors and scientists and grow plants from all over the world. They're trying hard to find cures for cancer, neurodegenerative diseases, addiction, everything."

"Who is 'they'? Who pays for all of it?"

"Loads of people donate. It's the best-known secret on earth. A lot of them donate in memory of family members. You know, like-minded people who believe life is more important than stuff. Right they are, huh?"

"Right they are, old chap."

Enzo looks down at his bee. "Oh, no. Astrid's mad at me."

Enzo had invited the entire ship: You are cordially invited to a pool party in honor of Maddie O'Neill Levine's 18th birthday. Cupcakes. Good music. 8 pm tomorrow.

Gram texted Enzo back: Enzo, we had planned to surprise Maddie with a formal dinner dance in the dining room and a proper cake for her 18th birthday. Astrid

I text, Gram, I want the pool party and cupcakes and 18-year-old music. Nothing proper. And no chicken feet. Love, Maddie

Gram texts, Suit yourself. But I'm bringing chicken feet.

Crisis averted.

−ξ◦⁊−

I officially meet Heinz in the poker room after dinner. He shakes my hand and tells me he's pleased to meet me. He and Vito are buddies now, and Vito has enlisted him to take down Dad and Bob in poker. I don't know what to make of him. He doesn't look like a scary Nazi. But nobody looks scary at ninety-three. He just looks like Gollum with heart failure.

When I stop by to tuck her in, Gram informs me that Gollum is kind of sexy. I inform her that slugs stuck to mushrooms are sexier.

−ξ◦⁊−

"Happy birthday, you big whore bag!" Janie tackles me.

"You're in a good mood."

"Of course. It's your birthday." She throws a gift bag at me.

"I kind of forgot to get you something. But this is from Rachel and the E's."

There are two boxes inside. One is a book of photos from the E's. The card says: *By now we are living in a postapocalyptic world and only Maddie can save us. Come home, birthday girl!*

The shower turns off. "Don't come out naked," I yell to Enzo. "We have a visitor."

"Come out naked," Janie yells.

I can tell Rachel wrapped her own gift because she wraps like a toddler. It's a pair of granny underwear. Very clever. *By now you've probably ruined all your pretty lace thongs with your Irritable Bowel Syndrome. Happy Birthday, Mads. Love, Rach.*

"You guys have to stop with the IBS jokes. I've practically outgrown it," I whisper.

"Oh, please. You're the IBS poster child," Janie says, just as the bathroom door opens.

Janie leaves me flipping through my birthday album with towel-clad Enzo.

"That's Lizzie on our first camping trip." I laugh. "This was taken after she got lost and claimed a possum showed her how to get back. And this is all of us at the lake."

"Who's the guy groping you?"

"That's Ethan, my ex. He's an idiot."

Enzo grabs his crumpled shorts from the chair and pulls out a red velvet drawstring bag from his pocket. "I saw this in London and thought of you."

It's a delicate silver bracelet with a single starfish charm.

My eyes start to fill with tears. "I love it."

"Why are you crying?"

"I just love it. Thank you for getting me."

"You're welcome, Maddie."

—⸘o⸘—

Gram has arranged a refined-young-lady lunch on her balcony. I can't stop touching my starfish bracelet.

"You outdid yourself, Astrid," I exclaim in my country club accent.

"Wes did most of it."

"Assy just barked orders from the chaise." Wes jumps up and lifts me off my feet. "Happy birthday, gorgeous."

They've hung tissue paper lanterns and set the long table with china and bud vases filled with flowers.

We eat omelets, potatoes, and fresh blueberry muffins. Mom and Dad sip "water with gas" and gaze at me with stupid smiles.

"I can't believe our baby is eighteen. We are so proud of the lovely, smart woman you have become." Dad raises a glass, and we toast to youth and good health and long life.

Uncle Billy sticks a candle in my muffin and they sing at the top of their lungs with Aunt Rose and Jeb two full beats off.

"Gifts, gifts," Mom says.

Bob gives me a picture of us all on the Spanish Steps in a silver frame, and Aunt Rose gives me a bejeweled bookmark she made in the craft room. Uncle Billy and Wes give me a "Welcome to New York" gift card basket, and Mom and Dad give me an IOU for a future road trip with the E's, all expenses paid.

This gift would have been a life-changer two months ago.

Jeb hands me a key.

"What's this, Jebby? The key to your heart?"

"No. It's a key to my apartment, in case you get lost in Brooklyn or chased by a predator."

"Aw. That's sweet. Thank you. Of course you know I'll be stealing food."

"I don't have food."

"My turn. It's age after foolery," Gram says. She hands me a package wrapped in plain brown paper. I open it slowly because I know it's the last birthday gift I will ever receive from my grandmother. It's a hard-cover, brand-new copy of Jules Verne's *Journey to the Center of the Earth*. I flip through and see that Gram taped a picture of the two of us in the lava tube inside the front cover. The words written on the next page pull at my heart:

Darling Maddie,

You are eighteen, which means you are still a baby and don't know a thing about anything. But trust me when I say you are special. There is a light in you that guides people through things they can't possibly get through alone. I know this, because I am one of those people. If Snaefellsjökull is a mystical place, you, my dear, are a mystical person. Be brave. Be adventurous. Let people come to you. You'll derive power from your own light. And I will be an eternal starfish chafing your ass all the years of your life. I love you, beautiful girl.

Gram

"Not fair, Gram. I can't sit on your lap anymore. You're too scrawny." I'm sobbing. I kneel down on the floor and plant my head on her bony legs and cry until she tells me to get ahold of myself. Janie and Wes are crying, too, raining tears on my birthday parade.

"Okay, stop. I'm dying, not paying full price for theater tickets. Enough with the tears." Gram pulls me up by my hair. "People are going to think I've pissed myself, and the one thing I have left is a stellar bladder. Light the muffin candle, Wessy. We forgot about the birthday wish."

I look around through my puffy eye slits. My family is trying their best to smile, to give me a good birthday. I don't want to screw up this wish. I got stupid and cynical and didn't wish for anything in Rio. I wished for Enzo to come back to me in Rome, and it came true. It's so much pressure. If Gram getting better were remotely possible, a wish might just make it happen, and the nightmare would be over. If only.

The logical answer hits me. I know my wish.

Enzo bursts onto the balcony. "Is there any food left?" Everybody shushes him.

"She's wishing," Wes mouths.

It's done. Now I wait.

Mom rests her head on my shoulder. I let her because Gram says I need to let the people come to me. Thanks, Gram. I can already feel the weight of the world on my shoulders.

—ε∘ɜ—

"How common do you think it is to get hepatitis from tattoo needles?" I ask Janie and Paige. We're in the cabin, getting ready for the party. Paige is mixing margaritas on the balcony.

"Not very," Janie says. She stops what she's doing and looks at me and my scrunch face. "Don't go there."

"Go where?"

"Enzo doesn't have AIDS, you freak."

But Paige nods at me like she understands. "I used to constantly worry about drunk drivers. I hardly went out at night because I didn't want a drunk to ram into me. And guess what? I ended up with a brain tumor. You never know what's going to hit you." She pours salt on her hand, licks it off, and throws back a shot of tequila. "The moral of the story is don't worry."

I shake my head.

"What? Do I sound too much like a mom?"

"No, you sound drunk," Janie says. "You're a lightweight."

"You just made me do three shots in ten minutes," Paige says.

"I don't like drunk drivers either," I say, before taking a yoga breath and following Paige and Janie to my eighteenth birthday party.

—ε∘ɜ—

The wheelchair brigade files in, with Gram now joining their ranks. She finally succumbed to the wheelchair, saying that she prefers to save her legs for dancing and lovemaking.

I stand behind the potted plants and take it all in for a minute. I had always imagined celebrating this birthday with my friends at the lake club under the stars. I would dance all night with the E's and make out with some guy and probably end up skinny-dipping in the lake.

But here I am. There's paralyzed Mark, and his oafish brother, and bald Gloria with her minister husband. There's Vito with his oxygen tank, and the Ornaments with their hearty laughs and Queens accents, and a guy who might possibly be a Nazi. And there's my thirty-three-year-old sorority sister, Paige, and Lane and Janie and Ty and my family—my crazy lovable family. I look at them all and then think about Enzo, who will be here any minute. And I can't believe I'm even thinking this, but this party is better than the one I pictured for all those years.

The crew set up a buffet with fried macaroni and cheese balls and sliders and chicken skewers and a giant cupcake tower. The deck is overflowing with silvery balloons and twinkly lights. I'm floating into adulthood on a magical ship.

"Here, honey. I found you a tiara," Mom says. She sets it on top of my head and steps back to assess me. She gives the familiar you-would-look-so-much-better-with-a-different-hairstyle nod.

"What, Mom? I'm not putting on Spanx under a sundress."

"No, no, honey. I just couldn't be prouder of the remarkable young woman you've become." She hugs me.

"Thanks, Mom. That really means a lot to me," I say, stuck in her uncomfortably tight grip. She adjusts my princess crown and makes her way over to Roberta.

Janie is already drunk. She and Ty are doing shots with Jeb and Camilla in the Grotto. Bob and Dad scurry back and forth to the wheelchair brigade, carrying plates and glasses of champagne.

Paige runs up and kisses me on the mouth. She reeks of tequila. "Sip?"

I take a swig from her margarita vat. It's so strong, I nearly barf.

"Where's Grace?"

"Uncle Babysitter is walking her around in the stroller, trying to get her to sleep. He's practicing for—" Her eyes go wide. "Uh-oh, oopsie."

"Don't worry. I know about the baby."

"Thank God." She smacks me on the back. "I've been keeping that secret for weeks. It was torture." She takes another drink. "Those two are going to be the best dads ever. I'm so happy for them. I am wicked drunk. When are we going to dance?"

"Soon." It's hard to be around drunk Paige without thinking about the seizure. Every time she looks at me funny, I'm afraid she's got one coming on.

"Will you keep in touch with Grace, Maddie? Will you tell her all about this"—she flings her hand toward the gathering crowd—"when she's old enough? Not the part about me being drunk."

"Of course. How about I take Grace shopping at Saks for her eighteenth birthday? I'll take her to the lunch counter and tell her about the Wishwell and her amazing mommy."

"Saks. Fancy. I like it." She puts her finger up to my lips. "Just don't tell her about the shots."

"I won't tell her about the shots," I say, as she runs over to tackle Lane.

Gollum comes toward me in a three-piece suit. He's combed his hair and slicked it back for the party. It might be the most pathetic thing I've ever seen.

"Happy birthday, Maddie. Thank you for inviting me." He shakes my hand. His fingers are like ice.

"Thank you, Heinz. Thank you for coming."

Awkward silence.

"Will you save me a dance later?" *Why did I say that?*

"That is kind of you, but I must decline. I'm not a very good dancer."

"Okay. No problem."

"Well, enjoy your party, Maddie. Happy birthday."

I don't say anything as he walks away. What do I say to a lonely old man who doesn't even know how to dance?

An über-cute baby in a purple party frock comes toward me in a stroller, flapping her arms frantically.

"Kiss Aunt Maddie, Gracie." Wes glows with daddy hormones. I lean over, and Grace holds her slimy mouth on my cheek. She hasn't figured out how to pucker, but she makes a *muh* sound.

"When are you going to tell everybody about the baby?" I say, grabbing Grace's bare feet and kissing her tiny toes. "Why are you keeping it a secret? It's the best news we've had, maybe ever."

"Billy doesn't want to tell until we're sure. It's like when a woman is pregnant. She waits until she's past the typical miscarriage stage. There's so much heartbreak in the adoption world."

"But you're slacking, Wes. I haven't had a status update since Italy."

"You've been shagging all day and night."

"Hey. Not cool."

"We are getting a baby girl," he says. "She's due in early September. We're going to have a baby, Gracie." Wes unbuckles Grace and picks her up. She grabs a big clump of his hair.

"So tell everyone before I explode. I'm a teenage girl—it's against my nature to keep juicy secrets."

"Soon. Very soon. Go have fun. Gracie needs to go night, night."

"How is it that Uncle Billy was the one pushing for the kid when you're so good with them?"

"I've always loved kids." He coaxes Grace back into the stroller. "I just didn't love *being* a kid. It wasn't easy growing up gay in cow country forty years ago. I don't want to screw things up for some other kid."

"You won't."

"How do you know?"

"Because you're Uncle Babysitter." Wes smiles wide before walking away behind Grace, who has decided she wants to push the stroller.

Enzo comes around the corner in khaki shorts, a faded T-shirt, and a red baseball cap.

"Hey, birthday girl. I like the crown. You're making me want to take you back to the cabin." He grabs my waist and pulls me toward him.

"Stop talking in that British accent. It's too distracting," I whisper in his ear.

"Burt and I got Mark so bombed he's giggling uncontrollably," Enzo says. Paige runs over, rips the tiara off my head, and puts it on top of Burt's cowboy hat.

"I'm glad this has degenerated into a frat party."

"Mum's here. Time to sing." He escorts me up to the Grotto.

Francesca kisses my cheeks and picks up the microphone. "Attention, everyone. May I have your attention?" After five minutes of trying to shut up the crowd, Bob Johns blows his trumpet into the mic. People cover their ears. Burt throws a beach ball at Bob.

"I'm going to play a little something for our Maddie girl." Bob's voice sounds even deeper over the mike. "Happy birthday to a lovely young lady."

Bob does a bluesy trumpet version of "Happy Birthday" and the entire Wishwell crowd serenades me. I scan the deck for Gram. She blows me a kiss, rests her hand on her heart, and mouths, *I love you.*

I love you too, I mouth back.

Ty's intern friend DJ Steve plays a reggae birthday song, and the dancing erupts like an Icelandic volcano. It's a whirling mass of stomping feet and shaking hips and spinning wheelchairs.

If only I could wrap up this moment and tie it with a pretty ribbon, I would give it to baby Grace someday.

-ξ∘ξ-

It's five AM, and Janie has puked and rallied so many times that I think she's finally sober. Only the strong have survived to settle into the Grotto with ganja and cold macaroni and cheese balls. My thighs are in spasm from all the dancing, and the hot water feels incredible.

"Oh my God, I am messed *up*." Lane slides in next to Paige and takes a long hit from Jeb's joint. "Macaroni and cheese in a fried ball. Genius."

Burt grabs the mic from Wes, the one-man karaoke act. "Mark wants to go skinny-dipping. Let's do this. Yeah!"

Burt yanks off Mark's shorts. Jeb and Lane jump out of the Grotto to help lower Mark's skinny, deformed body into the choppy water. Enzo holds one arm, Burt holds the other, and they pull Mark in circles around the pool. It's beautiful and grotesque at the same time. "Woo-hoo-hoo," Mark yells.

"How's that, little bro?" Burt says. "Hey, Maddie, how do you like your present? Mark's in his birthday suit for you."

"Ha-ha, Burt," I say before I cannonball in.

Wes gets the bright idea to have a chicken fight. Enzo hoists me up and barrels toward Ty. It's Janie and me in a death match. I'm fifteen pounds heavier and twenty shots lighter and Janie still shoves me into the water first.

We, the Wishwellians, purveyors of depravity, watch the sun rise, wrapped in towels. I shiver as the chill of dawn wakes me up and exhausts me all at once.

"How do we go from this to death?" We should be having sex right now. We should have gotten into bed and worked off all that crazy sexual energy. But I asked the question, and he is about to answer. It's stupid of both of us.

Enzo is on his stomach, facing away from me. His voice is hoarse.

"After Wishwell Island, it'll happen quickly, one patient after the next, in a matter of days. They will honor the patients and then there will be a grieving period. Mum always says grief is healthy. And that's it."

"That's it?"

"Yes. That's it."

I turn over. "I'm so tired," I tell him. I don't want him to talk anymore. I'm sorry I asked the question. He's asleep in two minutes, and I'm racked with anxiety.

It feels like the universe is punishing me for having the best birthday of my life.

-&° TWENTY °3-

SOMEHOW I GOT roped into typing Gloria's recipes, because Mom needs backup so she can laminate.

"I think it's time for Chicken Cordon Bleu," Gloria says. "Be sure to type it exactly as I say it, because this is a tricky one. Note that I use the heavy whipping cream and the good sliced ham, not the kind from the case."

Mom looks down at my text: Do you really think her grandchildren are going to eat this gross crap?

She texts back: Not nice, Maddie. It's Gloria's recipe book, not ours.

Gloria has a story for every recipe.

"Sometimes the minister and I took in homeless women and

children for weeks on end until we could find them a safe place. They loved my Cordon Bleu."

I text Mom again: You should be recording the stories for her kids. They would appreciate them.

She texts back: Already doing that. I'm one step ahead of you.

Gram texts me: Can you come up, honey? Need to talk.

I feel the instant stomach anxiety rise up into my throat. I don't like the tone of the text. I don't want her to die today. I'm not ready.

I recruit Roberta to take over, and I run the stairs to Gram's cabin. I'm getting the sharp stomach cramps. Damn irritable bowel syndrome. Gram answers the door in her housecoat and slippers. She must feel shitty.

"What is it, Gram? Are you okay?"

"I'm okay, honey. It's just time we talk about Grandpa Martin's service in Taiwan. I know it was a shock." She lowers herself onto the sofa. I cover her with a fuzzy blanket and sit at the other end. I lift her feet and lay them on my lap.

"It's okay, Gram."

"So here's the thing." She makes her humiliated-dog face. "We sort of didn't leave all of Grandpa in Taiwan."

"What?"

"There's a fabulous company that specializes in preserving ashes in handblown glass. And I had a marble made for each of you."

"Wait a minute. You made Grandpa into *marbles*?"

"Yes."

I can't believe she's keeping a straight face. She made her husband into marbles.

"I don't understand. I mean, why did you even cremate him in the first place? It's awful."

"One day Martin and I took one of those rowboats out in Central Park, and we talked about our wishes. Grandpa was like you; he avoided dealing with death. He wouldn't go to the doctor because he didn't want to hear bad news."

"I go to the doctor."

"Yeah, well, he didn't. Not smart."

I ignore a text from Mom: Thanks for ditching us.

"Your grandfather did not want to go into the ground. That gave him the creeps, with the worms and such. We talked about a family mausoleum, but Martin was too cheap for that. He settled on cremation, and once he decided, he was done. He wanted the ashes scattered at the temple. Then I found the marble company, and he loved the idea. 'I'll keep all my marbles even after I go,' he joked. He wanted this, honey. All of it."

I turn and stare out at the sea. Maybe I have been a brat. Maybe I should think about what other people want, even if it scares the shit out of me.

"So he wanted to be a marble?"

Gram laughs. "He did. And if you like, you can have the first pick."

"Now?"

"Sure." She struggles a little to get up, so I give her a push.

"Finally. Janie always gets first pick."

Gram sets a mahogany box on the table. Inside, eight marbles rest in grooves on a tray. I see mine right away.

"I'll take the blue one." I can't believe I'm doing this, but it feels like Grandpa Martin belongs inside these marbles.

"To match our eyes," she says. "See? There's one for your mom and Billy and Mary and the four of you. And I think I'll take the orange one. It reminds me of the temple roofs. That one goes with me."

I hold the marble against my cheek. I roll it between my fingers as we wait for the others to show up and claim their tiny round pieces of Grandpa Martin. For some strange reason, it's all okay.

$$-\text{{-}}\text{o}\text{{-}}-$$

Enzo persuades me to go running with him, even though he always wants to race and never lets me win. We get our smoothies from the Grotto bar and go down to see Mark. Enzo sees Mark a lot these days. On the Wishwell, every moment is a tiny glass ball we hold between our fingertips.

Burt is in the cabin, waiting for Mark to get back from group. I wonder if there's one nurse, a secret keeper, assigned to write thoughts on the Gathering Wall for the paralyzed people. Do they pick the nurse with the best handwriting?

Burt makes me uncomfortable, not because of the pockmarks and bulbous nose, but because he acts like the loser guys at the lake club who can't get girls and try too hard to be cool.

"Come hang out. I'm just playing a video game." Burt needs to put a shirt on. "Sweat much?" he says.

I want to say *Maybe you should try exercising once in your life,* but I hold my arm up and say, "Scratch and sniff."

"Good one," Burt says, laughing.

Burt and Enzo drink beers and tear open a bag of barbecue chips. I clear space on the cluttered balcony floor to stretch a little. They talk endlessly about sports. Burt chugs another beer and lets out a disgusting belch. He looks over at me.

"Can I tell you guys something fucked up?"

"Yeah," I say.

"My parents abandoned my brother. They fucking flat-out ditched him. They were all 'golden-boy Mark, superstar-surfer Mark, chick-magnet Mark,' and then he got the diagnosis, and they pretty much disappeared."

"That's terrible," Enzo says.

"Yeah, well. They hired nurses and then, when it got bad, they stuck him in a nursing home. He had me. As much as I bust on him, he's my little bro." Burt's voice cracks.

"You're a really good brother," I say. "I don't get how parents can just ditch their own son."

"Mostly because they're selfish pricks. Mark deserved better. That kid is golden. He'd do anything for anybody. Even now, he would if he could."

Burt's face is full of pain. The poor guy is forced to feed his little brother, and help the aides change his diapers, and watch hopelessly as Mark's body turns to mush.

"Do your parents even know he's here?" Enzo says. Burt tries to flip a quarter into a shot glass.

"Oh, yeah, they know. They think it's barbaric. The worst part of all is they refused to say good-bye. My brother has to go with that on his head. Plus, Mark's a surfer, man. His legs are his soul. He's got nothing left. Not even his parents."

"They're the ones who will have to live with that," I say. "Believe me, my aunt and cousin did the same thing. I wouldn't want to be them a couple months from now."

"Yeah, I hear you."

The nurse wheels Mark into the cabin. I can only imagine what that smile did to the girls back in his surfer days. I leave Enzo to talk surfing and go down for a shower.

-&o&-

The storm hits out of nowhere during lunch. All the plates and glasses fly off the table. We instinctively jump for the cutlery instead of the patients, who are left to fend for themselves. Gram, Gloria, and Vito roll around until we secure everyone against the inside dining room walls.

I would be even more terrified right now if Enzo weren't hugging me. The sky is night-dark, and we're still sitting here waiting out the storm. Enzo's hand roams beneath my giant beach towel, but I push it away. The rumbly noise of the sea crashing against the Wishwell isn't exactly putting me in the mood.

The ship hits a huge wave and goes airborne for a second, then plops back down. We scream. The lights flicker. "Are we going to die?" I dig my fingers into Enzo's arm.

"No. Relax. The ship has been through much worse than this. You should see the North Atlantic storms."

Suddenly it's gone. We get up and sort out all the ventilator equipment and canes.

"Oh, shit! Heinz," Dad yells. "We need to check on him."

Heinz rarely eats in the dining room. Other than the card games with the guys, he's reclusive.

A bunch of us run through the dining room, stepping over upturned tables and chairs everywhere. It's amazing how much damage a twenty-minute storm can cause. When we get to Heinz's cabin, the door is ajar.

"Oh, shit," Dad says again. "Don't move. We'll help you. Just don't move."

We need a bomb squad for this delicate job. Enzo calls the crew for canvas gloves and industrial trash bags. We pick up hundreds of pieces, one by one. Heinz has a look of utter despair. I'm not sure if it's because he's surrounded by broken glass or because his work is ruined.

He has spent all these weeks stuffing messages in bottles.

Paige, Mom, Roberta, and I collect the letters. They're in German, but some of them have sketches in the margins: a balloon, a teddy bear, and a little boy holding a book.

"This is so traumatic, I want to throw up," Paige whispers.

All I can think about is Paige going into a seizure on all this broken glass.

After hours of painstaking work, we've cleaned up most of the cabin and Heinz is talking to Vito on his balcony. My back aches, and I'm miserable. But we keep going.

Janie and Jeb and Wes and I swarm Dad in his cabin and grill him about Heinz.

"Come on, Aaron. You must know. You've been playing poker with the guy all these nights," Wes says.

Dad stands and smooths down the five hairs on his head. "I will tell you the story. But this is a judgment-free zone." He waves his arms likes he's clearing judgment out of the air. "Is everybody with me?"

"Yes, Professor Levine," Jeb says.

"Heinz was a member of the Nazi party when he was nineteen years old."

Janie punches Wes in the arm. "I knew it," she says.

"His job was to check passports on trains leaving Germany and turn in people with forged or missing documents."

"That's it? He didn't even kill anyone?" Jeb says.

"Oh my God. Shut up," I snap. Clearly Jeb has never read a book in his life.

"May I, please? He did the job for months before he found out he was sending people to camps. He was one of those kids who was bullied and tormented his whole life. He was a very sheltered young man, and thought he was serving his country by preventing people from defecting to the other side. He found out what the Nazis were doing at a picnic, of all places." Dad makes the scrunch face and shakes his head. "So Heinz went back and scanned the ledger of people he had turned in and realized it was five hundred thirty-one people. He fell apart and tried to starve himself to death. Most of his family was killed in the blitzkriegs, but his sister somehow got him to

Brazil, where he lived out his years with nieces and nephews. That's the story."

"So can he be considered a real Nazi?" Wes says. "I mean, he wasn't working in a concentration camp."

"The Nazis were a political party. Yes. He was a Nazi," Dad says. "Now you all know the truth. I'm going back up to help him with the bottles."

"What's he doing with the bottles?" I ask.

"He's writing letters to all five hundred thirty-one people he turned in, stuffing them into bottles, and throwing them into the sea."

"Isn't that polluting the ocean?" Janie says.

"Oh, come on, let the man be. He's not asking to snorkel or see volcanoes. He just wants to find a little peace by honoring those five hundred thirty-one souls. That's his only wish," Dad says.

Gram summons us before I can make sense of any of this.

-&o3-

The good news is we've recovered the 482 letters Heinz has written so far. The bad news is there are not enough bottles for 531 messages.

We leave Vito, Dad, Bob, and the minister with Heinz and call an emergency meeting in the café to figure out how to help him. Gram comes up with an idea.

"Papier-mâché. We're going to make five hundred and thirty-one fabulous bottles out of papier-mâché."

Thirty people file into the art studio to gather materials, and Gram crafts a prototype using balloons, glue, newspaper, and paint.

We stuff a paper inside and it works. We create an assembly line to slap the strips of tissue paper in layers. It takes every able-bodied person (and several not-so-able-bodied people) eight hours of work and large quantities of cookies and watermelon to complete and properly store all the bottles.

We take turns helping baby Grace crawl up the wheelchair onto Mark's lap and back down again. Then she wants to push Mark all the way down to the lobby. It's her baby obsession. She must think he's sitting in a giant stroller.

It's midnight when we text Dad to bring Heinz down to the ballroom. He's been dozing for hours, and Dad and Wes practically have to carry the disheveled, big-eared old guy. Heinz sees us standing behind 531 handmade bottles, and some extras, just in case. His eyes get wide, and for the first time I see his smile.

I never imagined I would help a Nazi try to make peace with the universe.

Enzo and I collapse into bed without even kissing. I'm beginning to feel like we're an old married couple. But I'm too tired to give it one last thought. The sound of a man singing wakes me up. Only it's not singing. It's Enzo yelling "no, no, no" in his sleep.

"Enzo, wake up." I shake him gently. "Enzo, it's okay." He wakes with a horrified expression. "What's wrong? What were you dreaming?" I ask.

He doesn't say a word, and I wonder if he's fallen back asleep. "I just...I haven't had that dream in a long time." Enzo sits up and blinks a few times. "I started having nightmares when Dad was sick.

Right before he died, he had tubes coming out of every orifice: his nose, his mouth, one stuck into his side. He choked and coughed and struggled all day. No amount of morphine could fully dull the pain, so he moaned and cried."

"Oh, Enzo, that's awful."

"I imagine if Dad was able to talk, he would have told Mum to keep us away. I imagine he was humiliated. Mum had her own dad dying at the same time, so she left us by Dad's side. He was our incapacitated babysitter. It was hell."

"Is that your dream?"

Enzo opens a bottle of water and takes a big gulp. "The dream is terrible. It's the way I saw the tubes when I was a kid, like serpents crawling into Dad and eating him alive. In the dream, the serpents are crawling into me." He shudders. "When you're sitting there for weeks, there's never a good-bye moment. It's suffering, and then relief when the suffering stops. We never had a good-bye."

I wrap my arms around Enzo and hold him as tightly as I can. I don't know what else to do. Nothing I say will exorcise that memory.

"Now you know why I used to avoid patients on this fucking ship. Or tried, at least." He gets up and walks out, leaving me to endure a miserable, sleepless night.

─ੴ TWENTY-ONE ੴ─

MY AUNT ROSE is dead in a freezer.

Uncle Billy found her curled up under the covers, dead and smiling. It's not that her dying was so surprising, but this was all about Gram's death trip. It's like when one sister elopes in Vegas days before the other sister's wedding.

Aunt Rose painted papier-mâché bottles for Heinz all day yesterday. She recited our family's plum pudding recipe—in perfect order, even—for Gloria's book. Now she's in a freezer in the underbelly of the ship because she wanted to be buried with Karl near their Charleston house.

Gram holds Aunt Rose's sweater to her face. "To be perfectly honest, my initial reaction was *Of course Rose dies smiling in her sleep. She's* the easy sister. But now I realize it was a gift. Deep down, Rosie knew I was worried sick about her. I know I had you people to look out for her, but we ate lunch at our place on Madison three times a week and talked on the phone every day. She was a pain in the ass, but she was my pain in the ass."

"She was a sweetheart," Bob says. "And a very pretty lady. I remember when we were young, she'd meet us for root beer floats and talk about her dates. She always wore red lipstick and smoked cigarettes."

"Aunt Rose smoked?" I say.

"Everybody smoked, Maddie," Gram says.

"How is this happening? She's gone, just like that." Wes shakes his head. "It's going to be strange not to hear her talk about Karl in Central Park."

"And how her plumbing didn't work," Dad says.

"And the dead dogs. 'Where's Tippy? Is Karl walking him at this hour?'" Uncle Billy imitates Aunt Rose's high-pitched voice.

"Is that you, Weebles?" Wes squints at Uncle Billy's face. Even Gram cracks a smile.

"You know, guys, those stories are silly to us, but she lost the majority of her mind, and those are the ones that stuck." Mom pauses. "Those were Rose's snow globe moments."

"See, people? We don't need to scale mountains. It's all about the little things," Wes says.

"Like reproductive problems and getting gas from kielbasa," Uncle Billy says.

"You're such a jerk, Billy. C'mon, Assy, let's have a service for her here," Wes says. "We'll do a luncheon because we all know Aunt Rose lived for luncheons. We can dress Easter chic and talk about all the fun we had in Charleston."

"Good idea, Wessy," Gram says. "Now, everybody clear out so I can mourn my sister in peace."

—ફ૦ર—

The luncheon is full of tea roses and Dixieland music. I wear my pink dress, Aunt Rose's favorite color, and Bob and Eddie surprise Gram with side-by-side enlargements of the old and new Bled photos. It's all very elegant, just like Aunt Rose. It feels like she went the way she was meant to go, on her expiration date.

Gram breaks down when Uncle Billy and Wes leave to pack up Aunt Rose's cabin. I watch her through the eyes of a little girl terrified to see a grown-up cry.

—ફ૦ર—

It's late, and insomnia is rampant on this ship. The closer we get to the end, the longer the line is for Whac-A-Mole. For a small woman, Paige can smack the hell out of those moles.

Enzo and I have spent hours on Mom and Dad's balcony, eating popcorn while Dad shows us the constellations in his fuzzy slippers.

It's almost midnight, and I get a text from Uncle Billy: Run?

"Be back in a little while." I kiss Enzo's cheek.

I pass the Skinny Dave chair and the Grotto and climb the stairs to the track. I walk up behind Uncle Billy, who's leaning over the railing.

"Hey, Mads. Thanks for coming up. I needed a running partner who can't talk and run at the same time."

I stretch out my calves. "Hey, I think that's an insult."

"Oh my God. Wes won't stop talking." He laughs. "I actually tried to stuff a sock in his mouth, but he managed to talk through it."

We sit on the floor and stretch in silence, bathed in starlight.

"I can't believe she's gone," he says, staring at his running shoes.

I nod. "You were her favorite," I say.

"You guys never knew the younger version of Aunt Rose. She was still sweet, but she was a force of nature."

"What do you mean?"

"Come on, screw the run. Let's walk and talk." We jump up and walk at a fast clip.

"As you might have noticed, Mother was not happy about Trish marrying a Jewish guy."

"Yeah, but Gram claims she was afraid Dad wouldn't see the value in her international Advent calendar collection. That can't be the reason."

"Actually, that was the reason. She was afraid he would ruin the North family Christmas traditions."

"Gram *is* pretty obsessed with Christmas."

"Yeah, but Rose convinced her to give Trish her blessing. You know how wishy-washy your mom is. I don't know if she would have married Aaron without that blessing."

"Damn. I never knew that."

"And then it happened again with Wes. Mom—and Dad, for that matter—were not cool with the gay thing."

"Oh, come on. Gram brags about how she loves the gays."

"Yeah, but she loved the idea of grandchildren more, and when she realized gay meant no grandchildren, she resented the hell out of Wes."

"No way."

"Yes, way. I'll never forget overhearing Aunt Rose rip Mom a new one. I had invited Wes to the Charleston house, and Mom was being rude to him. Aunt Rose told her to get over herself and welcome Wes with open arms, or she would make Astrid North O'Neill's life a living hell."

"I can't imagine Aunt Rose saying that."

"She didn't say it, she yelled it. The next morning, Mom and Wes hugged it out. And that was that."

"I'm going to miss her so much." The image of Aunt Rose in the freezer creeps me out. I want to remember her warm and smiling.

"Me too, Maddie girl."

We stop talking and run. I think about how Aunt Rose used to be—all the times she called us in for lemonade as she played her Dixieland music and how she wrote formal letters from Charleston to tell us how she couldn't wait to see us again. I had no idea behind all that grace and kindness was a quiet matriarch.

-&o&-

I get into bed emotionally drained and afraid it will be another night without Enzo sex. I snuggle into him and smell his neck. He pulls me on top of him, and I'm sucked into another dimension. It's all the senses and the breeze and the moon and his mouth. We keep going, swirling around the vortex of ecstasy and enchantment, until it finally collapses and we sleep fourteen hours straight.

─ॐ° TWENTY-TWO °ॐ─

ENZO DID NOT prepare me properly for Wishwell Island. I thought it would be a lab and a few scientists in cabins, but it is outrageous. Francesca showed us a lab complex that's bigger than three Target stores. It's divided into sections they call studios, named for famous places. Walden Pond, an outdoor lake in the middle of the complex, is the algae substation. The scientists here analyze millions of plants, fungi, insect secretions, leeches, and even shark cartilage.

My favorite part of the island is the shaman and faith healer village, where medicine people are recruited from tribes around the planet to share healing wisdom and hang out with priests and rabbis and imams. Outside the village, farmers grow superfoods for the people to eat. There are kids here and a small school and streets with quaint shops. The founders of the Wishwell movement wanted the people they recruited to be happy because happy people are creative people.

Mom is a nervous wreck, planning Gloria's recipe book unveiling with a feast for the patients, staff, and crew. Uncle Billy and Wes are up in the orchard right now, selecting fruits for the cobbler. I hope they don't make the Chicken Cordon Bleu.

Camilla figured out that Jeb's a douchebag, so he'll be our fifth wheel late tonight when Enzo takes us to Wishwell Island's bioluminescent lagoons. It's Jeb's own fault for screwing things up with Camilla, who is apparently getting her PhD in bioethics, whatever that is. Jeb has no ethics.

"Hey." Enzo smiles. I've been watching him sleep.

"Good morning." I slide over and lay my head on his chest. It feels unsettling to be docked and bobbing when we're used to moving with the sea.

"You have that look on your face," he says. His morning stubble is adorable.

"What look?"

"The same look you had last night when you were running around the island. Like a girl who's seen a fairy."

"I just can't believe a place like this exists."

"When we first got here, I was sure this place was magic and it would swallow up my father and spit him back whole. But it didn't quite work that way. They said the same things the doctors back home said: 'We're sorry, folks. He's riddled beyond repair.'"

"You know how Gram says we need to take the pain and grow beauty? That's what they're doing here." I'm quoting Gram a lot these days.

"That's exactly what funds this place. All those heartbroken people give money with the hope that other people won't go through what their loved ones have been through," Enzo says. He stops talking, and I hear his heartbeat. He leans down and tries to kiss me. I push him away.

"How do you not wake up with morning breath?"

"Caveman no care about breath."

"I need to get up. I'm helping Gram write Aunt Rose's obituary. She doesn't think anybody else will do justice to her memory."

"I bet those two were wild in the good old days."

"You know, I'm very close with my gram. We eat together, shop together, talk about travel and sex and movies. And yet I'll never really know what she was like seventy years ago. It's kind of bizarre."

"It's bizarre that you talk to your grandmother about sex. Have you told her about us?"

"Not yet. But it's only a matter of time. She won't be able to die without knowing how big your package is."

"Fantastic. Tell her it's thirty centimeters." He holds his hands an arm's width apart.

"How many inches is that?"

"You Americans and your inches. It's about twelve," he says. "That'll silence her."

"No. That'll just make her grope you more."

‑ξ∘ʒ‑

Jeb and Camilla made up in the middle of Wishwell Island's massive cannabinoid pasture. It took an entire field of pot to stop Jeb from being a douchebag. So Camilla will be joining our kayak trip tonight after all.

Dad and I are walking out of the invertebrate center. I haven't seen Dad this excited since the Roman ruins.

"Doesn't it seem like forever ago that Astrid told us her nutty plan? I gotta give it to her, this is the way to go out with a bang," Dad says, stopping abruptly to close his eyes and take a cleansing breath. I take a good, long yoga breath myself. It's as if the island is nudging us to breathe.

He leaps up and smacks the branch of a flowering tree. Tiny white petals tumble to the ground. "Think about it. Next time we're on the couch, zoning out in front of the tube, we'll be wondering why we're wasting precious time when we could be making extraordinary moments. It's as if all this death has given us the meaning of life."

"Dad, are you high?"

"High on life, maybe." He attempts to skip. I pull him by the shirt and make him stop.

"Have you ever seen Mom with such a spring in her step? I think she might have found her calling." Dad takes off his shoes and digs his hairy white feet into the sand. "She has loved every minute of helping Gloria with those recipes. She lies in bed at night talking about how she wants to visit nursing homes and record people's legacies."

"That's a perfect job for Mom. She actually has the patience to listen to people."

My toes make little marks as we wander on the edge of the beach. This island is a living organism, covered in sprawling vines and flowers. The birds and the bugs, the nectar suckers, hover and dart. The island is breathing, too, and we're stepping on it, tickling it. The lava tubes and the caves are arteries; the magma deep inside is its blood.

"There he is." Dad points down the beach to Enzo, talking to a woman I don't recognize. I get the stomach feeling. Who the fuck is she?

"Love you, Dad. That was fun." I make a beeline for my boyfriend.

"Hey, Maddie, this is Layla. She's a botanist here." A botanist? She's a hot girl in her twenties with olive skin, huge boobs, and a surfboard.

"Hi," Layla and I say. I think she just gave me the up-and-down bitch glance.

"Layla's been here awhile. She's researching indigenous flowering plants."

Awkward silence.

"That's really cool," I say. "I wish I could hang out, but I promised my uncles I'd help them before dinner. Nice meeting you, Layla. See you later, babe."

He could have followed me, but he let me go. He stayed with Tits Number Three.

I slam the plates down on the long tables in the outdoor pavilion and stick bunches of flowers in vases because God forbid Wes caters an event that isn't over-the-top perfect.

Enzo sends three What's going on? texts. I ignore them and the What's everybody wearing? text from Paige. Guests start arriving to crowd the bar and chug their mai tais, and I'm still in a sweaty tank top and running shorts. Mom's going to die of embarrassment on her big night.

Gram and Janie nibble buttermilk biscuits with honey butter and play the word game while I search the pavilion for Enzo.

"Honey," Janie says.

"That's an easy one. This story is rated R because I was topless. But everybody's topless in that particular village," Gram says.

"I like this game," Gloria says.

"Me too," Vito says.

I think of the Gathering Wall. *Me too. Me too. Me too.*

The steel drum band plays in the background as people from the ship and island mingle, and Francesca steps onto the stage.

"What a treat to see so many faces I love in one place. Thank you, Billy and Wes, for preparing this gorgeous feast. I will certainly hire you boys for my next meet-and-greet in New York." She claps her hands twice. "Now, before we begin, we have a little surprise for one of our beloved guests."

I spot Enzo sitting with Ty and a group of island people. I don't see Layla.

Francesca calls Mom up to the stage. "Trish, the floor is yours."

Mom takes the mic. Her hand shakes a bit, and her face goes red. I'm getting anxious watching.

"Um. Thank you, Francesca. Bear with me. I prepared something to read." She clears her throat. "Gloria is a Wishwell patient and a dear friend. She has lived a life of public service and devoted countless hours to helping those in need. One of Gloria's greatest gifts is her talent for creative cooking. The problem is she stored all her recipes in her head. Until now." Mom pauses and motions Roberta up to the podium. Roberta holds up a bound copy of *These Fine Foods*.

Gloria holds on to the minister with wide eyes and a cherry-lipped smile.

"I'm going to try to do this without tears," Mom continues. "Gloria, you may have recognized the biscuits and honey butter. They're yours. Everything Wes and Billy made today is from this book. Roberta and I wanted everyone to have a taste of your gift. We can't wait to give this book to your children and grandchildren. Each recipe comes with a sweet Gloria story. And each story tells us how you healed others with your food. Thank you, Gloria, for sharing your gift with us."

The minister takes Gloria by the arm and they walk slowly to the podium, where they embrace Mom and Roberta.

Mom looks down and scans the crowd. She sees me and waves, her face flushed with pride and contentment. There's not even a hint of *why are you dressed like THAT?* in her expression. I feel bad for making fun of Gloria's Chicken Cordon Bleu. It's actually delicious. So are the lasagna and the stuffed shells and the sweet potato casserole and the fruit cobbler.

I text Mom: I'm so proud of you. Remember this feeling, because Dad and I think you've found your calling.

As I hit SEND, I get a text from Enzo: Are you finished with your jealous teen rage? It's slightly endearing but let's not let it ruin my plans?

I don't reply. Why wouldn't Layla pounce? She's on an island in the middle of the Pacific, and he's fresh meat. I leave the table during a heated conversation about anal bleaching.

"Yes, Vito. They're all doing it."

"Why on earth would anyone put bleach on their anus?" Gloria says. "That is yet another reason I'm glad I'm on my way out."

Paige and her mom are at the playground near the beach, pushing Grace on a swing. Grace is shrieking with joy, unaware that her entire world is falling apart. Right now, life is a fast swing on a warm beach, and that's all that matters.

"Maddie, come to the beach with us. They do beach movies for the families here, and tonight it's *Winnie the Pooh*. It's Gracie's very favorite book. What are the odds?"

"I'll walk you over there," I say, looking down at a text from Janie. We're leaving. What are you doing?

"Isn't this the most amazing place?" Paige walks with an unsteady gait because of the sandy incline. Of course, the tumor pressing on her brain doesn't help. "It's spring break meets a science fiction movie. Did you know they have volcanologists in residence right now who go into the volcano and test a new theory about lava chemicals curing cancer? And they have a bakery where they make yam croissants, and they do poetry readings at Walden Pond every Friday night?"

"Don't you kind of feel like the island is alive?" I say.

"I totally know what you're saying. It's invigorating."

Several families gather on the beach in front of a giant inflatable movie screen. The sun, almost below the horizon line now, paints a purple-pink backdrop for *Winnie the Pooh*. Paige's mom and Grace plop down on a beach towel. Two bouncy-haired little girls run up and fawn all over Grace, who points at Lane and Uncle Babysitter as they walk our way with a big bag of popcorn.

Enzo texts a picture of a freckle-faced guy with a blond pubic-hair beard. The caption says Layla's fiancé Ted. Then he writes, Caveman wants woman in kayak now.

I'm sorry, I text.

Forgotten, he texts. My stomach feels instantly better, and I wish I had some of Gloria's buttermilk biscuits.

"Going kayaking, P. Don't miss me too much."

"Love you!" Paige snuggles in between Grace and Wes.

-&o&-

It's almost dark when I reach the bend in the beach and practically crash into Jeb wearing a forehead flashlight. They're all wearing fore-head flashlights.

Enzo hugs me hard and whispers, "I'm all yours, Maddie."

And I believe him.

We carry the kayaks over our heads. It's a long walk down the beach, and it's getting darker by the minute. We finally arrive at the mouth of the saltwater marsh that leads to the lagoons and get into the water. I've kayaked plenty in my life, always during the day and always at our rinky-dink lake club. Here it's dark and murky, and the trees cast shadow creatures over our caravan of wusses.

"Please tell us there are no sharks in this water," Jeb says.

"Not usually," Enzo says. "I mean, it's possible, but not likely."

"I prefer impossible," Janie yells from way behind us.

"How much longer? I'm dying back here," Ty whines.

"It's worth it. Stay with me, mates," Enzo yells. "When we get there, you need to be silent. The quieter we are, the more brilliant they will be."

"Okay," Jeb yells at the top of his lungs.

"God, you're annoying," Camilla says.

We settle into the rhythm of paddles slapping water. It's pitch-black now, except for the melon ball moon and the head flashlights. Enzo points out a bluish light. It gets brighter and fans out in front of us. "The phosphorescence comes from a colony of plankton that emit an eerie glow. They call them the fireflies of the sea, and they've found a home here on Wishwell Island," he says.

The lagoon feeds another larger lagoon and then one larger than that. They're all aglow.

"This is out of control," Jeb says. "This is a legitimate snow globe moment."

"Shh," we all shush Jeb.

We turn off the headlamps and Enzo and I paddle to the middle of the largest lagoon. We stop and rest the paddles on the kayak. The stars fan out in waves, brilliant against the night. It's impossible to know where earth and space begin or end. It's one fantastic stretch of dark and light and streaming, glowing blues and greens. I am awe-struck that life can give us such breathtaking beauty.

We turn and face each other. I look at Enzo, then out at the expanse of color radiating around us. Enzo dips his hand into the lagoon and drags it through the glow, making patterns in the water.

I press my forehead against his and we sit, knee to knee, forehead to forehead, breathing the same slow breaths. Suddenly he looks up, as if he just remembered something important. He stares at me with serious eyes.

"I love you, Maddie."

"I love you, too, Enzo."

—ᴈ• TWENTY-THREE •ᴈ—

ON THE WAY back through the marsh, Jeb and Camilla had a big fight after he tried to stand up in the kayak and tipped it over. He screamed like a maniac in four feet of water, and Ty and Enzo had to fish him out. Jeb should spend the rest of his life in Brooklyn.

We got back to the cabin, and Enzo said it again. Once might have been an accident. Twice makes it real.

Only two other guys have ever told me they loved me. Neither of them counted. My junior-year boyfriend, Brett, said it once right after I agreed to give him a BJ. My mouth touched his thing for less than one second before I bolted to Remy's bathroom to brush my lips raw with her toothbrush in an act of messed-up germ logic. Brett told everyone he got a BJ, and I let him have his moment of glory because I knew he was too dumb to go to college, the mythical land of bountiful BJs.

Ethan said he loved me every time he was drunk and suffocating me with his dry humps. I never bothered to say it back.

Janie helps me process my first real "I love you" over a breakfast of toast and frozen yogurt on our balcony. "A guy saying he loves you in the middle of a bioluminescent lagoon in Oceania, while sober, counts."

"What if he just feels sorry for me because of Gram?"

"That's stupid."

"What if he thinks it's love but it's only lust?"

"That's possible. But, really, how do you tell the difference?" Janie crumbles her toast and sprinkles it over her frozen yogurt. "Just go with it. I've never seen you so needy, Maddie. Maybe you're better off with somebody you can boss around, like Ethan."

"I didn't boss Ethan around."

"You made him go out of his way to pick you up for school so you could play on your phone."

"He liked picking me up for school."

"Just be normal. A perfect guy loves you. Deal with it."

Our bees vibrate at the same time.

"Uh-oh. Now what?" I say. "It's not even eight in the morning."

Wishwell guests, please come to the lobby. Pronto. Don't worry. It's all good. (You don't need to put on your face for this, Gloria.) Eddie

We wait in the lobby like sleepy hotel patrons during a fire drill. I almost panic a little when I don't see Aunt Rose, but then remember she's accounted for in the freezer. Heinz is the only one not in pajamas. Paige's dad and Lane drag a trunk off the elevator. Her mom follows them with Francesca, who is holding Grace. I have no idea what's going on.

"You had better give me a grandchild someday, Enzo. This is delightful."

She holds Grace's drooling mouth up to Enzo's cheek.

Paige texts me: Come meet me by the elevators.

I quietly slip away from the crowd and find a smiling Paige standing in the very spot I last saw Skinny Dave.

"Oh, you look so cute in your jammies," she says.

"What's going on, Paige?" I study her face. There's grief behind the unrelenting smile.

"Little sis, I'm staying here, on Wishwell Island."

I feel a massive sense of relief. "Oh, thank God."

My birthday wish came true.

"All along, this didn't feel right. Like I jumped into it too quickly." She looks down at her bee and texts Lane to wait a minute. "I was so angry, Maddie. When I had Grace, they told me I couldn't hold her, that it was too dangerous, because of the seizures. I was so mad at the universe, I just wanted to be done."

I nod.

"And then my parents were suffering; all the stress was killing them. And poor, wonderful Lane, I don't know, I just wanted to make it easy for them."

"I totally understand." I can't stop staring at her, soaking up every last Paige second.

"But even though all the doctors told me this is terminal, and I get what terminal means, I'm not ready to let go. I'm not ready yet. If there's a shred of hope, I'm going to hold on to it. Astrid convinced me last night that this is where I belong right now."

"I can't tell you how happy this makes me." I reach over and hug Paige for as long as I can before she pulls away.

"I have something for you." She wipes the tears with her T-shirt and pulls something from her shorts pocket. It's a tiny anchor pin.

"An anchor, that's so sweet," I say.

"It's my Delta Gamma pin." She smiles and pins it onto my pajama top. "It symbolizes hope."

"Oh, Paige." There are no words.

"Now, this is not a gift. I need you to hold on to it for Grace. Lane will never keep track of it."

I want to say, *Don't be ridiculous. You're going to be fine.* But I don't.

"I promise I'll keep it safe." I touch the pin. "Thank you, Paige, for being the best big sister ever," I say.

She holds my shoulders and stares into my eyes. "We're family now, Maddie."

We make our way to the emotional crowd.

Wes can't let go. He and Paige embrace Grace in a baby sandwich hug. Grace puts her pudgy little hand on Paige's face to sop up the tears. "It's okay, Gracie. We're going to the fun playground."

The engine rumbles, and they have no choice but to leave us waving frantically in our pajamas. We run up to the top deck and keep waving until Wishwell Island is a dot on the sea.

A group text comes just as Uncle Babysitter is starting to calm down. "'We'll be Friends Forever, won't we, Pooh?' asked Piglet. 'Even longer,' Pooh answered."—A. A. Milne

Janie and I discover the giant vat of jelly beans waiting for us in front of our door.

"I bet you can eat a bunch of those now, huh, you little ho bag?" Janie says.

I text Enzo from under the covers. Does Wishwell Island ever cure anyone?

Yes, he answers. I don't press for details.

Yes is good enough for me.

-ૐ૦ૐ-

Heinz finished the letters. All hands on deck in the ballroom. Aaron

"That's our cue," I say to Enzo.

We form an assembly line. Heinz is sitting at a table with a stack of letters, 531 to be exact, under a red stone paperweight. To add to the heartbreak, Heinz taped a sign to the table, written in shaky old-man script, that says *Thank you, Wishwell Friends.* For each letter, he lifts the paperweight, studies the paper, closes his eyes for a second, kisses the page, and hands it to Jeb or Janie, his trusty rollers. The next group neatly places them in the bottles.

The high-pressure tossing job goes to the young and virile team of Enzo, Burt, Wes, Billy, and me, which is a joke because Enzo is the only good thrower in the group. But we're very careful. We know what's in these bottles. We know they are the painful manifestations of a man's guilt and grief.

As we hurl each fragile papier-mâché bottle into the sea, I wonder which ones Aunt Rose painted during her last moments on earth. I wonder what terrible things happened to those poor people Heinz turned in. I know the act of throwing letters into the sea can't ever change anything, but somehow it matters. It matters to Heinz and it matters to the Wishwellians.

When we finish, there's a collective sigh and a palpable emptiness. Dad and Bob pull chairs close to Heinz and the three of them stare out at the waves in silence. The rest of us file past them. He shakes my hand and thanks me. I bend down and kiss him on the cheek. "I love you, Heinz," I blurt out. I rush away, wondering why I just told a man I barely know that I love him.

Gloria and Mom surprise Heinz with Gloria's signature dessert, a German cream-filled cake called Blitz Torte. Heinz eats his slice slowly, savoring each mouthful. The rest of us thrust our forks in like animals and squabble over every last crumb. It's heaven in my mouth.

Enzo and I walk Gram to her cabin so Bob can sit awhile with Heinz. Gram's room is cluttered with medicine bottles and heating pads. "Do you want me to stay, Gram? We can watch a movie."

"No, that's okay, honey. I'm conking out for the night. It's been a long day." I tuck her in like she's tucked me in so many times, kiss her cheek, and quietly shut the cabin door.

"I need a massage. My throwing arm hurts," Enzo says on our way to his room. We skip dinner and game night and karaoke and brunch. I blame it on the vortex, the most powerful force in the universe.

─&∘ TWENTY-FOUR ∘&─

WE GET A text to meet in the library. Heinz is already gone. He didn't want a funeral or any kind of service. But we need to do something to say good-bye. It's Gloria's idea to write him a letter.

> *Dear Heinz,*
>
> *You spent your long life steeped in guilt and regret. But to us you were gracious and kind. You allowed us to help you honor 531 lost souls, and we will carry you in our hearts always. We love you,*
>
> *The Wishwellians*

We all sign our names. Dad, Bob, Uncle Billy, Vito, and the minister sign *The Rat Pack Poker Club* next to theirs. Burt rolls the letter, and Dad places it in a papier-mâché bottle. Bob and Vito hold it for a minute and throw it into the sea. It is a perfect farewell.

When it's done, Vito and Gloria gather us in the library and tell us they're ready, and they want to go together because going together makes them brave. Vito's Ornaments lose it in a mess of muddy eye makeup and wailing. The minister's lower lip trembles. His hand shakes uncontrollably, and I feel sorry for him. I have a funny feeling it won't be long before he's next.

"Vito doesn't ever have to struggle for breaths again," Ty says, his head hanging low as he crawls onto Janie's bed.

I didn't know it would happen so quickly.

-&o&-

I haven't seen Gram undressed since Rio. She's a skeleton with a pregnancy bump, covered in purple scabby patches and needle marks. Mom and Janie and I pin her funeral dress behind her wasting frame and dot her cheeks with blush. Janie fluffs her thinning hair, freshly done at the salon, and I paint her nails seashell pink.

"Stop fussing over me," Gram says. "I'm fine."

"We love you, Gram. We're just trying to make you look pretty," Janie says.

"You're trying to make me look alive," she says.

We nearly crash wheelchairs with Mark as we round the corner to the ballroom. Enzo's pushing him, and Burt's bent down tying

Mark's shoe. There's an emptiness in Mark's expression, like he's tired of being fussed over, too.

I'm wearing red for the service in honor of Gloria's lips and Vito's love of Christmas. Enzo is wearing his Armani suit. I am an evil pervert for thinking about sex at a time like this.

"Bride's or groom's side?" Vito's son-in-law jokes as we file into the ballroom-turned-funeral-parlor. Roberta and one of the other daughters pass out programs. There are two screens, one showing photos of Vito's life, the other of Gloria's. Gloria's recipes are displayed on an easel for everyone to see.

"They were both attractive," Mom says. Mom has been crying off and on all day. "Who knows why I so enjoyed spending time with Gloria. Maybe it was that we both love makeup or that I have a passion for baking and she loved to cook. Whatever it was, I miss her. I miss her a lot."

Mom's lip quivers. I put my arm around her shoulders. "Isn't that what soul mates are? People who are drawn to each other?" I say.

"I guess it is. You are getting philosophical on me, hon. But, yeah, it's true. It's hard to put a finger on what connects people."

The minister talks about the power of family and friendship and how blessed Vito and Gloria were to have all of us. He tries to get through a story about when Gloria was diagnosed and the first thing she said was, "Who will cook your eggs, darling?" but he breaks down and Bob has to help him to his seat.

Roberta talks about her dad and how he supported all his

children through tough times. He was their rock. He was their Father Christmas.

Overall, it's a pretty painless service, maybe because it was exactly what Vito and Gloria wanted.

"It's so weird we'll never see them again," Janie says.

"Holy Christmas," Wes says as I elbow Uncle Billy out of the way so I can sit near Gram. I'm wearing the sapphire. I want her to see how much I cherish it.

The dining room is ablaze in twinkle lights. The crew moved Vito's Christmas village to the back wall near the giant heavily tinseled tree. I butter my roll and gear up for an Italian Christmas Eve with twelve trays of fish and Gloria's eggplant lasagna.

Uncle Billy clinks his glass with a knife. "I'd like to read our special message to Gloria. I hope we did our girl justice."

Gloria, Gloria, you bald beauty.

You swept us off our feet with your gorgeous face and knocked us off our feet with your fabulous recipes. We will never look at a lipstick without thinking of you, your quick wit, and your beautiful heart. We love you.

The Wishwellians

We clap and cheer when Jeb rolls the paper and sticks it in the paper bottle. Apparently messages in papier-mâché bottles is our new thing.

Dad stands up next.

Dear Vito,

*It is no wonder you loved Christmas so much. You
embodied the true spirit of Christmas. You were bright and
shiny, generous and charitable, and full to the brim with
love for family and friends. We will never forget the cheer
you spread every single day. We love you.*

The Wishwellians

We make our way out to the deck. The minister and the former
Mrs. Vito, who is more of a mess than any of his kids, kiss the bottles
and fling them overboard. We lean over the railing and watch the
bottles flip and flop until the sea swallows them up.

Eddie pulls out the karaoke machine. Our family can dance to
anything, but singing is a different matter. Nobody seems to care,
since "The Twelve Days of Christmas" was meant to suck. We take an
eggnog break while Bob sings "O Holy Night" with a voice as rich as
red velvet cake and the Ornaments deliver a moving rendition of "Ave
Maria."

For the grand finale, we sit Gram in a chair on stage and serenade her with "Grandma Got Run over by a Reindeer." It wouldn't
be Christmas without Gram saying "Thanks a lot, assholes," at least
once.

I get a knot in my stomach. It's easy to make fun of Gram while
she's still here. But when she's gone, swallowed up by the sea, with
the bottles and Heinz and Vito and Gloria, what then? Who will fill

the void she leaves in this world? Who will fill the void she leaves in me?

We linger, all of us, as if nobody wants to pull away from the comfort of the group. Janie and I wheel Gram up to her room and crawl under the covers like we've done so many times.

"When are you going to do this, Gram?" I blurt. I can no longer deal with the anxiety of not knowing. I push it away. It comes back. I do something fun. It comes back.

"I don't know, honey. Gloria and Vito said they just knew it was their time. She was in an awful lot of pain, and he could barely breathe. I'm tired and out of it and feeling pretty rotten, but I've still got a little bit left in me." She turns over and moans softly. "Bob and I want to watch the old movies one more time. It sounds trivial, but I can't enjoy food, so I might as well look at James Dean and Marlon Brando."

"Do you ever think about going back to New York and living until your body stops?" Janie says.

"No way, Jose. I'm more afraid of wearing a diaper and losing my mind than I am of death. This is the way to go, girlies. Haven't we had loads of fun? If you really want to get depressed, spend a month in a nursing home. You'll come out wanting to smother every bastard over eighty with a pillow."

She gets quiet. Janie and I stay up listening to her irregular, gurgling breaths. "What are we going to do without her?" Janie whispers. I don't answer because I don't know.

—ε·ο TWENTY-FIVE ο·ξ—

IT TURNS OUT Wes blabbed about the baby to everyone. He told Gloria and Vito before they passed. He told my entire family, then made each of us promise not to tell anyone. So when Uncle Billy gets us together for a "big news brunch" at their cabin, we all act abnormally surprised.

Uncle Billy passes around ultrasound pictures of a baby with a perfectly round head and a button nose.

"She's an adorable fetus," Mom says.

"We're going to name her Tessa Astrid O'Neill Parker," Uncle Billy announces.

"Can I make a suggestion? A revision, if I may?" Gram says.

"What's your revision, Assy? There's always something," Wes says.

"I adore the name Tessa. But how about Tessa Rose? I have you people, and I'll surely have buildings named after me. Rose didn't get to have children. She would have been tickled pink."

Uncle Billy and Wes exchange looks. "Yes. I love it," Wes says.

"Me too." Uncle Billy kisses Gram. "Tessa Rose O'Neill Parker it is."

"Now we have a question for Bob," Uncle Billy says.

"Sure, Bill, shoot," Bob says.

"We would be honored if you would be Tessa's godfather. We want you to be part of our family officially, forever."

Bob's eyes fill with tears. "I've been a lot of things in this life," Bob says, "but I've never been a godfather." Wes and Uncle Billy get up and walk over to Bob, and the three of them embrace.

"I've raised good boys," Gram says.

"You didn't raise me, Assy," Wes says.

"Yes, but I taught you everything you know. That dowdy back-woods mother of yours didn't know a thing about raising a gay. It's not all musical theater and decorating, Delores," Gram jokes.

"I love you, Assy."

"I love you more, Wessy."

Gram and Bob don't seem thrilled about me following them to the theater. Gram wants to watch a movie from 1949 because Celia Hobbes has a bit part. I don't want to leave Gram. I take in every gesture, every smile, every word. I hold them for a second and stuff them into my mental file, already overflowing with Gram memories. I don't want to miss a single one.

"Go, Maddie. Read a book. Bob and I have a date. No kids allowed."

"Fine, Gram. Go have your date. I love you."

"I love you, too, stalker child."

I wander aimlessly. Mom and Roberta are playing Scrabble in the library, and what's left of the poker guys are down in the card room. I bang out a few rounds of Whac-A-Mole and go up to the cabin. Janie's on the balcony bawling her eyes out.

"Janie, talk to me. Is it Gram?" She nods. I slide next to her, hold her head on my lap, and stroke her hair like I did in Charleston after her parents' divorce.

After a long silence, I ask, "Do you want your worry doll back?"

"No." She laughs a little. "I still have Maria and Conchita and Claudia and Rigoberta and Missy."

"All right, then," I say. "I think you're good. I'll keep Esperanza for now."

Mark wants to have his memorial service before he dies. He doesn't see the point in not being there to enjoy it. He wants old-school music and a burger bar and an endless stream of Mark's greatest surfing moments.

I take a shower and put on my funeral sundress and flip-flops and starfish bracelet. I go over to Wes and Uncle Billy's cabin and lie on their bed while they share a bottle of wine.

"It's just so unfair," Uncle Billy says. "It's bullshit."

"He told me as soon as he was forced to wear a diaper, it was time to book the ship," Wes says, polishing off his wine. "There's no dignity in diapers for a guy like Mark. Come on, peeps. It's time to let Mark go."

We enter Malibu Beach circa 1987 and take in the surfboards and strings of hanging paper lanterns and the barbecue smells. Mark's surfing videos play on the screen to Pink Floyd's "On the Turning Away."

Bob tells me he's worried about the minister, who has been sitting in the old-fashioned car on his balcony and won't get out. They have to hand-deliver him soup and tea through the car window.

We eat burgers and fries and ice cream sundaes and wait for Mark and Burt and Enzo to arrive. It feels flat and empty without Paige and Grace and the others.

I've barely talked to Vito's family, other than Roberta. They look alike and talk alike and move in a group like zebras. It takes too much energy to figure out how to separate them. But they're funny and sarcastic and smart, just like Vito. Mark's right, they are Christmas ornaments. One of them alone isn't very exciting—together they're so much fun. But even the Ornaments are quiet tonight.

Finally, Burt comes into the ballroom with a red, swollen face. He asks Eddie to turn off the movie and the music.

"Can I have everyone's attention?" We freeze.

"I, uh, Markie can't do the party. He's having a tough time. He wants me to tell you he loves you guys." Burt can barely get the words out. His face is twisted in anguish.

"He says you are his family now and forever, and he just can't say good-bye to each of you so he asked me to say good-bye to all of you." Wes and Uncle Billy embrace Burt's heaving body. "He can't do it."

"How about we text him messages?" Wes asks as Burt blows his nose on a napkin.

Burt nods. "I think he'd like that."

We give Burt hugs and deliver quiet whispers. Wes and Uncle Billy offer to walk him to his cabin, but he wants to go by himself. On the way out, Burt tells me Mark has asked Enzo to be with him in his cabin.

We bend over our bees and text Mark messages of love and comfort. We tell him how he inspired us, moved us, and made us braver. One by one, we get up and walk out, deflated.

Burt texts us all the photo of laughing Mark sprawled out in the wheelbarrow in Jamaica. This is how I'll always remember him.

Paige texts me right away. You okay?

Yeah. I'm okay.

She sends a picture of Grace blowing a kiss, and I wish I could have that slimy baby mouth on my cheek right now.

I lie on the lounge chair, wrapped in my comforter, and think about the time when I was four or five and Gram screamed at Jeb and me for leaning over her penthouse balcony. It was the only time she ever yelled like that. I hid in the bookcase passageway, ashamed and afraid. I'm not sure why that memory came up. All the memories are swimming to the surface now.

The door opens, and Enzo comes out and slides silently under the blanket. I cradle him, his head on my chest, our legs intertwined.

"Do you hear that?" he whispers, his voice hoarse.

"What?"

"The music?"

I don't hear music. I only hear the waves.

Mark belongs to the sea now.

-ε∘ჳ-

Jeb and Enzo write the note.

> *Dear Mark,*
>
> *You will always be our superstar. You showed us all that it's not how long we live, but how well we live that counts. You are in good hands with Marley and Hendrix and all the righteous ones. Surf on, good dude, surf on. We love you.*
>
> *The Wishwellians*

—᠂ TWENTY-SIX ᠂—

BURT HAS TAKEN to sleeping on Wes and Uncle Billy's floor. It started the night Mark died, and it's been going on for a few nights now. They're cool with it as long as he gives them space to get to the bathroom.

It's too quiet. I wander the ship, sometimes with Enzo, sometimes with Janie or Mom or Dad. We sit with Gram in her room, but she's sleeping a lot now. We visit the Ornaments at the pool or flip through magazines in the café. I pace. I fidget. I don't know what to do.

At night, I burrow into the vortex and stay as long as I can with the waves and my Enzo. He spoons me facing the moonlit water, and we talk about college classes and music and our friends. Regular things.

"When are you going to start running?" Enzo blows past me. It's raining, and the upper deck is empty. We stop for water, and there it is, a little green light on the side of my buzzing bee. I know what the message is before I pick it up.

Hello, babies. I have a dinner date tonight with Martin and Rose and Karl. I'm looking forward to it. It's been too long.

My knees buckle, and I sink down to the floor, a shivering, pathetic little mess of fear and grief. Enzo sits next to me and holds me as tightly as a person can hold another person. He wipes my face with his shirt and doesn't say a word because there are no words.

I'm too weak to get up. Enzo holds my hand and walks me around a little, gives me sips of water, and kisses my forehead.

"I'm okay." My voice barely works.

"Do you want to lie down?"

"Yeah. I want to lie down and then I want to see my gram."

We lie in bed with the curtains drawn. I doze off for a few minutes, and I wake with the feeling that everything is fine. Then I remember.

"Can I be alone for a little while?" I say to Enzo. "I'll text you in an hour."

He doesn't press me. He cradles my face in his hands, kisses me on the lips, and gets up to leave.

There's a wailing noise coming from the hallway. Enzo flings the door open and runs out. I jump up and follow him. Gram is hysterical and heaving on the floor in front of Jeb's open door. Enzo kneels on the floor next to her while Jeb leans against the wall.

"Jeb, what did you do to her?" I scream. I've never seen Gram this upset. She's the stoic one. She deflects with humor. She tells us to get ahold of ourselves.

The whole family comes running. Bob steps out of Jeb's room. "Come on, Astrid." He picks her up. "Show them what got your panties in a bunch," Bob says.

"Jebby," Gram sobs. "My genius, Jebby."

I haven't ventured into Jeb's cabin since the first day. I figured it was just a trash heap of masturbation tissues and empty pizza boxes.

"Oh my God, Jeb." Wes freezes as he walks into Jeb's room. The rest of us are stuck behind him. He moves and we see. My stupid, gross brother is a genius. Gram made his walls out of canvas in case he was inspired to paint, and I guess he was inspired to paint.

Snow globes.

He painted our entire journey in snow globes on the wall. There's Jamaica on the beach with Tits and Mama and the bat cave and us on top of Corcovado Mountain and the Rio waterfall. There's Dad hang gliding and us in the Blue Lagoon and standing inside the lava tube surrounded by a rainbow of elves and Jules Verne himself. He painted Mom in a gondola and Dad with the telescope and Gram and Aunt Rose in front of the forever tree with the castle in the background. There's the Colosseum filled with cats and Celia Hobbes on stage and a snow globe for each of our Wishwell friends. Heinz is inside a bottle, and Dave is hugging his mom, and Gloria's wearing a chef's hat and purple lipstick. Aunt Rose is smiling in a tangle of roses. Vito is an elf grinning near the tree, and Mark's on a surfboard, and Holly is in plié pose. Paige's family is waving from Wishwell Island, and Enzo and I are waving from a kayak surrounded by bioluminescence. And the one in the middle is of Gram and Bob holding baby Tessa's ultrasound. The one of Camilla in the Grotto is such a flattering likeness, it hits me just now that my brother is in love.

Jeb filled his room with snow globe moments for Gram. For us. He must have spent every free second he had to give Gram the gift of memories. He's sitting on his bed, limp and teary-eyed as we study each snow globe. The moment is so ugly and distorted and full of primal sounds and deep pain. Yet it's the most beautiful moment my family has ever shared.

-&o3-

I am a pumpkin. A metal scoop is digging out my insides. Soon there will be nothing left but dangles of slime and rotting flesh.

-&o3-

Gram blows her nose. "I need a macaroon," she says, struggling to get up from her chair.

"The canvases on those walls are going home with us," Dad says. "I'll be damned if I leave the artwork on the *Titanic*."

Bob brings in a case of macaroons and rips it open. They stuff their faces. I can't even think about eating.

"It's going to go like this, kids." Gram talks with her mouth full. "I'm going to have a bath and a champagne. Then we'll text you, and you can sit with me if you want. If you don't, that's okay. And that's it."

"Wait, Gram. Don't you want to spend time with each of us? To say good-bye?" I'm panicking.

"Maddie, that's what this trip was all about. We've had our time, honey. I'm feeling too rotten now. We need to rip off the Band-Aid. I used to tell your parents to drop you at preschool and run." She waves her half-eaten macaroon toward Mom and Dad. "But no, you two had to stick around and hang all over the kids and drag them into your anxious frenzy. The one day you had the strength to drop Maddie and run out without looking back was the day she didn't cry."

"We're still going to cry," Janie says.

"Yes, I imagine. You are a bunch of criers. How did I end up with all the crybabies? Ruth's kids were troupers."

"We just love you," Wes says.

"Okay, I'm pulling off the Band-Aid. Billy, help me up. I might vomit the macaroons. Wow. That was a binge." She leaves, and I get a text. Wear the blue dress.

"She wants us all in blue," Mom says, looking at my bee. "She 'doesn't want to die surrounded by mismatched ragamuffins.' That's more unsettling than the prospect of no longer living."

Mom talks Janie and me into spending the afternoon at the spa getting manicures, pedicures, facials, blowouts, and makeup. She wants us to be our most beautiful selves for Gram.

We get the text just before sunset.

It's time, my babies.

Mom lets out a shaky breath and puts her arms around us. "Come, girls, let's go see our old gal off."

-&o&-

Gram is tucked into her bed on her favorite pillow. She's wearing a blue satin robe with one sleeve rolled up, and she's holding a tiny drawstring bag with her marble-shaped husband inside; the IV port is already nestled into her wrinkled stick arm. Wisps of white hair frame her face. She's barely there, a ghost of a woman. She doesn't look like the Gram I've always known. But her eyes are every bit as blue.

She smiles up at all of us hunched over her like children studying an injured mouse. "Come sit." She pats the bed. The nurses and doctor busy themselves with the business of death.

Mom climbs up next to Gram. I want to fight her for the good spot, but it's only right for the daughter to sit next to her mother. We look like idiots, dressed in shades of Bermuda morning blue. But she wanted it this way, and today is her day. The last light of afternoon bathes the room, the purples of the sunset filter in through the open balcony door, and the filmy white curtains move to the swish of the waves.

Gram has her family and her fresh orchids and a lit candle from her favorite store on Madison Avenue.

"Come on, Aaron, you crawl up here, too." Dad slides awkwardly between Jeb and me. Out of nowhere, Ella Fitzgerald and Louis Armstrong's "Dream a Little Dream of Me" comes on.

313

"I want to go before the song ends, Doctor." She must feel a collective stiffening, because she says, "It's okay. I've said and done and lived everything. And what's left, I've left for you. I love you all. Thank you for making this life so very rich."

The doctor injects a clear liquid. Mom strokes Gram's hair and Uncle Billy holds her hand. Bob sits on the other side and smiles at her, tears streaming down his face.

"Sleep now, Mommy," Mom says softly.

Her eyes close, and then she's gone. Just like that.

We sit a long time. We don't want to disrupt her departing soul. We get up, one by one, and kiss her cheek. She's still warm. Mom and Uncle Billy stay alone with Gram. They help the nurses wrap her in her sheets from home, and tie her body with white ribbons made of sugarcane so the dolphins don't get stuck. We wait, stiff and sad, in Mom and Dad's cabin until they come back. Uncle Billy tells us he carried her all the way to the stern of the ship and set her on a soft belt that gently pushed her through an opening into the sea.

-ξoζ-

Now I'm the fully hollow pumpkin. The one all scraped out and left to rot.

-ξoζ-

Dad guides me down to the ballroom, where the last of the Wishwellians have formed a perfect horseshoe surrounded by a thousand candles. We walk from person to person like we're doing a morbid

314

folk dance, hugging Vito's family and Burt and Francesca and Eddie and Camilla and Enzo.

I can't do this. It's too hard.

It gets blurry when they show photos of Gram on the big screen. There are lots of them from when she was young and in the thick of the jazz years. They play Otis Redding's "Remember Me."

Why are they trying to make it worse?

I can't eat. I'm so tired and thirsty. People around me talk and joke about Gram as she's floating, floating in the ocean. It's dark and cold, and I'm so afraid she's not quite dead. I'm so afraid sharks are ripping my gram apart and we're here in this grotesque display of disrespect. Enzo keeps a hand firmly on my leg and squeezes every few minutes, pumping life to my heart.

Roberta and Ty step up to read:

> *Dear Astrid,*
>
> *You taught us that age is an illusion steeped in bullshit. You showed us that even the smallest adventures count, even the briefest human interactions matter, and there are no limits to the joy this life offers. You are not just an unlikely revolutionary and a remarkable woman, you are everybody's gram, and we will miss you terribly. We love you.*
>
> *The Wishwellians*

"I'm going to bed," I say. I lean on Enzo and stumble to the cabin. I'm halfway to sleep, my head pressed against the picture of Gram holding me on her lap, when I hear thumping. I imagine it's Gram slamming up against the ship.

"No, no, no, no."

Enzo is having the serpent dream.

$$-\xi \circ \xi-$$

We hide again in the vortex. It feels selfish, indulgent, but being with Enzo is the only thing that makes a dent in the pain.

My family pesters me to see if I'm okay. I put a sign on the door. I'M OKAY! *Okay* is a ridiculous word.

We're in the middle of the Pacific and won't reach Hawaii for another week.

Gram died two days ago already. I've had two milk shakes and a bag of chips, but I've had sex eleven times. When I went to get the chips, Wes and Burt were on the balcony with a case of wine and a picked-apart chicken.

"What do you mean you've never seen *Sixteen Candles*? It's a classic," I say. Enzo hasn't seen any classic American movies. I get a burst of energy and text Jeb and Janie. Movie marathon? We meet in the theater, and Eddie sets up *Sixteen Candles* and tubs of popcorn. The theater fills with people who actually saw eighties movies in the eighties.

After movie number three, Francesca texts us: We need Astrid's family in the library.

We file in and sit in front of a movie screen. The anxiety overtakes me. I know what this is. It's her "group" project.

"Hello, lovelies. I've called you all here because Astrid made a video. Before I play it, I want to let you in on a little secret. You should be very proud of Astrid. She came to me during her trip with Ruth and badgered me about financials to the point where I thought she might be working for the IRS. It turned out she was deeply moved by our mission, and asked me to identify people she could sponsor. She asked that I choose people who had reached out to me and who deserved to be here, but couldn't afford it otherwise."

"Astrid paid for all the patients?" Dad says.

"And the families. All of it."

"Well, I'll be damned."

"Please don't mention this to the others. Astrid wanted them to think it was an anonymous Good Samaritan. But I thought you should know Astrid is a Wishwell angel."

Gram is an angel. I picture her winged raisin body floating around in a thong bikini.

"It doesn't surprise me," Wes says. "Not in the least."

I'm not surprised either. I'm just grateful.

Francesca dims the lights and starts the video. I have no idea what to expect.

Gram's face pops up. She's wearing the green cardigan that hangs past her fingertips. She's looking past the camera, squinting her eyes. "Is it on?" she says. "Is this taping?" A voice from behind the camera says, "Yes, go ahead."

Gram shifts in her seat, clears her throat, and begins. Not one person in the room is breathing right now.

If you're watching this, I'm dead. I hope you are surviving without me. I was the glue that held this family together. That's not up for debate. But stick together, and you'll be just fine. Oh, and please be nice to one another. That includes Mary and Brit. Don't argue. Just be nice.

So let's see, a wise young lady—thank you, Maddie—gave me the idea to do a Loose Ends list. It didn't make sense to start a bucket list when I was dying. But tying up loose ends, that's what I needed to do. So I came up with some good ones, and I checked them off one by one. I have to say, I had my reservations. But you all behaved marvelously. I'm proud of you. I'm going to share the list now.

She unfolds a piece of paper and starts reading.

One. Smoke marijuana. *It didn't do anything for me. I prefer a good glass of champagne and a macaroon.*

Two. Visit Rio. *I loved it. Especially the beach scene.*

Three. Find Sneffels and prove Mother wrong. *We sure did that.*

Four. Take Rose back to Bled, where it all began. *What a thrill to find that tree!*

Five. Spend one more unforgettable night with Celia. *We've still got it, Bobby.*

Six. Something old, something new, something borrowed, something blue. *At least one of my grandkids better carry on the bloodline.*

Seven. Lay my dear Martin to rest. *I apologize one more time for not telling you all in advance about the ashes.*

Eight. Make peace with Aaron. *I'm sorry for being difficult, Aaron Levine. You're a good man, a great husband, and a fabulous father, and I love you.*

Nine. Watch the old movies. *Bobby, you and I fell in love in the jazz clubs and movie houses. I'm in love all over again. Better and deeper than ever, baby. That's a private joke.*

Ten. Forgive someone unforgivable. *That was Heinz. I knew he was a Nazi all along, and I chose to forgive him. I hope you all will work on forgiving people sooner than I did. And forgive yourselves. Life is too short.*

So I've done what I set out to do. We crammed a lot in, didn't we? I hope you all do big things. Make them count. When it's all over, you'll be sad, but not nearly as sad as if you screw around and sit on your behinds.

By the way, there's plenty of money to go around, so there better not be any squabbling. Wes and Aaron, the North

Foundation is yours if you want it. You'll be able to help plenty of poor kids in Rio and all the caged animals of Taipei if you are so inclined. And Billy, I'm so glad you're taking on the Taiwan scholarship program. Your father would be so proud of you. I'm giving Titi and Joe Rose's Charleston house, and Billy and Wes get Bermuda. Take Tessa Rose to play in the pink sands. Trish, you get the apartment. I hope you'll get out of the insufferable suburbs and do what you were meant to do. Mary, you get a big wad to squander as you wish. No regrets, darling.

She sets the paper on the floor next to her and stares into the camera.

Maddie and Jeb, Brit and Janie, money isn't free. You don't get a cent until you finish college. Do you hear me? And remember: Sex is not love, drugs don't make you happy, and the only real music is jazz music.

Don't waste too much time grieving. You've got a lot of living to do. And as much as you love me, I love you more.

She blows a kiss. The screen goes black.
We're still not breathing.

−ξ∘ζ−

"How about a smoothie with your old buddy?" Bob says, putting his arm around me as we walk toward the elevator.

I have a feeling Gram set this up.

We order smoothies and find a corner on the pool deck, somewhere between the Grotto and the Skinny Dave chair.

"I'm sad, Bob. I just can't stop being sad." The tears come again.

"Be patient, kiddo. It'll come." He turns and faces me. "You know when you fall and get a big old bruise on your leg? That bruise isn't going anywhere for a while. But it takes longer to heal if you're pressing on it all the time."

I motion for him to wait while I grab napkins from the bar and blow my nose.

"Be gentle with yourself. Listen to good music. Eat good food. Nourish your body and your spirit, and you'll be all right." He gives me a big Bob Johns grin.

"How do you smile all the time? You've lost practically everybody. How are you not miserable?" I shouldn't have said that. Stupid Astrid-blurt gene.

"I haven't lost everybody. Sure, I've lost my parents and two sisters and my wife and Astrid. But I have children and grandchildren, and look who I gained by losing Astrid: you." He lays his hand on my arm. "That's how life works. The pain of losing doesn't get less with each person I lose. But I have the wisdom of knowing the pain isn't forever. That fades. The memories stay. And the love isn't going anywhere."

I study his silver-and-turquoise rings.

"What was it like when you and Gram broke up?"

Bob laughs. He tells me about how he fell into a deep abyss and thought he would die of heartbreak. He flew to Jamaica and sat on a banana crate in front of his uncle's store for a year, drinking rum and peeing his pants until his sister yanked him up by the hair and told him to do something with his life. That's when he went back to New York, met his wife, and dusted off his trumpet.

"Do you ever regret not spending your whole life with Gram?"

He slurps his smoothie and waves to Eddie.

"You know what? I don't. Astrid and I always said this was our one great love. But we said that because we didn't have to live together and fight over who takes out the garbage or how to squeeze the toothpaste." He shakes his head. "Astrid kicked me out of bed after a week on the ship. Couldn't take the snoring. That's life, Maddie, garbage and toothpaste and snoring."

His face softens.

"If you think about it, we had the best of both worlds. Passion and romance were the bookends of our lives. But the books, well, your family and my family and all those messy, fantastic years were the books."

"You're one of my books now, Bob," I say.

"That's good to hear, Maddie girl."

I reach over and give Bob a big hug. He smells familiar. He smells like Gram.

-ɜ∘ TWENTY-SEVEN ∘ɜ-

FRANCESCA WANTS US to go to the grief circle to help process our losses. Mom and Dad aren't making me go yet. The grief hits worst at night, when I'm left alone with Enzo's sleep sounds and the ship's creaks. I lie on my back, choking away the tears, paralyzed in the darkness.

I feel her. The air is heavy. I know she's beside me.

I want to touch her one more time, to feel the bones popping out of her frail hand. I want to kiss her cheek and hear her call me Maddie girl. The worst part of all is I'm terrified I'll forget her.

-ɜ∘ɜ-

Enzo and I pull the lounge chairs up to the balcony railing so we can lie on our stomachs and scan the sea for dolphins. The pods sometimes follow us in the morning.

"Let's order pancakes," Enzo says. "Soon I'll be eating fava beans and pita for breakfast."

That's his way of saying it's almost over.

I get up and go into the shower. We knew it was coming. He's going to Egypt, and I'm going to New York. This has to end.

I stand in the dark under a warm stream, trying to rinse the pain away. The door slides open.

"Can I just have a few minutes?" I say feebly.

"Maddie, I know you're pissy. I'm coming in." He throws off his boxers.

"I'm not pissy. I'm sad," I whisper. I don't want to cry, but I can't control it. I can't control anything.

"Come here." He pulls me toward him, and we stand naked and still.

After a long time, he says, "Do you remember before Brazil, when we thought we only had Rome to look forward to and we were determined to make our time in Rome fantastic?"

"Yeah. I remember."

"So wouldn't we have given anything for a week? We still have a week, Maddie."

"That's true."

"Isn't it better to end on good terms? Let's admit most relationships die of boredom or resentment."

"But maybe we would be different."

"Nothing this good lasts forever, Maddie. Let's enjoy this good now."

"This good?" I kiss him softly.

"Yes. This good."

He turns me around so the stream hits my face, and presses lemony soap against my back. The soap glides over the tiny starfish and down my leg.

It hits me. I know what we need to do.

—§o3—

We make a list of seven Loose Ends. Seven for luck.

One. *Shag a thousand times.* (Modified to shag as much as possible.)

_____

Two. *Be nocturnal.*
We've stopped sleeping at night. We're defying the demons and the dreams and staying wide awake. We sleep all day with the sunbeams sneaking through the blinds, bathing our naked bodies in warmth and light. We rise in time for dinner, ready for adventures.

_____

Three. *Have a picnic.*
Enzo waits until midnight when the Ornaments are finished with their biscotti and gossip. He blindfolds me and leads me through decks and corridors to the bow of the ship. We lie on a pile of blankets surrounded by twinkle lights and eat seven kinds of cheeses and warm bread and olives with sparkling pomegranate soda and a

chocolate cake so fancy it could be our wedding night. We toss the leftovers overboard and dance in silence until dawn.

Four. *A night with the kids table.*

It starts in the game room as a rowdy billiards tournament with Camilla, Ty, and me against Enzo, Jeb, and Janie. Their team wins. We run around like twelve-year-olds, raid the vintage wine cellar, and sneak into the chapel. We lie on the pews, watching the moonlight through stained glass. We make bottles in the craft room, three times the size of the Heinz bottles, and stuff them with things we find along the way.

We end up in the Grotto choreographing a hot tub dance to that U2 song "Beautiful Day."

Before dawn we use our last burst of energy on wishes. We write wishes on napkins, stuff them into our bottles, and, one by one, throw the bottles into the sea. We hold hands and watch a rogue wave gulp them up with one big swallow. If somebody discovers mine on a faraway beach, they'll wonder why anyone would fill a soggy paper bottle with a hibiscus flower, seven jelly beans, a squirt of sunscreen, and a wish on a napkin.

My wish is simple. The sea will decide if it's meant to come true.

Five. *Leave our mark.*

There's a nook in the underbelly of the ship, not far from Aunt Rose, between a broom closet and a boiler room. Enzo used to go there with his sister to escape the sadness surrounding them. We find a spot and scratch our words into a painted metal beam. *Maddie and Enzo beneath the sea, bound by this ship eternally.* Enzo came up with that himself.

Six. *Be eternal.*

We summon the family and Francesca to the telescope to stargaze and tell stories about our lives before the Wishwell. We laugh more than I have ever laughed with my family and discover a meteor shower impressive enough to make Dad say, "Holy fucking shit." Then we surprise them. We show them a star-naming website on our bees and choose the bright and spectacular Wishwellian as our very own. We are officially eternal.

Seven. *Do something extraordinary.*

This one's my secret. It's happening tonight, and I'm getting nervous.

The ship slows to a stop somewhere off Hawaii.

"Do I need to wear anything special?" Enzo asks.

"Shorts and a T-shirt. Maybe a sweatshirt."

"I figured you'd want me in Armani."

"Not this time."

We wait in the lobby armed with a stuffed backpack and a jug of water. Paul the dinghy guy motions us out the side door, where the dinghy is revved and waiting.

"Maddie? What is this?" Enzo says.

"We're going for a ride."

"It's four o'clock in the morning. It's pitch-black out there."

"Relax. Paul is a master dinghy driver. And your buddy Eddie gave his blessing. He's the Wishwell dream master, right?"

It's freezing in the musty dinghy as we tumble along the choppy sea. "You'll have to get out here," Paul says. "This is as close as I can get."

I panic. I can't believe this was my idea. I didn't realize we would be jumping into chest-deep, murky cold water in the dark.

Enzo sees the fear on my face. "It's okay, Maddie. We don't have to do this. Let's just go back."

I take a yoga breath. "No. We're doing something extraordinary. Help me get the surfboard."

"What surfboard?"

Paul slides open the life jacket storage closet and reveals my surprise—a surfboard and a wetsuit. Somehow we manage to lower the surfboard into the water and paddle together to the shore without being eaten.

Paul takes off. We're alone on a beach, wet and cold, but invigorated. I pull soggy towels out of my bag and we sit on the sand.

"You know, we'd be less cold if we took these wet clothes off," I say.

"That is true," he says. He pulls my T-shirt over my head.

We merge with the sand and the tide and the briny breeze as light creeps up on the horizon. It casts an eerie halo over our ship.

"Come on, you're going to Egypt. Get out there and surf," I say. He grabs the board and paddles into the strong but steady breakers. He flies in and paddles out, flies in and paddles out.

We stand knee-deep in the water, bodies swaying, foreheads touching. I play with his damp hair and tell him he's an amazing surfer and Mark would be proud. The waves swell stronger, the sting of the water chills us to the bone. And still we dance.

We watch the sunrise enfold the Wishwell.

I say it first this time. "I love you, Enzo."

He tilts his head and looks at me. "I love you, too, Maddie."

-&o3-

I don't go with him to pack or eat or field the swarm of mosquitoes gathered to see him off. I kiss him. It's gentle and warm and just right.

"He's just a boy," I whisper. "He's just a boy."

It doesn't work anymore. I'm floating. I'm falling. I'm falling apart.

⟡ TWENTY-EIGHT ⟡

AFTER BUB THE dog was killed by the bus, Gram took me to Bermuda. Titi fed me crepes, and Gram buried me up to my head in pink sand. The sadness was still there, but Bermuda and crepes and sand made it more bearable.

Enzo was my Bermuda and my crepes and my pink sand.

And now he's gone.

I crawl to the bed and scream into the pillow and cry until my face swells and my nostrils swell and I can't breathe.

I'm a pumpkin rotting from the inside out.

⟡

They swarm. My bee buzzes over and over again. They bang on the door, but it's bolted and I can't get up. I can't humor them.

Nobody is ever getting in again.

Eddie breaks down the door. Mom rushes in.

"Oh, Maddie, look at you. You need to eat. Please. I know this is so hard, but you need to eat. Oh, honey, you've had your period all over the bed. Let me help you."

"Mommy, I'm weak. I can't."

Mom comes back with Janie and Camilla. Together they lift me and put me in the shower. I sit under the warm spray and shiver like the first time with Enzo. Mom puts a straw to my lips, and I drink for her.

They dress me and change my sheets; Janie props me on pillows and combs my hair. She's gentle and loving, and it makes me cry a torrent of silent tears. The nursemaids surround me. I smile a little, sip more ginger ale, take Esperanza and hold her to my cheek as if a stupid cloth doll could make me better.

But I trick them into leaving.

They won't put the door back up.

"Maddie, it's Dad. Come on, talk to me. I need you to eat some soup. It's chicken noodle. Please take a bite." He's sitting on the edge of my bed with a silver tray and a basket of rolls. They sent a little flower in a vase and a pot of tea. I hate it.

"One bite, Maddie. Please." I bite. I eat the whole roll smeared with an inch of butter. Or maybe it's a centimeter. How would I know? I'm a stupid American.

"Good girl." He kisses my forehead and leaves me alone.

I wake to the sound of someone shouting, "No, no, no, no." It's dark except for a dim light in the hallway. It was me. I was dreaming of Gram dancing the tango with Grandpa Martin. She wore a flower in her hair and a red dress, and Gloria was there in the background like a photo bomb. Their faces changed, and they were covered with tubes coming out of all their orifices.

Janie holds me tight and strokes my hair. "What is it, Maddie? Tell me."

"Just a nightmare," I say.

Enzo left behind his fucked-up dream.

—ༀ०ༀ—

I wake in the morning to Uncle Billy reading a *Scientific American* and sipping espresso. "Hi, Sunshine. Trish says you need to change your feminine hygiene. Will you eat a doughnut for your handsome uncle?"

"Stop, Uncle Billy." I shuffle to the bathroom. A fungus has invaded my teeth so I brush and floss. I eat half a doughnut to get rid of him, but he doesn't leave. He recruits others.

Paige texts me another inspiring quote. I love her, but it's not working.

Wes climbs into bed and turns on the TV. "We're watching *The Breakfast Club*. You can watch or not, but we're staying." I roll over. I can't help saying the lines in my head. It's distracting, and it's the longest movie in the history of movies. When it's over, Uncle Billy shoves the rest of the doughnut in my face. "Finish it, and we'll leave you alone."

I finish in one bite.

I lie here, my body shaped like a C. The only tolerable moments are when I first wake up. I forget, just for a second, that this is happening. Then I remember, and it's maddening every single time.

$$-\xi \circ \xi-$$

"Maddie, can I just examine you? I want to make sure you're not dehydrated." That's all I need, perfect Ty playing doctor while Janie stands behind him gloating. He pokes me and tells me I need to drink or he's taking me to the infirmary. I chug half a bottle of Gatorade and wrestle with my stomach to keep it down.

"Sips, Maddie. Tiny sips." He's nice, but I can't take him seriously because he's a pickle.

$$-\xi \circ \xi-$$

"Okay, Maddie. It's time to stop the 'woe is me' and get up." Wes steps through the doorless doorway, yanks off the covers, and pulls open the blinds.

"What the hell? You're blinding me."

"Billy and I are making a party for the staff and crew. We need all hands on deck."

"I'm not going."

"Look, I get it. You're depressed. I once refused to leave my closet for the entire month of August because of somebody named Sasha. People tried to force me to feel better. But the only things that worked were time and distraction. Distract yourself. Stay busy. Count marshmallows, study frogs, whatever it takes. Time heals all wounds. It just does."

"But this isn't somebody named Sasha. It's Gram. She's gone, Wes. She's never coming back."

"I do not believe she's gone," he says, staring right into my eyes. "I felt her last night when Billy and I were sitting on the balcony. You're going to think I'm nuts, but I felt her sitting there between us. I am telling you, Assy is still with us."

"I know," I say.

We sit awhile.

"Wes?"

"Yes, Maddie girl?"

"Was Sasha a guy or a girl?"

"Sasha was a guy in love with a girl, and I was a teenager with a lot of issues."

"I see that."

"But look at me now, about to be a daddy. The world is bizarre, Mads. In a good way."

-ξ∘ξ-

Bob texts me: Hi, Maddie. Wes says you're feeling better. Can you meet me in Gloria's wing? I'd love some help coaxing out the minister.

Bob gives me a pity smile outside Gloria's cabin and gently pushes the slightly ajar door.

"Hey, wait," I call out. "I don't want to give him a heart attack."

"He's still in the car. We're thinking maybe a fresh face will talk him into getting out."

The room looks sterile and untouched. I walk through to the balcony where they've somehow managed to fasten an antique car to the beams. The minister's head is sticking up behind the steering wheel.

334

He's a sad, scraggly-bearded statue of a husband pining away for his wife of sixty-two years.

"Hi, Minister. It's me, Maddie."

I can't read his expression. I'm not sure if it's surprise or indifference.

"Wes and Uncle Billy are throwing a party for the staff and crew tonight. They're making me go. You should go, too. Gloria would want you there."

The minister looks me in the eye and nods slightly. There's an unspoken recognition, as if we are mutually bound by unrelenting grief. He turns his gaze back to the water, and I leave feeling just a tiny bit better for some reason.

"Well?" Bob says.

"He looked at me and nodded," I say.

"Okay. That's something."

I'm in the elevator when I get Enzo's text. It's only fitting since this is where I first saw him.

1. I found a place in Cairo that serves something that almost tastes like macaroni and cheese balls. I plan to go there a lot. 2. I dreamt of Astrid last night. She was eating watermelon and spitting the seeds at Mark. He was catching them with his hands and flicking them back at her. 3. You are the only woman I have ever loved.

$$-\math{\large\,\circ\,}-$$

I agree to wear a yellow lei for the hokey luau theme. Gram would have preferred me in blue.

The doctors and nurses sip their drinks and chat with the crew. Janie tells me she and Ty have made a commitment. They're going to try to make it work. I'm giving the union a full month, or until the first big fraternity party at Janie's school. But who knows? Strange things happen every day.

I eat a little, but there's a perpetual hairball of anguish stuck in my esophagus. A slouched figure shuffles in from the other side of the deck. It's the minister. He shaved and put on a white dress shirt. I wonder if Gloria ironed it for him before she died. The Ornaments fuss over him and bring him food.

Eddie gets up and thanks Wes and Billy for their generosity. He reminds us to stay in touch and that our bees are our lifeline to the other Wishwellians. Wherever we go, we're never alone.

"Every trip, the crew chooses a bee screensaver for the guests to take home. I think you'll like this one. Francesca, go ahead and do the honors."

Francesca does something on her laptop and raises her hand. The crew starts a countdown. Five, four, three, two, one. Our bees buzz. A video screensaver pops up of our conga line from the night on the equator, with the quote streaming along the bottom. *And Still We Dance.*

I smile my best smile because I need air, and I don't want them chasing after me. People are cheering and laughing at the video. They're jumping up on cue as the music starts. It's as if nothing has changed. It's as if everyone is still with us. But they're not with us. They're on Wishwell Island. They've gone home because their loved ones are gone. They're shoved in a drawer on the ship. They're in Egypt. They're suspended beneath the waves.

Nobody notices me slip out. I don't know where to go. I can't go to bed. I can't play Whac-A-Mole or sit in the café. Everything reminds me of them.

There are too many stairs, too many memories. When I get to the Gathering Wall, I feel for the light. I have to know what she wrote. I have to know how she really felt right before she left us.

The first words I see are tiny words scribbled against the groove of the wall.

I gave all my money to a street family in Morocco.—Pete

I've never felt more at peace.—JSY

There's a drawing of a little girl peeking through a window. And a drawing of an owl on a branch made of Christmas holly.

I want to die to a rock-and-roll song.—AY
Me too. Me too.

I've never paid attention to the way the sky changes a
thousand times a day.—R

There's a flock of angels drawn with purple wings. I get lost in the wall and forget why I'm here. I begin to wonder if I'll know when I see it. Then I see it, and I know.

It's a snow globe scrawled in a low place, like she did it from the wheelchair. It's not nearly as pretty as Jeb's. She drew a circle and a base and inside she wrote one simple sentence:

What a way to go!

I laugh. She didn't have any deep regrets or twisted secrets or musings. This was Astrid's Last Hurrah, just as she had said. It's okay. It's all okay.

–ε∘ʒ–

I slip back into the world of the living as the party is winding down.

"There you are, honey. We were afraid you went back to bed," Mom says.

I realize I haven't seen Mom drunk since our first night on the Wishwell. I don't know if this Mom will stick, but I like her, and I hope she does.

Dad extends his hand, and we dance to Frank Sinatra's "The Best Is Yet to Come." Jeb and Mom dance, too. He dips her, and she laughs.

"Dad, I have to tell you something. But I don't want you to get mad at me."

"Uh...Maddie. Dads don't need to know certain things. We like to pretend our little girls are virgins forever."

I shove him away. "Dad, that is mortifying. That's not it. Come on."

"Oh, okay. So what is it, then? I'm bracing myself."

"I got a tattoo when I was in Rome with Gram. She talked me into it."

"Oh, boy. You and your brother and these tattoos. Where is it?"

"On my tush. It's a little starfish."

"I guess it's not as bad if it's hidden. Do you know people aren't allowed to be buried in traditional Jewish cemeteries if they defile their bodies with tattoos?"

"Dad, after this trip, why would anyone want to go into the ground?"

"Good point," he says. "I read an article that said the formalde-hyde from dead bodies is poisoning the earth."

"Gross. Don't tell me that stuff."

"I like it, Maddie."

"Like what?"

"The starfish. You know I have a soft spot for stars."

"Aw. Thanks, Dad. Me too."

-ξ○ξ-

I'm already in bed when Francesca walks in. Now that I have no door, people think they can come in whenever they want.

She sits on the edge of my bed and tells me she's sorry for Gram, for Enzo, and that our bees will always connect us.

"Your bee even sends birthday alerts."

"That's how Tits and Mama remembered my birthday," I say.

She laughs. "Those two never forget a birthday. And they say marijuana makes people forgetful. Anyway, every day you'll feel a little stronger, and one day you'll feel like you again." She gets up to go. "Thank you, Maddie."

"For what?"

"For bringing my son back."

-&o&-

I shove a heap of dirty clothes into the suitcase and pull out the electric-blue flamenco dress. I hold it to my nose, searching for Enzo's scent, but all I smell is the perfume Janie lent me that night.

The Jules Verne book and Aunt Rose's bejeweled bookmark go into the carry-on bag. And one by one, I take out the treasures from my velvet drawstring pouch: the worry doll, Paige's Delta Gamma pin, the key to Jeb's apartment, the sea star bracelet, the sapphire, and the Grandpa Martin marble. I add the tiny glass soccer ball. I never got around to giving it to Enzo. I hope I can someday.

I eat the last of the jelly beans and hold the framed picture of Gram and me when I was three in my lap. I look out at the sea and try to remember what the world sounds like without waves.

I need to go home. I need to unpack.

-&o TWENTY-NINE o3-

I'VE GOT ALL the E's in the van. We're cruising with the windows down, primped and ready for Last Bash. We get out, link arms, and head toward the music. It's unusually cool for August. It's sweatshirt weather.

Of course, we're not wearing sweatshirts. We're wearing obscenely short dresses. *Those are blow-job dresses.* I can hear Gram now.

"Maddie, you're back. You're so skinny. You look a-mazing," somebody says. Two people tell me their grandmas died this summer, too. And three people act as if their Disney Cruise experiences somehow mean we have something in common. I play along, pretending my "family cruise" was just like theirs. And I find myself wanting to share things, as if any of them will care that the minister died or that Gracie is saying lots of words or that Janie broke up with Ty or that I miss my smoothies and frozen yogurts almost as much as I miss sitting in the Grotto.

It's good to be home, with the chill in the air, the doting acquaintances, the familiar sand under my toes. Yet it reminds me of when I was seven and insisted on wearing my size 4T pants to school. I could barely squeeze into them, but I wanted to wear them anyway. It all feels smaller, or I feel bigger, like I'm squeezing into something that will never quite fit again.

—ξoξ—

On Tessa Rose O'Neill Parker's baptism day, we walk through Central Park. We show Bob Johns the spot where Karl allegedly proposed to Aunt Rose. Bob sits on the bench with Tessa, who looks like she could be his own granddaughter.

Aunt Rose would adore Tessa. Gram would call her delicious and divine. She would let Tessa suck on the sapphire and play with her pearls and slobber on her knobby hands. She would say, "Look at this child. Is there anything more precious on earth?" She would tell Wes to stop dressing the poor thing like a doll and put her in a cotton romper. And Wes would say, "Mind your business, Assy." And Gram would say, "Shove it up your ass, Wessy, and hand over that baby."

—ξoξ—

I leave Gram's apartment, Mom and Dad's apartment now, and get on the downtown bus. I don't know what I'll be interrupting in Cairo, but I take a chance.

Me: I actually witnessed a chipmunk couple shagging.

Him: See, I said you would just know.

Me: Right you were, old chap.

Him: Celia Hobbes is boarding the Wishwell.

Me: Performer?

Him: Patient.

Me: Gram must need music.

Me: On a brighter note, Burt has a girlfriend.

Him: Yeah. I heard that from Wes.

Me: You won't believe this one. Jeb has convinced Camilla to move to Brooklyn.

Him: Yes. Wes texted me.

Me: Of course he did.

A few minutes later, my bee buzzes again.

Him: Miss you.

Me: Miss you more.

I look up and see a pretty older woman staring at my bee. I don't know if she's staring because it's a strange yellow device or because I was just laughing out loud. She smiles through the crowd, digs around in her bag, and pulls out her own bee. I smile back. She waves as she gets off at the next stop. It almost feels like this woman and I are the only people in the world who share a secret. But I know better.

We, the Wishwellians, are everywhere.

-&∘ ACKNOWLEDGMENTS ∘3-
(LOOSE ENDS)

I had a snow globe moment in a room overlooking the sea when I read the first pages of this book to my husband, Michael Firestone. Thank you, Michael, for being eternally wonderful. You are my muse.

I had a second snow globe moment in a restaurant overlooking Central Park when I had lunch with two extraordinary women: my agent, Sara Crowe, and my editor, Lisa Yoskowitz. Thank you, Sara, for helping me find the heart of this story. Thank you, Lisa, for making that heart beat with your remarkable precision, dedication, humor, and wisdom.

Many more thank-yous go out to Jon Appleton, Kristin Dulaney, Maggie Edkins, Sasha Illingworth, Annie McDonnell, Kheryn Callender, and the rest of the Little, Brown and Hodder teams for transforming the beating story heart into an actual book.

The following people have kept me happy, grounded, and sane, and have inspired the stories inside me. I am deeply grateful for you all.

1. **My parents, Faye and Fred Eichholzer and Ray and Kay Lenarcic, and my in-laws, Paulette and Jerry Firestone.** Mom,

you've encouraged me to write since I scared myself with my own Halloween story. You even got a seahorse tattoo to celebrate this book. Dad, you've taught me, through your own tireless work, that writing can be a powerful vehicle for change. Kay and Fred, everyone should have a second set of parents as stellar and loving as you. And to Paulette and Jerry Firestone, thank you for being anything but "chopped liver."

2. **My sister.** Jennifer Snyder, you are the strongest, bravest person I know, and my life is exponentially richer thanks to you and Tim and Devin and Lindsay and Andrew.

3. **Four Unrelated Women.** Abigail Esty, Nancy Krick, Laura Radmore, and Ellen Posner—you may not know this, but long ago, the four of you gave me the encouragement I needed to write bigger, better books. Thank you all.

4. **My friends.** You guys are my E's (and my Rachels), my secret keepers, and my cheerleaders, and without you I would be a one-woman conga line.

5. **My writing partners.** Thank you Jennifer O'Dea, Juliana Mills, Cindy Rodriguez, Christy Yaros, Eleni DeGraw, and Denise Alfeld for totally "getting it."

6. **My girls.** Emily and Lauren Firestone, I can't wait for more amazing family adventures. I love you both so much.

7. **My grandmothers.** I lost my beloved grandmother, Vivian Lenarcic, while editing this book. She was my grandma and my dear friend and I miss her every day. Both my grandmothers were strong, resilient women who plowed through adversity and grief and still found grace and meaning in simple things. They taught me to take the pain and grow beauty. There's nothing more healing or more powerful than that.